The Wolf-Mate Trials

THE WOLF-MATE TRIALS

THE PACK MATES OF LUNAR CREST, BOOK TWO

by

GINNA MORAN

ISBN 978-1-951314-33-0 (soft cover)
ISBN 978-1-951314-34-7 (hard cover)

Cover design by Silver Starlight Designs
Cover images copyright Depositphotos

For Inquiries Contact:
Sunny Palms Press
9663 Santa Monica Blvd Suite 1158
Beverly Hills, CA 90210, USA
www.sunnypalmspress.com
www.GinnaMoran.com

Dedication

To Felicia Schuster, You are amazing and so supported. I appreciate all your enthusiasm for my books and your invaluable support. XOXO!

1

Stranger Danger

"DON'T STOP. PUSH THROUGH IT. You've been hurt worse." I chant the words over and over again, listening to the sound of tires crunching on the asphalt road that I pray to be nearby. They're a flat out lie, but I will tell myself anything to keep my body moving.

Clutching my shirt to my abdomen, I try to staunch the blood as it seeps into the fabric. I grind my teeth, my jaw aching from the gesture. It's the only thing keeping me from screaming in agony. From giving up and just curling in on myself to die alone on the quiet forest ground.

"Fuck. Shit. Son-of-a-bitch. Cocksucker. Douchebag." My mind decides that chanting I'm fine is worthless. Swearing is where it wants to be. If I keep saying every bad phrase I can think of, I might make it farther. Or I'll just keel over with my final declaration being something along the lines of twat-waffle, cunt, piece-of-shit, taint-loving, dickhead, hag-biscuit.

Because if I survive, auntie shit eater is going to suck on her bowels as I rip them out of her and shove them in her bitter mouth.

Harsh? Yeah, no. I'm pissed.

I'm bleeding.

I'm fucking stumbling from tree to tree. I might not make it to the road, let alone return to Lunar Crest to seek revenge.

"Fuck!" Burning pain sizzles through me. If I don't find help soon, I'll go into shock from blood loss. The edges of my vision darken, and my stomach twists with nausea. The cool air does nothing for my clammy skin. I shiver and blink my eyes, desperately trying to clear my vision, but nothing works.

Dizziness slows me down, and I brace against a tree, trying to get the world to stop moving and shaking and blurring. Fear tightens my chest. All I can think about is how much I don't want to die, especially alone and in the woods where I might never be found. The idea of losing my life scares the shit out of me more than I realized. I've always felt invincible. In control.

Like my dad taught me enough that nothing could ever hurt me.

And now, if I die, everything my parents went through to get me away from the packs of Lulupoterra, the spelled land protected from the rest of Magaelorum, and to the Mortal World would have been for nothing. Many wolves would've died for nothing. My dad will be forever lost, and my future pack mates? Fuck. I can't die. I can't. They need me.

My mouth dries, and I lick my lips, trying to get my voice to work. My tongue sticks to the roof of my mouth. It's painful to even stretch my lips to speak. "Help! Help m-me." My throat burns, my words coming out as a croak.

Not a croak—a gurgling mess. Inhuman.

Light blond fur prickles across the tops of my hands. I close my eyes, trying to get my human form to cling on for a bit longer, but my she-wolf turns desperate to break free. Pain lashes through me, sending me to the dirt. I face-plant, searing pain leaving me gasping. I think I pass out for a few seconds from the agony. The sudden feeling of experiencing a void of nothing pushes me to get off the ground as best as I can. I crawl forward on my hands and knees until I can't anymore and fall to my belly again.

"No-o-o-o-o-o." A howl rips through the air with my word as my whole body explodes in torturous anguish. The world shifts, the colors of the forest turning more vibrant with my wolf vision. Bright crimson blood coats my paws, dripping to the dirt. It squishes like mud on the pads of my paws. The strange sensation helps keep my focus, the pain not as intense in this form.

The scent of the sugar pines blends with the gasoline fumes wafting through the air. I know I'm near a town in the Mortal World, but even if I make it to the road, how will I get help? I'm in my she-wolf form for fuck's sake. If anything, humans will call animal control.

A whimper escapes my muzzle, and I blow air through my nostrils, stirring up the dirt. My mind tumbles with different ways to save myself—like going back to the creek and jumping in, hoping to access the portal—but damn it. My wolf body refuses to move. The pain gripping my stomach burns up to my heart, knowing that this might be it for me.

"Help!" I call through my mind, praying that maybe the old woman was wrong about the competitors remaining knocked out for hours. Along with my thought comes another whimpering howl.

No one responds, and I can't stop the hopelessness from pouring through me. I might not have wanted to find myself in Lunar Crest, competing in a crazy-ass mating game to find pack mates for my supposed next season, but I've come to realize that even if I don't agree with the pack leaders' ways, I've grown accustomed to my new life already.

Adapting had always been easy for me. My dad ensured it. Because if I was quick to adapt, I could learn to get through the unexpected—and not only when it came to fighting. It's how I managed to get my shit together after he was taken from me.

Having a pack of men who don't think of me as their baby-making, species-saving bitch also helps with my acceptance of my she-wolf nature and all the customs that come with it. Dax, Bastien, Sagan, Sterling, and Caz want more. They want to change things. They've spent their lives preparing for a life by my side and are ready to follow wherever I lead.

Which might not be anywhere now.

The old woman tried to ensure it, claiming I will be the death of many wolves like my mother. Fuck her. I'm going to kill her for doing this to me. For ripping me away from a place starting to feel like home to abandon me to die alone in the woods.

My anger is enough to get my body to cooperate, and I manage to push up on my front paws and stumble forward. I make it all of ten feet before I crash to the ground again. Numbness tingles in my paws, and my vision dims. If my wolf doesn't release my human side soon, I'll die out here. No one will ever know what happened to me or how one of the she-wolves who was supposed to be by my side and guide me betrayed everyone. She unfairly sentenced me to death. She made herself the judge, jury, and executioner, and what she'll do now? Shit. I don't know.

My muscles suddenly tense with my spiraling thoughts, and my howl turns into a cry as I shift into my human form. I hate this. I can't seem to control anything, and I'm so afraid of what will happen to me if I do survive. I need to get my shifting in control. It's more spontaneous than ever.

I kneel half-naked in the dirt, my clothes torn and tattered from my wolf form. My body is much larger as a wolf, and the fabric of my sleep shorts and lace panties ripped at the seams. Only my bra survived, though the straps hang broken. I don't even know where my bloody shirt is. I'm a fucking mess.

"Help me! Please! Someone, help me!" I call the words out as loud as I can. My chest heaves, and I cough from the exertion. I should be dead. I feel as if my body shuts down with every passing second, and if I were human, I know I would've died. But my wolf keeps pushing me forward, my strength coming from every moment in my life adding up to remind me of what I have to lose. People depend on me. I depend on me.

Using the trunk of a tree, I hoist myself to my feet, my legs wobbling. My whole body struggles in this position. Trembles steal away my mobility. It's going to be one hell of a bad time to keep going, but I have to. I can't give up.

I push off the rough bark of the tree to get my ass running. I can't feel my feet sinking into the ground, though I know I'm moving. My body runs on my last ounce of energy, my legs stumbling as far as they can go before giving out. I nearly eat shit on the ground, tripping over a tree root, but I catch myself on another trunk and rest against it. The sound of passing cars pushes me to keep going. I'm getting close. A few dozen feet feels like miles. I spot the glow of a streetlight, illuminating the two-lane road. The sign of civilization strengthens my body. I'll drag myself if I have to. Because I'm not going to die. Not now.

"Almost there," I say out loud, clutching my stomach.

The wound doesn't bleed like it had been, and to my horror, I realize fur sprouts from my skin. I must not have transformed completely like my body knew what it had to do to give me extra time before I bleed out. It's freaky as hell, seeing my wolf peeking from the wound the way grass can grow between sidewalk cracks. It's unnatural and eerie, but I'm so thankful for this nasty new look.

If only my vision didn't blur or I could feel my feet slapping the dirt.

If only I didn't have to risk my safety by begging a human to help me—the freaky, bloody, beastly monster coming from the forest.

Fuck. No one will stop for me. I know I wouldn't.

But I have to try.

Pushing from another tree, I half-jog, half-stumble toward the asphalt. Headlights illuminate the forest road in an area I'm not familiar with. Evergreen Beach had a road like this, but it wasn't empty, even late at night. There were tons of businesses open through the night, including the gym I worked for. But this place? Shit. I might be near civilization, but I'm still far away.

I cover my face with my hands, inhaling a few deep breaths, trying to catch any sort of familiar scents. If we were near the

Pacific Ocean, I'd smell it. I could smell the salt and feel the moisture during the cool nights, and now that my she-wolf has been freed, I think I could recognize a thing like that now.

The rumble of an engine draws my attention away from trying to orient myself to my location. A car speeds by, the stereo blaring loud enough to hurt my ears. The bass thuds in sync with my heart. I had no idea how noisy the Mortal World was until I was taken away to experience the quiet of Lulupoterra and the pack territories. There aren't any cars in Lunar Crest—not really much of anything. Dax said it'll be up to us to make it into a place we'll call home, at least when we're not in the Mortal World. I never really thought of what that meant until now.

I lean on a tree near the guardrail to catch my breath. How I'm still managing to stay upright is beyond me. Blood streams down my hip and to my leg. If I weren't used to being naked in the competition, I'd freak the hell out now that I'm about to flash the driver of the next vehicle my damn ladybits.

Closing my eyes, I listen to the world around me. I don't know how far the town is, but I know it's nearby. The subtle sounds of nightlife hum in the distance. A car horn blares, startling me, and I snap my eyes open. I lie on the asphalt in the middle of the road. My body screams in pain, my muscles refusing to move. How did I get on this side of the guardrail? I must've blacked out.

"Shit, what the hell is it?" a masculine voice draws my attention to the idling car a dozen feet away. Headlights obscure my vision, shadowing the man. Boots crunch on the loose gravel of the worn road, but the man doesn't move more than a few feet closer. "Is it alive?"

A deep, guttural noise reverberates through my bones, coming from my mouth. Ah, hell. My mind struggles to grasp what's going on. I didn't realize I transformed back into a she-wolf, and my instincts rattle like crazy to keep these strangers away. Baring my teeth, I snarl and scramble back, half-dragging myself to do so.

"Get back in the car, Lonnie. It could attack," a woman says, her shadowy face hard to see as she sticks her head out the window. "We'll call animal control to put that poor thing out of its suffering."

Oh, fuck.

Fucking fuck.

This was exactly what I was worried about.

Her words set me off, and I howl through intense spasms, my she-wolf and humanity warring for control. My body feels better, more stable as my wolf, but I can't stop thinking about how I'd be safer if I were a woman. They don't put people down like they do animals they don't think they can save or don't have the means to. And I didn't make it this damn far to put my fate in anyone else's hands, especially not these two strangers.

Agony steals my vision, and I crash to the asphalt on my stomach, splaying my legs out but unable to get up. I can't do anything as my body gives up. I've never felt this utterly helpless.

Weak. My breathing quickens, my lungs burning with my struggling breath. Ice coats my skin, freezing me to the core. Numbness follows, and I lose every sensation buzzing through my body. I thought I wanted the pain to stop, but now I pray it returns. The pain means I'm alive. The pain means I still have a fighting chance.

But nothing.

This is it.

Change, damn it. Change. The words swirl over and over in my mind.

Transform. I can't die as a wolf. I can't—

A spark of warmth blossoms across my spine as the universe shows me one last mercy. But no matter what I do, I can't get up. I can't even turn my head as I shift completely into a human before the strangers. I should panic. I should try to open my mouth to beg for help. I should try to do anything. Instead, I remain naked on the cold ground, staring at the dark, still forest. At least now I won't die as an unknown beast. Maybe someone will put effort into finding out my identity. It's all I can hope for.

The man gasps at the shifting of my form. "What the—"

A bright flash of light turns my dark lids red. I brace for the car engine to roar as the strangers try to run me over to kill me. Squeezing my eyes closed tighter, I send out one final plea to the universe to end things quickly. To please give my future pack mates some sort of answer. To allow me justice. I beg and pray that there might be more than this end.

The world turns silent and still, and I wonder if this is what dying is like—alone and afraid, cold and miserable, thinking about everything I should've done to save myself. An image flashes through my mind, a single memory of my mom smiling at me. I don't know where it comes from, but the snapshot fills my thoughts. I grip it tightly with my very being.

"Teg kcab ni elcihev." A velvety smooth whisper trickles through the air, prodding at my very essence. It's strange yet comforting. The masculine voice wraps me in warmth, soothing my fear of dying. The foreign words pull my attention away from the heavy realization that there's nothing else I can do. "Tegrof eht flow. Tievinitatia vals pu."

Someone slams a car door before the sound of tires rolling over the road hums through the air. I remain on the ground, my body uncontrollably trembling as the headlights fade. The absence of the strangers fills me with relief. I won't die in front of them, leaving this world weak and powerless and always remembered that way by people who don't know me.

Except I'm still not alone. I sense a strange presence nearby, watching me. I can't see him, but my body tingles under the weight of his stare. If I could open my eyes, I could confirm what I know is true. But by who? Who stands there in silence to watch me die? I'm afraid to find out.

The soft thump of footsteps draws closer, breaking the overwhelming silence hanging in the air. I try my best to get my shit together, but it's no use. I can't even do anything as a big, warm hand slides under my side and flips me over, gently positioning me on my back.

Fear seizes my very being as I flutter my lashes, trying to get my shit together.

This isn't an ordinary man. He's something else.

Shit. He looks ready to take me.

2

Magical Intervention

WORK, DAMN IT. FIGHT. FIGHT. Come on body, don't let me down. The words swirl through my mind over and over again. But no matter what I think or pray or demand, my body refuses to cooperate. I'm too tired and injured. I can't even open my mouth to scream.

The man intakes a sharp breath, raising his hands between us. Sparks flicker in his palms, setting my face aglow as he leans in to get a better look at me. "I don't believe it. Where the hell did you come from?"

I don't respond and instead close my eyes again. There is nothing I can do but put my life into the universe's hands.

Touching my cheek, the man pulls my hair from my face to get it out of the way. The heat of his fingers blazes in hot trails as he peels the strands from the mud and blood on my face. I shouldn't enjoy the sensation, but it feels so incredibly good. I almost wish he'd pick me up and cradle me in his arms so that I can borrow his warmth. I'm so cold. So numb. But something about his touch stirs my very nature. It warns me to keep my guard up.

"My fates. Who did this?" His voice drips with concern, his surprise fizzling into something I don't recognize. Anger, maybe? But why? "What kind of monster would do this to such a magnificent creature?"

I can't tell if he's asking himself or me, but either way, I won't tell him anything. The old woman was wrong about me. I won't endanger the packs, even if it means I have to take this secret to the grave, which I might. Because the man is obviously not mortal. No mortal would ask these kinds of questions. They wouldn't sound so intrigued and calm. They wouldn't just kneel beside me, staring and listening and not rushing to help. This guy must be from Magaelorum.

And now I'm even more afraid.

"I want you to hold on. I don't have everything I need here, so I'm going to relocate you before someone else sees you." The man drapes something over me—his shirt—and the soft fabric engulfs me. It smells of spice and mint and something I can't put my finger on. I've never smelled anything like it. "This might hurt a little bit, she-wolf. You're injured badly, but I have to pick you up."

His calling me of what I am sets me off, giving me a burst of energy to fight. I knew he wasn't human, and this proves it. If he knows what I am, he might be one of the witches from the Fire Mountain Clan or some-shit. They're one of the few who knows of the wolves' existence when the rest of the universe thinks we went extinct. He could be acting nice just to capture me.

Jabbing my fist, I punch the man in the thigh, missing his groin by inches. My sudden movement startles him, sending him falling back on his ass. Muscle spasms seize my body, freezing me in place. Ah, hell. Not again.

I don't get a chance to complete my transformation before the man tackles me. He pins me down, straddling my body and holding on to the scruff of my neck. I release a growl and snarl, trying to twist to bite him anywhere I can. I can't let him take me. I need to fight any way I can.

The clink of him unbuckling his belt scares the shit out of me, but not for the same reason it would if I was in my human form. Shifting his weight, he uses his knees to hold my head in place while he slips the belt over my snout, tightening it like a muzzle. Nothing I seem to do can stop the man from hoisting me from the ground and into his arms. Pain bursts through my abdomen, and I whimper and slacken my body. Without my teeth, I can't fight. He's far stronger than I thought possible, outmatching me.

"It's okay, she-wolf. I got ya. I know you're scared, but you don't have to be. I won't hurt you. I'm only trying to help. Just hold on. I'll be fast." Static hums through the air, sending my fur on end. It crackles but doesn't shock me. I blink my eyes, the glowing light spinning around us, cutting off my view of the world.

"No," I whisper in my mind because I can't say anything. A whimpering sound trickles from my muzzled mouth. I wish I could speak with the man telepathically. Then I could tell him to just take me to a hospital. Because I don't want to go with him.

A dozen thoughts swirl through my mind as I think about everything to try to calm the anxiety crashing through me. I can't believe this happened to me. I can't believe that just when I thought my life was starting to get better and make sense, my world comes crashing down again. And I'm scared. Terrified. Where this man plans to take me—oh, shit. My guys won't be able to track me down. They might never find me again.

Bright blue light illuminates the night world around us. From my spot in the man's arms, I manage to tip my head up slightly to peer at what reminds me of the streams of Lunar Crest. The glow looks like the exact color of the gateways into other wolf territories, but this one is different. It's not a blue light beneath the icy water. It's a magical doorway to who the hell knows where.

And it swallows the two of us whole.

I think I blackout from fear, pain, and exhaustion. One moment, I'm in my wolf form in the man's arms in the middle of the road. In the next, I jerk upright on a bed in a room full of so many different aromas that they overwhelm my senses. Pepper, burning sage, something salty, mint, and a dozen other things I can't pinpoint.

"Docante florbita." The man's voice draws my attention from the glittering light fixtures hazed in smoke from whatever burns nearby. He stands a foot away, mixing something in a stone bowl, his gaze trained on its contents. "Cod fi abolies tor."

Swiveling on his feet, he meets my gaze. Strange lavender light flickers in his eyes as he rubs whatever the stuff is in the bowl between his palms, coating them in the black substance. My eyes widen, and I try to swing my arm to fight him off, but my wrist jerks against a metal restraint. I'm fucking chained to a damn bed, unable to move or fight him off.

"Please, n-no," I say, kicking my leg next, only to discover my feet are bound to the bed too, the cuffs on my ankles biting my skin. "Please. Please. You can't do this to me."

The man doesn't stop, stepping forward with his scary eyes, similar yet different to the witch doppelgangers they've sent through the weakened shield and into Lunar Crest. But they were smoke and fire and something monstrous. He's electricity and light, and it fucking doesn't matter, because he doesn't stop striding closer. His eyes narrow on mine, searching my face for something.

Raising his hands, he says, "Almost done, she-wolf. This will hurt a bit, but I need you to try to stay still."

My chest clenches, my whole body screaming with my voice as it echoes through the small room. Clapping his hands together, he sends the black liquid splattering on my stomach. He chants something low and indecipherable, his velvety voice turning breathy, husky, nearly enchanting.

"Ki tud alar tiena," he whispers, his chest heaving as hard as mine.

Liquid continues to pour from his hands, the amount seemingly impossible as it cascades across my body in a black waterfall that smells of smoke. Fire explodes over my skin, shadowing the edges of my vision. I jerk and fight the restraints, the pain sending my body into a panic. I need to break free. This is torture.

I scream again, yanking at the restraints binding me to the bed. I squeeze my eyes shut and will for my transformation to grab hold on me. I might be able to free myself if it does. For the first time, I feel like I'd be more powerful in my wolf form, the need to embrace who I am far greater than it has ever been.

But I don't get the chance.

Lavender electricity explodes against my stomach as the man releases his strange, cracking magic. It sparks across the black liquid, igniting it in purple flames that eat across my skin. I tense, bracing for more pain, but it doesn't worsen. My vision turns white, my screams cutting off with the sudden wave of ice washing over me. The pain fizzles out completely with the bright light, and I blink through the stars peppering my vision. The sweet relief automatically relaxes my muscles, my body turning to jelly. I sink back to the bed and stare at the ceiling above, the smoky haze now gone from the air.

The bed shifts next to me and the man draws my attention to him as he pulls the gross strands of my hair from my face. "Please forgive me, she-wolf. I know you thought you could heal yourself, but your injury was far worse than you were probably aware. Whoever stabbed you wanted to ensure a slow, agonizing death, poisoned by a blade infused with banned magic. You're lucky I found you when I did."

My mind whirls with his words. I can barely grasp that the world I grew up in wasn't even my own. I've just accepted that I'm a she-wolf, and one day soon, I'll have my own pack and territory, and a life unlike I imagined. But this? Poisoned with magic by one of my own relatives? Healed by whatever the hell this guy is? My. Fucking. Luck.

"You don't know what I am? How interesting," the guy murmurs, answering my silent thoughts. Shifting, he meets my gaze straight on. His eyes remain lavender in color, but they no longer glow with his magic. The lines smooth from his face, and he releases a breath from his nose, offering me a tease of a smile.

"My name is Flynn of the Tenebris Coven. What is your name?"

I blink a few times, realizing he responds to my thoughts with his own. He not only heard me, but he can speak to me telepathically just like the wolves. I might have wanted him to do so before, but now? Shit. I can't have this guy eavesdropping on my mind.

He stands and raises his arms, putting a couple feet of space between us. "I'm not a threat."

Squeezing my eyes shut, I concentrate on putting a mental block in place to shut him out like I do with most of the competitors of the games. With my injury and desperation, my guard crumbled. But now? Fuck this.

I flail my body, trying to snap the restraints, his comment pissing me off. How can he claim not to be a threat? Everyone seems to be a threat, but especially someone like him. How can I think otherwise? "You're not a threat? You fucking tied me to a bed. You act as if this is normal. Now, let me go. Unchain me."

The fuckhead has the nerve to raise his eyebrows in surprise and release an exasperated laugh like my request is ridiculous. He brushes his chestnut brown hair out of the way, leaving a streak of what might be my blood across his forehead.

"Release me!" I yell, flailing on the bed, my strength returning to me. Now that I'm not on the verge of collapsing, my body finally gets its shit together to cooperate with me.

"So you can transform and attack me?" Amusement lines his voice, lighting up his handsome face. I've never wanted so badly to punch anyone in my life. I can't believe he thinks this is funny. Only twisted assholes laugh in the face of people they claim to be helping. This douchebag isn't helping me. He wants to hurt me.

I was right. He will try to use me. The thought angers me even more. "Let me go!" I scream again, fighting the restraints.

"I don't think so. But if you will just tell me where you came from, I will help return you if that's what you want...though, I'm not sure why you would." He waves at my bare stomach, drawing my attention to the fact that I'm still half-naked. At least he covered me in a sheet. "All things considered."

"Just let me go," I say again, tugging my arms against the restraints, determined to pull my hands out of them even if it means dislocating my damn thumbs. "I'll find my own way home. The packs will surely come looking for me."

"The same ones who tried to murder you? Why would you want to do that?" Flynn takes a seat on the edge of the bed again, keeping his hands to himself this time. "Don't you think it'd be in your best interest to, you know, ask me to cast a protection spell on you? Shield you from whoever did this. I'm sure we could negotiate the cost such magic would involve."

Is he for real?

I remain frozen, his suggestion swirling a dozen thoughts through my head. It sounds a lot like what my parents did to me, taking me to the Mortal World and having a coven suppress my nature with magic. But now knowing exactly what I'd leave behind, what kind of risk I'd face with my dad's captors still after me, and not to mention the lycans who want to exchange me for a cure...

"It was one woman, and I'll take care of her. So let me fuck-ing go, you bastard!" My voice rings through the room, and I jerk my whole body against the restraints, managing to snap the chain connected to my right wrist from its anchor in the wall.

Flynn widens his lavender eyes and hops up, summoning electricity in his hands with a few unfamiliar words. But fuck him if he thinks that's going to stop me. I'm not afraid of getting shocked. What I'm afraid of is him keeping me locked up here, pretending as if he's doing me a favor. I'm afraid that restraints on the bed are just the beginning, and he'll summon a damn cage next.

I swing out my arm and whip the chain across his chest. It snags the fabric of his shirt, startling him. Clenching his teeth, he stumbles back toward the wall of the small room and just out of reach of the chain. I take advantage of the space between us and grab the chain hooked to my other wrist cuff. I yank and thrash, using all of my strength to rip that one free from the shoddy wall anchor as well.

"She-wolf, please. Settle down," he says, raising his arms in surrender. "I know you're nervous, but I'm telling you the truth. I won't hurt you. I'm trying to help you."

Backing himself into the corner of the room, Flynn watches me without acting. I expect him to throw his magic at me at any moment, but he remains frozen in his spot, his frown puckering his lips. And what the fuck? Why does he look so pouty? What the hell did he expect? He kidnapped me and relocated me to who-knows-where instead of just taking me to a Mortal World hospital. He claims I was poisoned, but he could be lying. People have been lying to me all my life. I'd be stupid to think any differently, but especially from a witch.

I don't wait to find out what he plans to do next and yank open the buckles on the leather cuffs around my ankles. My tender skin aches, bruises already tinting my skin bluish-black. I suppress the annoying sensation as best as I can, keeping my expression stern, so he doesn't think I might be weak enough to challenge again.

"You have ten seconds to send me back to where you found me," I say, wrapping the chains around my wrist. I stand up and get into my fighting stance, studying his position for any openings to the spots that will take him down. His magic seems to come from his hands, so I must injure those. I narrow my eyes on his knee, knowing that if I lash at his leg, he'll fall to the ground and clutch his legs. The reflex will help me get his hands.

"You don't have to do this," he says, raising his hands in front of him.

He sweeps his gaze down my body, the sheet that was around me now in a pile on the floor. And damn it. He's totally checking me out. An indecipherable look darkens his eyes, and he swallows, his Adam's apple bouncing with the gesture. With the way he continues to drink in the sight of me, I'd think he's never seen a woman's body before. Or maybe he's just not used to women breaking free of his freaky-ass bed restraints. Either way, now I will gouge out his damn lavender eyes first.

"Five," I say, preparing to pummel him with my fists. "Four."

Striding forward, I rush to close the distance between me and the witch. Flynn tenses his muscles, his eyes flickering with lavender light. The second I swing my fist, he locks his fingers around my wrist, stopping me. I swivel my body to throw off his balance to break free of him, but he expects my move and flings his arms around me, pinning me to him.

I try to head-butt him. I try to stomp his boots with my bare feet. I even try to sink my teeth into his neck even though I'm not in my wolf form. But nothing works. He chants something into my ear, the words seizing my muscles.

"I'm a warlock, she-wolf. Fighting me is pointless and un-necessary," he murmurs, adjusting me in his hold. "If I wanted to hurt you, you'd already be dead. Now hold your damn ass still and stop it. You're getting your wish."

Once again, light swallows us whole.

3

GATEKEEPER

I HEAVE A BREATH AND clutch my knees, my brain refusing to orient itself from the dizzying relocation. Flynn takes advantage of my weakness and steps a few feet away before I can launch at him. Wind whistles through the dark night, and I shiver, wishing I had grabbed the blanket.

"Here, put this on. I'm sure it's normal for you to be naked all the time, but it's against the Mortal World law to expose yourself like this in public." Flynn tosses me his long, black muscle shirt, which leaves him now bare-chested since he lost his overshirt when he found me in the road.

My. Damn. Eyes. I flick my attention from his eyes and to the rest of him, drinking in his subtly muscular form. He's fit and toned and covered in tattoos, the strange patterns popping with bursts of bright colors shaded within the black ink. I forgot how much I liked tattoos until this moment. I was even saving up to get one before getting taken to Lunar Crest.

Flynn tilts his head under my gaze, shifting on his feet as I continue to devour every detail mapping across his chest with a geometric, abstract heart over his pec like he wanted to display a twisted version of one of his most vital organs for the world to see.

He clears his throat and waves his hand to his discarded muscle shirt. "Please, put it on and stop looking at me like you're going to rip my stomach open and devour me. I did what you asked, despite not wanting to just put you in danger all over again."

Devour him? He might be right. Just not the way he suspects.

And I'm annoyed with myself for letting my mind wander. I shouldn't let his sexy body distract me from what's important. It's just—fuck. I'm so used to men stripping down to give me a show on purpose. To let me peek at what they have to offer. But Flynn? No. He's only shirtless because he doesn't want me to be exposed. I appreciate it more than I realize.

I inhale a few deep breaths, afraid pain might explode through my middle if I try to reach for his discarded undershirt by my feet. Thankfully, I feel fine. Better than fine, actually. I feel as if I was never stabbed at all.

"Why are you doing this?" I ask, needing to figure out exactly what his intentions are. Twisting the shirt between my fingers, I shift my eyes from his tattoos and back to his lavender eyes, which almost look light blue in the faint light of the streetlamp a couple dozen feet away.

"You're really questioning why I'm helping you?" Flynn rubs his stubbly chin with his hand. "You can't just accept that I'm kind?"

I scrunch my nose. "No one is this kind without reason. What do you want from me? Why did you help me in the first place? And this—" Straightening my back, I scrub the fabric of the shirt over my stomach, cleaning off some of the black residue to examine my body more closely. "Shit—why and how did you do this?" I ask, inspecting my smooth stomach. "There's not even a scar."

"She-wolf, please. Put on the shirt," Flynn says, snapping his fingers at me like I'll just suddenly jump to his commands like a dog. The gesture annoys the hell out of me. "The Mortal World rules are—"

I whip my head up to glower at him when he snaps his fingers again. "I know the damn laws. I grew up here."

He raises an eyebrow and thins his lips. "You what? I don't

believe you. My coven would've known. We're the gatekeepers of the access portal to Shalawood Forest and have been for a century. I felt your disturbance to the shield, which means you came from somewhere else, and I want to know where. It was something I've never felt. There are no gates to Magaelorum in this area."

I tighten my mouth and shrug the muscle shirt over my head, pulling it down as far as it can go. My cleavage bulges from the neckline, but it's better that than having my vagina on display, because clearly, this warlock struggles to keep his eyes to himself. It's nearly laughable how his gaze constantly flicks to the night sky only to drop right back down to my body. I can't tell if he's turned on or not through his pants, but either way, I feel like calling him out about it.

"How about instead of checking out my body and accusing me of lying, how about you tell me where I need to go? I came from Evergreen Beach," I snap, swiveling to peer around the forest. We can't be too far from civilization since I can hear cars on a nearby road. "That's all you need to know. Now, if you can point me in that direction..." Shit. I can't go there. It's too dangerous.

He groans. "I'm sorry. I don't mean to look at you. It's just—I've never seen a she-wolf, and you are...never mind." Flynn lifts his arm and points behind me. "Head west until you reach the road. It's thirty miles north of here. But please, take caution. Stay out of sight."

His sinewy, muscular arm flexes, his body not quite as buff as what I'm used to seeing but still attractive enough for me to take an extra second to trail my gaze down his tattooed chest again and to his toned abs with a trimmed happy trail that disappears into his pants. Which I stare at next. Am I still really checking him out? Damn straight, I am. I can't help myself. Now that I'm no longer in excruciating pain, and he's no longer restraining me to a bed...

He shifts under the weight of my gaze and tips his head back to look at the dark sky. Thankfully, he doesn't call my ass out about checking him out now, because I totally deserve it. Instead, he tries to ignore my scrutiny and waits in silence for me to release him from my stare.

His unfinished comment suddenly feels important, and I lick my lips, and say, "Are she-wolves that fascinating to you? I thought I was normal."

"You're magical," he says softly, sneaking another look at me.

I shake my head, snapping out of it before I fucking smile. My damn lips need to behave. He doesn't mean it in the same way most men complimenting a woman do. He's being literal. I can tell.

"And you're—you need to chill out. Don't think I won't punch you for thinking about whatever the hell magic you think I possess. You clearly have your own, so—" I close my mouth and wave my hand, motioning for him to step back. "Go away."

I don't know what is wrong with me. Am I going through some kind of lust-induced curiosity because he saved me? Does my desire go beyond the competitors because it's close to mating season? Does my supposed pull work on anyone? I have no idea. I couldn't tell during my supposed last heat because I was screwing one of the guys at my dad's fight gym all the time. He didn't seem hornier than any of the other guys who hit on me.

What. The. Fuck. Am. I. Thinking?

I mean, I have some very sexy, protective, and a mixture of playful, broody, and sweet men to entertain me for the rest of my life—not to mention the dozens of other men who still carry hope to win a day-claim on me in the competition like they even stand a chance. I don't need to give this warlock any more of my attention. He might only be nice now, so he can turn against me when my guard is down.

I realize I continue to gawk at him and manage to shift my feet to stare at the thinning forest behind me. "Thank you for your help," I spit out, the words sounding as awkward as I feel, trying to figure out how to gracefully and fearlessly strut away from a man who can drag me through strange portals.

"You're welcome, she-wolf. Stay safe. There has been a lot of unsanctioned magic use causing problems nearby recently." It's like he purposely tries to scare me into asking for more of his help, but I know better than accepting anything from a guy that said we could work out a damn price for his protection.

"Thanks for the warning. I can handle myself," I call over

my shoulder, striding away from him.

"I'm sure you can," he responds.

A bright flash of light erupts in the dark forest, illuminating the world around me. I crane my neck to see what the hell Flynn is doing, but he vanishes with the glow. Releasing a breath, I calm my nerves the best I can and trudge through the forest. An eerie sensation sets the hairs on my arms on end, and I hug myself, picking up my pace. I feel like such a wimp, constantly peering around me. A part of me hates that Flynn just left, and a more dominant part of me despises that I even consider the idea of asking him for help.

"Fucking, fuck," I mutter under my breath, saying the words out loud to help ease the fear coursing through me. "Fucking she-wolf games. Fucking pack claiming. Fucking stupid rules and mating season." I check off each thing with an invisible line across my palm. "Fucking coven bargain. Fucking Fire Mountain Clan. Fucking lycans. Fucking no cell phone or psychic calls. Fucking old she-wolf and her thinking she could murder me. This fucking night."

The more I think about everything that has happened to me over the last few weeks, the angrier I become. Without the constant presence of the guys who swore loyalty to me, I can finally process everything that's gone wrong in my life. And thinking about their absences hurts my heart more than I knew it would. I guess I accepted things more than I realized. Now that I almost lost my life, it makes me want to fight harder—not just against my expected duties and those who want to see me fail but also against an entire world that stole my chance at a normal existence. That ruined my parents' lives and killed the fathers of the men who want me to rise as their leader. And a leader I will be.

My confidence pushes me forward toward the road, strengthening my resolve with each step.

But then a damn car horn blares and headlights engulf me. Screeching, I spin away and dart behind the nearest tree like it can somehow shield me from the asshole who purposely swerved off the road to skid to a stop in the dirt. I'm so over this bullshit. I am better than this fear.

"Hey, she-wolf. It's me." Flynn's voice echoes over the hum of his car's engine. "Why don't you stop being stubborn and just get the hell in? I don't want to be the one responsible for leaving you to the Dark Ones who mess with the fates, when it was the fates that drew me to you."

What the hell is he talking about?

He clears his throat. "I mean, I didn't save your life, which cost me at least a damn year of my own life, just to have you waste it. If that isn't proof enough that I have no ill intentions, then—"

"A year of your life?" I ask, peeking out from behind the tree. "I don't understand."

Flynn leans against a black Corvette, still shirtless with his jeans slung low on his hips. "You really are from the Mortal World, aren't you?"

I rub my lips together. "Until a couple of weeks ago, when the packs sent their fiercest members to bring me home after a witch sent monsters after me. So, fucking sorry if I have a hard time believing you're not one of them."

He stares at me without a word, processing everything I say. A strange look crosses his face, scrunching his brows and pouting out his bottom lip slightly. Scrubbing his fingers over his stubble, he releases a long breath.

"This is still so unbelievable. The wolves of Magaelorum still exist. Everyone thought your species to have gone extinct after the territory wars," he says.

I puff air through my lips and step out from behind the tree. "Yeah, that's what they told me. Apparently my dad screwed up, breaking their traditions, and attempted to raise me elsewhere. It got him nowhere but indebted to the witches of the Fire Mountain Clan and me alone to deal with what he left behind. And it's been hard as hell. I thought I was finally getting used to being a she-wolf when I thought I was human my whole life...and then this shit happened." I don't know why I tell him. I mean, it's stupid of me to say as much, but my instincts no longer panic. I no longer feel threatened by this man who saved my life. "I just want to return to Lunar Crest. My soon-to-be pack mates are probably going crazy."

He tilts his head. "Soon to be? The wolves I know of are born into packs."

I shrug. "Not she-wolves. At least, not anymore. We're

supposedly born to all the packs…it's complicated. I haven't gotten to learn much yet because of the—"

A howl echoes through the air, sending my heart soaring. I don't believe it. I'd recognize Sagan's call anywhere. It's the most musical sound I've ever heard. Relief washes over me, and my body quivers in anticipation for his arrival.

Flynn stiffens, his lavender eyes sparking with magic as he gathers it between his palms. Another howl cuts through the air—Bastien—as his wolf responds to Sagan. They're separated, probably following my scent.

"You found me," I say the words out loud, even though the howls still sound a good ways away in the distance. "How did you find me?" Because I really want to know. I'm nowhere familiar to me and thirty miles from where they might have looked for me at my old apartment.

"You know, she-wolf. I feel bad for you," Flynn says, shaking his head. He groans and scratches the back of his neck. "You say you've been with the packs for weeks, yet you speak as if they've taught you absolutely nothing. Are you not afraid that perhaps they're keeping you ignorant for a reason? Are you even sure you really want to go back there? Someone stabbed you and left you to die. Why risk your life all over again? Let me get you out of here. I will find somewhere safe for you to go."

I don't get a chance to open my mouth to argue with him that I know more than he thinks, because a deep growl reverberates through my bones. Sterling's massive silvery gray form pounces on the roof of Flynn's car, denting the metal. His coat gleams metallic in the streetlamp overhead, and he bares his teeth, preparing to launch. Flynn reflexively throws his power at Sterling, sending him skidding off the roof of the car and onto the street.

My heart sinks into my stomach, my shock of seeing Sterling hit with magic setting me off. I stride forward to get between them. "Don't hurt hi—"

Another growl rumbles through the air. Soft fur caresses the side of my leg as Dax slinks around my body to stand in front of me protectively in his wolf form. He bares his teeth and snarls, his hackles standing on end. I link my fingers into his mahogany coat, stopping him from abandoning me to collide into Flynn.

Swiveling on his feet, Flynn jerks his attention to where Caz launches at him from the trees, trying to do what I prevent Dax from doing. I open my mouth to call him off, my mind whirling at the sight of four more wolves surrounding Flynn's car like the pack leaders sent everyone they could from the sanctuary of Lulupoterra to come after me. Tension runs hot through the pack enough to heat up my core. I know they're protecting me, but Flynn saved me. I owe him.

Blinding light flashes through the air, stealing my vision. I tighten my fingers more into Dax's fur, steadying myself against his hulking form. Haze obscures the night, making it harder to see anything. I blink my eyes a dozen times, trying to orient myself.

"Shit, he's gone." Sagan's voice draws my attention in his direction, and I spot him standing in the spot I last saw Flynn before he disappeared into his light portal. "We almost had—"

My body kicks into action, and I launch myself at Sagan, my heart screaming that the only safe place in this moment might be in his arms. He catches me and hugs me to him, nuzzling his nose into the crook of my neck to breathe in the scent of my hair. He embraces me for a long moment, just letting me squeeze him as hard as I can. Someone might need a crowbar to pry me away. I've never felt like a damsel in distress in need of some serious taking care of until now, but I don't even give a shit. I'm happy to let someone else take care of me. I've been stabbed. I deserve man snuggles.

"Are you okay? Did he hurt you?" Sagan asks, setting me on my feet for a better look. He gathers the chains still dangling from the cuffs on my wrists, so I don't swing them into his legs by accident.

"Let me see her." Bastien's voice draws my attention away from Sagan and his thrumming heart, pounding like crazy against my chest as I press myself flush against him. Reaching his hands out, Bastien gently touches my shoulder, combing my disgusting hair out of the way. "Ma Belle, where are you injured? There was so much of your blood..."

"I—I—" My. Fucking. Eyes. Just the reminder of my injuries sends tears welling in my vision, the phantom pain of being stabbed burning across my stomach, though I know it's no longer there. I blink as fast as I can, but it does nothing to stop the tears from escaping, making me feel dumb for crying so late after the fact. I'm not even hurting anymore. Flynn fixed me up just fine.

"Here, give her to me. I'll take her back to Lunar Crest," Bastien says, stroking his fingers along my back and between my shoulder blades, trying to smooth away my trembles. "It's not safe for her out here. She's cold and shaking so much. Pale. She lost a lot of blood. We have to get her home and safe before anything else."

"Caz, back him up. The rest of us need to comb the area. The warlock must be found," Dax says, his deep, sultry voice caressing my ears. I sway in his direction. My body goes crazy for his closeness, but he keeps his distance like he's afraid if I touch him, he won't be able to leave me. And he might be right because I don't want him to go. "He cannot go back to Magaelorum or to his coven to notify the High Council of our existence. It's bad enough that Fire Mountain knows."

Dax, Sterling, and Sagan morph into their wolf forms and charge away with a dozen other wolves behind them before I can argue. My heart aches at their disappearance. I know they think they need to do this, but I need them to be here. I feel as if things will fall apart if they're not.

"I'm here, Ma Belle," Bastien says, rubbing his warm hands up and down my arms. "The others will be back soon. We'll all be okay. Your safety is what's most important."

A soft whine draws my attention to Caz as he circles Bastien and bumps his big, furry head against my dangling hand. I automatically scratch my fingers between his ears, though I stare after the others as they disappear into the forest.

"Lyric," Bastien says softly, caressing my cheek. "Will you look at me? What happened? What did that bastard do to you? Was it so bad that you're afraid to let any of us in? You don't have to protect us."

I lick my dry lips. I hadn't realized I had been shutting everyone out and that Bastien probably felt my concern of watching Dax and the others abandon us to hunt who they think was responsible. "It w-wasn't Flynn. He saved me," I manage to say. "Call the others back. I just want us to all go home, so I can tell you everything in the privacy of our den."

Bastien touches the streaks of blood on my arms until he reaches the cuffs and lifts one of the chains. "But the blood. The restraints—"

"Please, Bastien. Call them back. It wasn't Flynn. He saved my life." I purse my lips, begging him with my eyes. "He only chained me because...I was fighting him a lot, thinking he was going to lock me up."

"I'm sorry, Ma Belle. He must be found regardless." Bastien adjusts me in his arms, positioning me to face him. His lips pout at my expression, and I can feel his inner conflict over doing what I ask or disappointing me. "The pack leaders will make the decision about how to proceed. They—"

"They'll kill him." I know it's not what he was planning to say, but I already sense where his thoughts wander. How else will the pack leaders deal with him? They'll consider his knowledge of us a threat. And it's my fault. I just couldn't keep the information to myself. I might've doomed a person that might have been able to help me in the future. I hadn't even thought about that before now. Fuck.

"Lyric." Bastien exhales a breath with my name. He knows this situation is screwed up. I can see it written on his face, yet here he is, contemplating what to do.

"Bastien." I don't mean to say his name so sharply, making him flinch like me saying his name this way is some sort of punishment. But I can't help it. "Please. I'm going to be your pack leader. Don't you think you should treat me as such by placing the decision in my hands?"

Did I just go there, pulling the alpha card? Yup. He can't believe it, either. I can nearly hear the string of swears flitting through his mind with my question.

His eyes search mine, a dozen unsaid thoughts swirling through his head. It only takes one flick of his gaze to Caz for me to know he's having a silent conversation with him, leaving me out. I want to assume it's because I keep them out of my mind, my thoughts not ready to let anyone in at the moment, but I know that's not the reason. They could let me hear them if they wanted me to. And hell.

Annoyance rushes through me, because he—and all of my

guys—promised never to leave me out. They were to always include me in even the smallest decisions. They weren't to block me from their minds, allowing me to listen if I so choose. I know it's unfair of me to get upset since I'd be a hypocrite, but this is different to me. These are my personal thoughts and not something I'm excluding some of them from. That was part of the deal they made with me when I agreed to give them a chance. This whole arrangement of rigging the She-Wolf Games won't work otherwise. I will not stand by and let anyone make decisions without me.

Shoving my hands to Bastien's chest, I push myself away hard enough that he drops me. He swears with my action, growling at himself for not being prepared. I instinctively land in a crouch, flashing Caz the perfect view of my damn vagina in the process, now that I'm at his level, but I manage to stifle my groan and hop to my feet. Dodging around both Bastien and Caz, I bolt away from them in the direction the others ran. I have no idea where the hell I'm going, but I need to get close enough to yell for them. If Bastien doesn't call them back, I will.

"Dax!" I shout, both out loud and in my mind, easing down my guard just enough to keep everyone else out. I don't want all of the competitors who joined the guys to know my request. They'll use it against me or some bullshit. Anything to make them look great to the leaders. "Dax, get your sexy ass back here." That should work. He likes when I compliment him.

A howl rips through the night, but Dax doesn't respond

with words. In fact, I'm nearly certain he cuts me out too. The unnerving silence digs under my skin to burrow inside me. I need to transform into a wolf if I'm going to hunt the guys down. It'll be a bit easier with my enhanced senses, though I don't exactly know how to track. Not like they do.

With my thought, the thing Flynn said about them purposefully keeping me ignorant flashes through my mind. He can't be right, can he? We've been so focused on getting through the games and the competition that it's not like they have time to teach me such a skill...right?

Damn Flynn and the doubt he roused inside me. Now I need to prove him wrong and one of them to teach me. Until then, I'll just wing it.

Closing my eyes, I concentrate on my transformation. My body aches with exhaustion, but I ignore it the best I can. I'm not returning to Lunar Crest unless everyone comes with me. I don't care if they feel me remaining in the Mortal World is dangerous. It's dangerous in Lulupoterra too, even with the magic shield protecting the place. It can't protect me from the strange rogue she-wolf who only returned to kill me. How did she know I was there? I need to find out. Someone had to tell her.

Bastien snatches the chains dangling from my wrists and pulls me back to him, not giving me a chance to embrace my wolf-form. "Lyric, I know you're upset and scared and angry, but please, think about the packs. I know it's hard for you to really understand the gravity of the situation, but all our lives depend on remaining hidden. We're not ready to face the battles that will occur if word got out. It's bad enough the Fire Mountain witches know. Look how often they attacked over the last couple of weeks."

"That's because the shield was weakened. You guys said so yourself," I argue. "Flynn—"

"Just because that bastard saved your life doesn't mean anything. He could've been doing so for selfish reasons and not from the goodness of his heart." Caz's words trickle into my mind, interrupting me, my guard cracking a bit with Bastien's words.

I cross my arms over my chest and grab Caz's fur between his ears, holding him still while I get in his face. "I just—you can't kill him if you find him. You can't drag him to Lunar Crest and in front of the pack leaders until I get a chance to talk to him. Please. I've been through a lot. I need you to stand with me on this."

Caz sighs through his nostrils and noses my cheek before licking me. "I'll always stand with you."

"Even so, the others won't go for it," Bastien says, winding the chains as he closes the space to me, getting me to straighten my back. "Their loyalty remains with their packs until the end of the She-Wolf Games. Some of them will use the circumstances to make an impression on the leaders, trying to secure a spot." He's not talking about Dax, Sterling, and Sagan—at least, I think he isn't—but the rest of the competitors who left the sanctuary to look for me.

"Then figure something out," I say, swinging the chains back and forth, wishing I could get them off already. "Please."

"It could risk my standing, Ma Belle. I won't do it. I thought I lost you tonight, and it killed me. I will not jeopardize my chances of winning a permanent claim on your pack. Not for the warlock I know did at least some of this to you. These chains have a Magaelorum High Council insignia. They're used by gatekeepers. You said it yourself. He restrained you because you fought him. You sound like you eventually stopped. So why didn't he remove them? Why are they broken? Did you escape and he gave up?"

"It wasn't like that. And the Magaelorum shit? It means nothing to me. I don't even know what that is. I don't know anything. I don't even know how to get home or what to expect anymore. I felt so helpless tonight, like everything my dad taught me was useless. I need to learn more." I clench my fingers into fists, my whole body tensing as the night keeps replaying in my mind over and over again. "The only thing I know is that I can't even trust my life in Lunar Crest. You stand here arguing with me when the whole reason I'm out here is because of—" I growl, snapping my mouth shut. I don't want to say the words.

I'm afraid to speak about the she-wolf. What if someone helped her? It wasn't the first time someone in Lunar Crest tried to kill me.

A cool nose pokes me in the back of my leg as Caz circles

around me. He rubs his body to my calf like he needs my closeness. I automatically pet the length of his back, feeling his nerves trickle to me. "Lyric, I'll do it. You don't need Bastien or anyone else to risk their chances. I'll interfere if the others catch the warlock and bring him to you." His voice hums through my mind, and he sits in front of me and looks up with his wolfie eyes. It makes me want to snuggle him. It's the most we've done together, but I enjoy it. I've been slowing things down a bit with everyone, and suddenly, I wonder why. What's the point? My life proves that it could be too damn short.

"My loyalty is to you, and I trust you as my pack leader," Caz adds, nudging his head to my hand. "The only risk I have is failing to keep my vow to stand by you as your pack mate and be the best damn one I can be."

I blink a few times as he paws my foot. "Are you sure?"

His ears twitch. "Yes, but please. Let Bastien take you home. I can't focus on my task unless I know you're safe. I just want to know you're being taken care of. Seeing you like this—fuck. I can't—" His voice fades as he lets his words trail off. He's cautious with what he says to me, knowing that things were shaky between us. And I'm thankful for his consideration, for him never pressuring or pushing me even though he was given an official claim and spot on my pack.

I sigh a breath through my nose, a dozen emotions running hot through me. I want to hug and assure him I'm okay, but I'm not sure I am.

I no longer believe anywhere in the universe is safe for me, and it sucks. Not the Mortal World. Not Lunar Crest. Nowhere.

"I will only feel safe with the six of us together," I manage to say, shifting on my feet. "So hurry, okay? And bring Flynn to our den. Tell the others to meet us there too. There's something more important we need to worry about."

"The reason you're out here?" Bastien asks, finally speaking up. He tightens his jaw, searching around the forest like the shadows cast from the trees in the moonlight will somehow give him the answers.

I nod, stepping close to get close to his ear. I fear thinking the words. I don't think I project my thoughts, but I'm afraid to chance it. "There is a traitor among the packs."

Bastien tenses at my whisper and growls. "Who? He's a dead man."

Standing on my tiptoes, I brace myself on his shoulder and caress my lips to his earlobe. "Not a man. A she-wolf. One I've never seen before. She claimed she had been in the Mortal World searching for me."

"What? Do you know who?" Confusion puckers his brows as he leans back to meet my gaze, trying to decipher if he heard me correctly.

"My great aunt," I say, my heart beating wildly. Thinking about her putting the cursed muzzle on me, whipping me with chains, and stabbing me steals the warmth Bastien's closeness creates. I wish I could suppress the memories. Pretend they didn't happen. But I'm sure they'll continue to haunt me.

He frowns, his brown eyes narrowing into slits as he lets my revelation sink in. "Your great aunt? Are you sure?"

I nod, sliding my arms around him to keep myself steady. "She told me. Her scent even reminded me of my mother. We were definitely related."

"Shit. I don't believe it," he mutters, combing a hand through his hair.

"Well, it's true. She—"

He shakes his head and quickly scoops me off my feet. "No, Ma Belle. I believe you. What I struggle to believe is that Paige is alive. I mean, every damn one of us watched her die."

4

REUNITED

"ARE YOU SURE NOTHING ELSE hurts?" Bastien asks for the tenth time, even though I lie naked before him, so he can see mostly every inch of me.

"Just my wrists and ankles. Like I said, Flynn restrained me because I scared him. How is that any different than when the leaders shoved me in a cage? At least he was saving me. I was bleeding out. What is the leaders' excuse?" I stretch my leg up and stare at the slight bruising and scratches on my shins. I know

It's unfair to throw this in his face, considering it wasn't his decision, but still. I want him to know my feelings on the matter.

"You're right. It's just...he didn't look afraid. He didn't look like he was trying to help you," he mutters under his breath, his emotions still running hot from everything I told him. "What he looked like was ready to kidnap you after you broke free like the badass you are."

I lift an eyebrow at him and playfully kick his chest with my foot. "Like you kidnapped me, Bastien? Some people wouldn't see it any other way. Humans might consider me brainwashed or something for not holding it against you. They'd think I was crazy for bonding. So please, you have to understand." I keep my voice light, teasing almost, because we both know things didn't go according to plan. I wasn't supposed to be dragged to Lunar Crest, but the doppelganger sent after me by the witches would have killed or taken me to the Fire Mountain Clan. As for the She-Wolf Games, I can thank the damn leaders for that. I'm sure the guys would be happy with not having to play.

He groans and snatches my foot, holding it between his hands. "You know I had to relocate you to save your life. Anyone who thinks otherwise can fuck off." Uh-oh. He's still too emotional to see my point.

"Exactly. That's what Flynn did. He saved my life. He was concerned about sending me back because of, you know, getting stabbed and poisoned." I touch the smooth skin on my stomach. "Which he lost a year of his life to fix."

He kneels in front of me, tugging me closer to the edge of the bed. Dipping his hand into a container of some sort of cream, he scoops up a palmful and coats it over the top of my foot and around my ankle. "You say that as if you want me to thank him."

I smirk and lift my leg, swinging it onto his shoulder. I hope giving him a better view of my body distracts him from his broody mood. I'm over discussing Flynn and tonight. I just want him to join me on this bed and cuddle me. "You sound jealous that someone else mended me, Bastien."

"And if I am?" He tips his head up to peek at me, his brown eyes catching the soft glow from the wall sconce.

"Don't be." I flop back on the pillow with a sigh. He's currently in doctor mode, which he won't stray from without being nudged or knowing I'm good. "If you must know, I didn't enjoy one second of it...not like this." I wiggle my toes as he holds my foot between his hands. Using his thumbs, he massages the arch of my foot while rubbing in the cream, the sensation feeling so amazing after such an awful night. "I also lied about the pain. I ache everywhere. Every inch of me."

I smile with my words, watching his eyes darken with the wave of his desire that crashes over me. My playfulness pushes the jealousy and anger from his mind so that it knocks him out of doctor mode and into mate mode. It's been days since I've had much alone time with Bastien, and I hadn't realized how much I missed it. We've all been so concerned with the games and the possibility of lycan attacks that I might have been unintentionally stopping any sort of real progression in my relationships with each of them.

"Do you think there is anything you can do about it?" I add, stretching my arms over my head and arching my back, knowing his gaze smolders over the curves of my hips and to my breasts, drinking in every inch of me as I remain exposed to him even though I can cover up. I want nothing more than for him to give in to me and enjoy our alone time. Who knows when we'll get it again.

He rubs his lips together, shifting straighter to rest his hands on my knees. "Are you sure you want me to? I don't think you realize what you do to me, Ma Belle. I've craved a moment alone with you for days."

"Then maybe you should take advantage of it, because once the others return, it might be our last." I reach my arms out to him, getting him to set the cream aside and pay more attention to me rather than the bruises that will fade.

Bastien climbs closer, his desire growing between his legs, his muscular body as naked as mine, seeing as we came straight here instead of stopping for clothes. I hum under my breath as his cock grazes my hip, and he nestles next to me on his side, sliding his hand under my back to get me to roll over and face him.

His gaze trails to my mouth. His desire to kiss me captures me in a gravitational pull, drawing me to him first. I brush my lips to his, kissing him slow and sensually, savoring the sensation of his body pressed to mine. How his warmth blankets me. How his scent alone can turn me on. Slipping my tongue into his mouth, I taste and explore his soft tongue, stroking mine against his. I rub my hands over his taut shoulders and trace his muscles. His sexy body captures my complete attention, and I hook my leg over his, wanting to feel as close as possible. He lets me lead, staying with my pace instead of unleashing the wild desperation boiling in his soul. He wants me, craves me, but his caution keeps him holding back from just rolling on top of me and giving in to our natures.

And I appreciate and love it. This is exactly what I need in this moment—just to feel his adoration and care, his desire to give me what I need instead of taking what he wants. I know the idea of claiming me runs through his mind, bonding our bodies and souls on an intimate level, but a part of me hesitates to allow such a thing. I'm too scared of what can happen, especially after tonight.

Sagan and Dax have already done so, not caring about the consequences of such a bond before the leaders agree on the winners of the She-Wolf Games. And now if either of them loses a spot on my pack, or if something happens to me, they will never be able to bond with anyone else. Their hearts and souls are in my hands.

I'm nearly certain that's what happened with my dad and one of the reasons why they chose to leave besides my mom's pregnancy with me. I'm afraid of it happening to anyone else. I've grown to care about Bastien, but it's too early for such a commitment. I'd have treaded more cautiously with the others had I known the extent of such a claim.

"That's not your fault and a risk they were both willing to take," Bastien whispers, our minds opening completely to each other. He runs his fingers over my jaw, cradling my head. "Your arrival was just so exciting for all of us, but I understand your hesitation and respect your wishes."

He touches my cheek and smiles at me. I wish my mind hadn't wandered, because I really don't want to think about the claims or anything else besides Bastien for that matter. I feel bad that I do.

"Don't be," he murmurs, responding to my thoughts again. "It just means I need to do a better job of distracting you...if you'll let me."

My vagina clenches in good anticipation at his comment, my mind already imagining his mouth all over me as he kisses the aches away. He moans under his breath, the noise sexy as hell, and kisses me again, deeper, more fervently, rolling me onto my back to get on top of me. The heat of his muscular body presses against mine, pushing me into the bed. I comb my fingers through his hair and to his back, grazing my nails over his muscles until I squeeze his ass to pull him harder into me, feeling the length of his cock rub between my legs without entering.

And now that it rests on my pelvis, teasing my body and so

close...fuck. I wonder what it would feel like sinking inside me, how his balls would feel tapping my ass with his thrusts. I wonder if he'll like it slow or fast, rough or sensual. My wandering mind sets me off, and I shove him over and switch places with me on top.

Bastien releases a playful growl and pinches his fingers into my hips, not allowing me to align my body. He slides me up his pelvis, the sensation of my slick body rubbing his raging hard-on sending tingles through my legs. He doesn't let me grind against him as much as I want to and pulls me the rest of the way until my knees hit the pillow at the sides of his head.

I gasp and arch my spine, leaning back to open my hips wider instead of bowing forward to brace on the rock wall. Bastien tightens his grip on me, pressing his thumbs into my hips and the rest of his fingers into my ass cheeks. He flicks his tongue against my clit, the sensation incredibly intense in the best way, the constant rhythm dragging a loud, uncontrollable moan from my mouth. I wiggle, my body unable to stay still, but he ensures I remain in place as he rolls his tongue and makes me gasp. He sucks me harder, sending an explosion of pleasure zinging through me. A whimper of a moan escapes my lips, the intensity of his mouth mind-numbing. It takes everything in me not to scream my enjoyment, my body on the verge of ecstasy.

And now I can't stop thinking about pleasuring Bastien, tasting him with my mouth, wanting to see if I can make him cum, how long it might take, how smooth his balls will feel if I sucked them. I want to enjoy him like he does me. Take care of him how he takes care of me.

Bastien reacts to my thoughts, his moan vibrating against my body in a shockwave of pleasure. It's enough for him to flip me off of him only to have him pull me back so fast that I laugh at my stomach pressing to his as I face the opposite way. His cock flexes with his anticipation for me to act on my fantasy. The hot, raw, deep-seated craving to get him off courses through me. Excitement pours through my core at even the thought of tasting what I will do to him.

I lace my fingers around the base of his shaft, holding him in place as I bow forward. He moans between my legs as I lick the ridge of his tip and down the underside to his balls. I glide my tongue over his smooth skin and back up, my own body reacting to the wave of his pleasure crashing into me as he thinks about how mind-blowing my mouth feels on him, how intoxicating he thinks my body tastes, how much he enjoys every second of being with me.

I smile at his thoughts and lick my lips, pursing them to suck his tip into my mouth to feel his reaction to the tightening sensation. It sets him off in lustful determination, and he works his mouth over me, sucking my clit in a way that tenses my muscles. I dig my fingers into his thigh and pull away with my orgasm, using my hand to stroke him blindly, desperately.

He moans at my reaction, slowing down but not stopping like he's determined to bring me to my peak again and again.

And fuck, I'm not so sure I can survive so much pleasure, but my body is fully dedicated to finding out.

Bringing my mouth back to his body, I suck him off, rolling my tongue and bobbing my head up and down a bit faster, his moans letting me know how much he enjoys my mouth. I massage my fingers into his balls, working him over with my tongue, loving how he slows his own mouth to enjoy what I do to him. Stroking his fingers up and down my hips, he touches me and memorizes my body with his hands.

"Lyric, I'm going to cum," he murmurs, his breath panting against my thigh.

I ignore his warning and suck a bit harder, my hand slippery with spit as I hold his base and work him over until he moans and tightens his fingers to my legs as he orgasms. Slowing down, I swallow and lick my lips, excitement still rushing through me. He gently eases me off of him and sits up only to move next to me, pulling me into his arms and meeting my eyes.

"You are everything I've ever dreamed of, Ma Belle. Your desires...I look forward to proving we're meant to be together beyond our duty to help our species. It's more than getting us out of hiding from the rest of the universe."

"And what about our supposed duty to re-populate?" I tease, cupping my hand to his face, just feeling the prickly stubble on his cheeks.

"I must admit. I love the idea. You will surely be the best mother, mate, and leader with your fierce convictions, need to take care of others, and desire to fight for more than what you've been offered." His eyes light with his words, his mind wandering to a place I want to savor and enjoy alongside him as he imagines our future together.

Who knew I'd start to want such a thing...

But then darkness sneaks up on me, a wave of heated emotions breaking through the protective shield I put into place to be and think and enjoy Bastien alone by pushing the rest of the world out. And damn it. This isn't what I wanted from the others coming back. I wanted nothing but relief. Happiness. Not the annoyance and anger the guys still carry from the night.

Grabbing the blanket, Bastien covers the two of us, his own comforting thoughts darkening with the muttering voices echoing through the den as the rest of my guys arrive, splashing their way through the naturally heated pool in our direction.

If Bastien wasn't so set on using the blanket as a protective shield from their wild emotions like it could actually keep their moods out, I'd rip it off and greet them naked to distract them.

"Fucking hell," Sterling says, darting around Dax, who looks broody as fuck, to rush toward the bed. His gaze darts over me in Bastien's arms, and he pouts out his kissable bottom lip. "My beautiful, bombshell blondie. This night has been utter torture. I was so worried."

Flopping beside me, Sterling's damp body sandwiches me to Bastien. He inhales a deep breath of my scent, drawing his nose from my hip to my neck. I laugh as he curls around me from behind, his bulge pressing into my ass, probably the first time since we met that he doesn't have a boner testing the barrier of the sheets. Groaning, he shifts my hair from my neck and peppers me with kisses between my shoulder blades.

"Let me love up on you next," he murmurs, locking me in place. "You smell like my last wet dream."

I squeeze my eyes shut, scrunching my face. If I react, he'll continue with his playful teasing. Right now, I need answers.

"Did you find Flynn?" I ask, wiggling in his embrace until I can shift to face him. Bastien snuggles against my back this time, the two of the smothering me with their affection. Sterling doesn't respond and kisses me over and over, just light pecks of our lips together.

"No, the warlock got away. We lost his trail," Dax says, answering for Sterling. His golden eyes sweep across my body like he's inspecting me like Bastien had done. Heat blossoms over my skin under his scrutiny. I'd prefer he look at me like he wants to rip the sheet away to ravish the hell out of me and not see if I have any injuries. I hope their protectiveness doesn't become a problem. Because I'm tough. A little bruising from restraints hasn't ruined anything. If anything, I'd prefer for someone to replace the bad experience with a good one.

Dax cocks his head, surprise softening his face as he hears my thoughts. I blush under the idea. I'm not exactly the submissive type, but I'd be willing to try...especially if Dax looks at me like he does right now, his concern morphing into desire and maybe annoyance like he wants to bend me over his knee to spank my ass for making his mind wander to turn my fantasy into his own when he clearly wants to remain focused.

"Damn it," Bastien says, his muscles rippling across his arms. His comment yanks Dax's attention from me, killing our silent fantasy, which I only share with him.

I imagine him using his massive cock to spank me instead, trying to get creative with my fantasy to hold his attention.

His body hardens, his nostrils flaring at my grin. "Damn it, is right," he mutters, shaking his head while narrowing his eyes at me. "Someone needs to be punished."

Yup. Me.

He doesn't say it though.

"We'll have to continue the search later." Sagan meanders closer and whacks Dax on the shoulder as he passes by him, not realizing Dax's comment was a tease to me. Water drips off his skin from the pool, sending rivers over his abs to drag my attention to his naked body.

And fuck. Nearly dying has given me a new zest for life. My desire burns in my core, begging me to take advantage of all these sexy men while I can.

Sitting on the edge of the bed, Sagan reaches out and sneaks his hand under the blanket to stroke my bare leg like he needs to touch my skin to reassure himself I'm here and okay. "He'll be back for his vehicle, so Caz stayed behind to keep watch."

"I think you should call him back. I need us all to be here

together. I don't think Flynn is the threat you think he is," I say, tipping my head back to meet Dax's stern gaze. His lust over my dirty thoughts dissipates with my words.

Dax's eyes search mine, his forehead wrinkling with his frown. And fuck do I want him to quit it. I want nothing but smiles right now, but I understand. He wasn't there. He'll only ever think the worst. "How can you be so sure, Lyric? You don't know him or what he's capable of."

"Should we be worried that you speak as if you're worried about him?" Sagan asks softly. His concern digs at me. I never really thought I'd have to be cautious about how I speak of others outside our pack, even if nothing is there to freak out about, but I guess I do, especially with his claim on me. "Seeing you in those chains—"

"Sagan, please relax. It's not like that," I say, knowing that Sagan and Dax's claim on me affects their feelings more so than Bastien and Sterling. I can't imagine it being easy for any of them, considering how hard it was on me, but I need them to know that things could've been much, much worse. "I'm fine. You guys are thinking the worst about the wrong person."

"Highly doubt it, but okay. I might argue with you more if you didn't smell so damn good." Leaning in, Sterling kisses me, pulling me closer until his thick cock taps against my pelvis, his mind settled enough to tease me. "My one-eyed anaconda wants nothing more than to make a home in your love glove, blondie...not to mention how much I want to cuddle the hell out of you to assure myself that you're not faking it."

I nip his lip and stretch it with my teeth. "So poetic, you horn-dog. Makes me wish I could turn my body into a snake-trap."

He flexes his cock. "I could work with that."

"So can I...if you believe me when I say I'm okay." I arch my hips up and down to mess with him.

He groans and breathes in another breath of my hair. "Good. I needed that confirmation before I dry hump the hell out of—"

A heavy body lands on top of me and Sterling. Dax hooks his arms around Sterling and throws him off to take his place. His surprise tackle triggers my fight-mode. I shove my knees into his gut and use the strength of my legs to flip him off. The world spins as he holds onto me, giving in to my move instead of re-sisting. He huffs as his back hits the cold rock floor with me on top of him.

And now that I am...

Shit, I need to jump into the icy river. All of their scents mingle and wrap around me, prying at my innate nature as a she-wolf. It doesn't help that I'll come into heat. I nearly fear such an occurrence, considering how fucking horny they all make me now.

I can't stop the image of each of them taking turns to train bang the hell out of me even though I doubt that's what will happen, and I wonder how much I'll need to stretch if my out-of-whack hormones change my mind about the whole...nope. Not going there. Being stabbed and poisoned, left to die in the Mortal World by one of my own relatives, really solidifies my stance on the matter.

Dax stiffens under me and not in the way I like, his golden eyes widening as they search my face. I twist my lips as he listens to the thoughts rushing through my mind. Silence falls through the den, the burning intensity Bastien roused in me, kindled by Sterling's endearing comedic honesty, now fizzles out.

My tears pelt Dax's face, everything sneaking up on me at once as I realize I totally crushed all their dreams and expectations for that kind of future with me. One I might have even started thinking about for myself the last few weeks because of their confidence in us as a pack and me as their leader. I know it's what Dax wants. He was clear about it. I wish I could be too, but I can't help it. If this is the life I'd have to give my children, I'm not sure I want them. Almost dying tonight was enough.

"Fuck." I roll off of Dax and push to my feet, turning my back on the four of them. Their whirlwind emotions trickle to me—confusion, anger, heartache—in a wave I can't decipher. I know it's not about my decision and more about the circumstances that settled it. But still. "Fuck!" My voice echoes through the den, my rage about everything leaving my body tense, stealing away the good feelings I had from my delicious moment with Bastien.

Sagan gets to his feet and comes to me, grabbing my hands

before I slice my palms with my nails. "Gorgeous, it's okay. We've all been through a lot. Just take a breath with me."

I squeeze my eyes shut. "It's not, though. My fucking relative just had to ruin everything. She killed my hope and needs for our future when she tried to kill me."

Dax pushes from the floor, his lips hidden in a thin line. He comes up next to us, standing super close, his body grazing mine. "Who are you talking about, Lyric? You don't have any blood relatives in Lulupoterra. You and I are the last of our fathers' bloodlines, remember?"

Bastien groans, scrubbing his face. "It's not her father's bloodline."

"Her mother's bloodline? There are no females. It's why Lunar Crest is hers, and the leaders haven't given a new territory." Sagan looks at Bastien.

"Lyric thinks it was Paige," Bastien says, drawing everyone's attention to him. "She said the old woman smelled like her mom but called herself her great aunt. I can't think of anyone else. It has to be Paige. She didn't die after all."

Dax whips his attention towards him. "Are you absolutely sure?"

"I believe Lyric, so yeah. It would make sense if she's been in the Mortal World. Paige probably had a deal with a coven. The leaders wouldn't let any she-wolf leave like Melody, so she probably figured out her own way to follow. You know how crazy things were as kids." Bastien scoots to the end of the bed.

Rushing from the den, Dax abandons the rest of us without a single word. Sagan runs after him, and I listen as the two of them splash through the pool. The silence that follows from them diving into the river to return to the forest kicks my ass in gear. Fear tightens my chest. My bare feet slap the wet rocks, and I stand on the ledge, staring into the glowing river water.

"Dax! Sagan!" I call, sending the thought to them. "Stop."

A warm hand touches my shoulder, and I turn to face Sterling. "Let them handle this. If she is out there, they will find her. Why don't you come and let me and Bastien snuggle with you a bit longer?"

"Handle it? Handle it, how?" I ask, searching his gray eyes.

He doesn't have to say anything for me to know. They will handle my wicked aunt in the same way they wanted to handle Flynn. It's written all over his sullen expression. How he can just stand there and be okay with letting his brother and Dax risk everything? Ugh.

"She tried to murder you," Sterling says softly, linking his fingers around my wrist, responding to my thought. "There is only one way to handle that kind of treachery, especially if she's suddenly appearing when everyone watched her die. Something is going on, and—"

"Hurting a she-wolf is punishable by death for any wolf responsible," I say, shivering at the memory of the death sentence Hendrix received for attacking me. And with thoughts of him come Flynn, telling me that the poison Paige used was created by the Dark Ones and banned magic. What if Hendrix was too? This has to be connected. It has to.

"Relax, blondie. If no one finds out, we'll be fine." Sterling tries to tug me from the ledge and back into the natural pool. He groans and pouts his lip when I resist.

"Seriously? So you're saying if they do find out—damn it, Sterling. I'm not letting anyone risk anything." Tugging from Sterling, I dive headfirst into the freezing water. My body tenses under the change in temperature. Shit, it's cold.

Kicking my aching legs as hard as I can, I swim down until it feels like I'll crash into the bottom of the river. Instead, I break the surface to air. I flip my soaking hair from my face and gasp a few deep breaths, peering around the quiet forest.

"Sagan. Dax. Damn it, you two. You better stop right now. I know what you think you have to do but like hell is it going to be you who does it. I command you as your pack leader to turn your cute asses around right now and return to me." I think the words, afraid that if I say them out loud, someone will hear me. I wish I didn't have to pull the pack leader card at all.

A whistle rings through the air, calling all the packs to gather like they do before the start of the She-Wolf Games. And hell. My heart sinks into my stomach. I have a terrible feeling about this—enough of one that I spin to run without waiting for the guys to respond.

I crash right into Dax's muscular chest. Slapping my palms to his pecs, I try to shove him back for scaring me. He catches my arms and pulls me into him, engulfing me in a hug I can't help but sink into. He's driving me crazy today.

"You think I'm driving you crazy, Lyric? Do you know how hard it was for me to stop myself from seeking Paige out?" he mutters, lifting me off my feet so he can press his nose into the crook of my neck and breathe in the scent of my skin. His embrace soothes the wild beast inside me who wants to fight him. His concern and need to take care of things has left me starved for his affection more than I realized. He feels it too. He's starved himself and now that I'm within his arms, he's realizing it. "Nearly impossible. I was so caught up in my anger that had you not reminded me, I would have broken my promise. And I'm sorry for that. I just—you mean so much to me. But I'll do better. I swear."

My heart fills with something indescribable at his words. I appreciate him holding himself accountable and not twisting the blame on something else.

"Do you remember why I asked you to make me that promise, Dax?" I slide my arms down his neck, rubbing my fingers into the taut muscles of his back, now in serious need of a massage to loosen them up.

"Because I'm yours. I'm here to back you up despite how much I crave to protect you," he whispers, repeating our conversation from the moment he decided he didn't need to win the competition to announce a claim on me, one I also announced on him before I truly knew the extent of it. Like before, the words ignite something raw and deep-seated in me. It's unexplainable how perfect such a promise feels on another level.

"I know you do. I know you want to create this life together and make sure everything is right for me. I love that and want that too. But Dax, you need to remember that it's my duty to ensure the safety of our pack. I can handle my own. I also desire to protect you, and if I allow you to seek justice or revenge or whatever on my behalf, I could lose you. I'm not willing to risk it." I ease away, craning my neck to look behind me as I sense Sagan, Sterling, and Bastien all closing in behind me. "That goes for all of you. I will handle this shit myself. If Paige thinks she can just come here and force us back to the dark times my parents barely lived through, she will be sorely disappointed."

"Damn, she's so fucking sexy when she gets like this," Sterling murmurs to Sagan. He drapes his arm over his brother's shoulders and gives him a shake, getting Sagan to smirk and nod his head.

I lift an eyebrow at both of them, their brotherly love so sweet that I can't stop my mouth from smiling when I'm trying to channel my badass side. "You mean it's sexy that I act as your leader?"

Sterling bites his bottom lip and nods his head. He shudders at some thought swirling through his mind that he keeps to himself. "It gives me the urge to wrestle with you."

"Do you like getting kicked in the balls, brother?" Sagan asks, clearing his throat. His voice deepens with his words, and he tightens his mouth, trying to hide the fact that Sterling's comment distracted him from his need to back Dax up. But I caught him. He knows it. I know it. It's enough to make me stick my tongue out at him, making him laugh at my playfulness.

And thank the fucking universe.

"Hell-fucking-yeah, brother. I don't care which part of her touches me, how, or where. I think she likes me enough to feel bad about it. And when she feels bad..." Sterling releases a sexy growl, meeting my eyes, his smoldering thoughts whispering to me that he'll accept his punishment because I might lick his injuries. The bastard.

I narrow my eyes at him, trying to keep a straight face. Sterling always knows exactly which of my damn buttons to push to get a reaction out of me. Wiggling from Dax's arms, I face Sterling and place my hands on my hips. "I won't feel bad about bringing you to your knees," I say, locking my gaze to his. I give him a slow once-over, drinking in every inch of his body. "That's where you'd prefer to be anyway."

He chuckles, his face lighting at my insinuation. I can already imagine all the dirty thoughts coursing through his mind. He's shared them enough with me over the last weeks, while trying to seduce me that my vagina tingles in expectation. "Says the woman who loves the idea of my bean tickler getting near that sweet seed that makes your rose bloom." He flicks his tongue between his index and middle finger, getting my filthy-hot imagination to project the fantasy for him.

Fuck. Me. He's right about his comment, and he knows it. Bastien knows it too. He smirks at me from a few feet away, dragging his gaze down my naked body, reminding me exactly how much he enjoyed making me moan and forget the world. Now I can't stop staring at his mouth. How he teases me by gliding his tongue over his bottom lip.

Heat builds between my legs, my damn body declaring my shift in mood. I hate thinking about it, but I know they can all sense it. Smell the chemicals my body releases in what they consider a mouthwatering fragrance that gets them wild.

Everyone stares at me, noticing my reaction. And talk about their bodies pointing it out, because damn. Dax stands close enough behind me that his massive cock grows even more to rise right between my legs as I keep my fighting stance. I clench my thighs together, trapping him in place. He freezes under my gesture and slides his big hand down my stomach, sending an explosion of tingles through my body. I'm pretty damn sure fireworks will crackle and burst to announce just how thrilled my vagina is about the idea of Dax bending me over to screw me from behind. I can imagine it already, feeling his hips hit my ass as he holds me in place. How my leg muscles will tighten as I stretch to plant my palms flat on the ground in front of me. Fuck. I'll probably scream my pleasure so loud that the Mortal World would hear me.

Dax releases a deep, throaty, breathy moan against my ear, his chest grazing mine with his deep breaths. He's fully ready for my word, waiting for me to give in to the fantasy burning through my mind. He doesn't care that we're in the open in front of Sagan, Bastien, and Sterling...and I might not either.

"Damn," Sagan murmurs, shifting closer. He traces his finger from my shoulder to my elbow, getting me to look at him. "Gorgeous, if you have even an ounce of doubt, you might want to take a breath and ease away from Dax. He won't deny your thoughts. None of us would. It's getting too close to mating season."

"You're intoxicating just to stand next to," Bastien adds.

"I'm already drunk as fuck on that sex potion I need to feel dripping from between your legs." Sterling flares his nostrils and sniffs the air. "Come here, blondie. I'll give you what you want. Just let me taste that sweet cream first."

I consider his words way longer than I should, finally shaking the fantasy from my mind as blush burns across my neck and chest.

"Someone needs a cold shower," Bastien says with a laugh. I expect him to push Sterling into the river, but Bastien playfully kicks ice water from the river at me. I squeal and spin away, trying to use Dax as a shield from the freezing water. Dax surprises the hell out of me by diving right in, cooling the hot desire coursing through him. I think Bastien is right. An ice bath is exactly what I need as well.

Howls echo through the air, the call of the packs drawing our attention toward the community once again. If only it didn't turn into a place I'm afraid to return to after everything. It doesn't help that I have no clue what this is about. It couldn't possibly be the games. I'm not sure I even want to find out. I'd prefer to head back to my parents' old den and stay where no one can get to me, since it only opens to me and those loyal to me. Maybe all of my hot emotions and my getting taken from here was a sign that I need to fully embrace my position as pack leader. That I need to give in to my innate she-wolf needs that want me to take things to the next level with each of my pack mates.

"I agree," Sterling says, ruffling his fingers through his hair as he responds to my thoughts. "We should just accept our lives in the den with Lyric, kneeling before her while she yanks my hair as I make her scream by kissing her peach pit."

Sagan growls deep in his throat. "Sterling, we can't. You know we have to return. The leaders will want to speak with Lyric. They've probably been alerted that we've found her by the other competitors."

I bounce on the balls of my feet and turn to Bastien. "Will you go get Caz? I need him to stand beside me. I don't want to face them alone." Because the rest of them can't. They'll have to fall in line with their current packs until the end of the games and the winners are announced. Caz is my only official pack mate, which I thought I'd hate, but he's been so supportive and loyal, acting as the friend I knew and cared about when we worked together at Ripped Fitness.

"I'll be as quick as I can, Ma Belle." Bastien brushes his lips to my cheek and transforms into his beautiful white wolf. His eyes flash gold with the glow of the river water, which is the only thing illuminating the forest around us.

I hug myself, staring at his form disappearing into the trees like a beautiful phantom gliding through the forest to protect the night. He howls once, his call to me stirring my wild emotions. I wish I could follow him and lead the others away from here. I wish I didn't have to separate from Bastien at all.

My heart feels as if it follows him even though I can no longer see him, my she-wolf suddenly desperately craving to take control of my being. I close my eyes, giving in to my need. I don't have to be in my human form to face the leaders. And right now, I want to take on the form my pack mates feel the most powerful. With their strength, I gather even more of my own.

Dax pads his way from the river's edge, his coat damp from changing in the water, and he rubs his body along mine. Sterling circles us before playfully pouncing on me, trying to pin me down. Sagan nudges his nose into my hindquarter, and I yip and dash away, knowing if I don't run, they might start ganging up on me in a game.

"You're going to have to run faster than that, blondie!" Sterling calls into my mind, releasing a yip. "If I catch you, don't think I won't nip your ass. It's still cute, you know."

I bark in response and dart through the trees, weaving around them as I push myself faster. Voices hum through the air the closer we get to the community in the eclectic structure, housing all the packs' competitors in the middle of Lunar Crest.

"Everyone, settle down," Trista, Dax's mom, says, motioning the crowd of guys in human and wolf form. "We knew the possibility of this happening. Lyric was clear about her dissatisfaction with our way of life. Try not to be alarmed. Our best warriors will bring her home."

I slow down, confusion swirling in my mind. And fuck. Anger rushes through me at her words. She thinks I ran away. Probably all of the leaders do...and I can't expect them to think anything more, but the fact that she commanded the fiercest of the packs to drag me back? Ugh.

Sagan circles in front of me. "Antone was supposed to inform them you'd been found...I don't understand."

Sterling releases a low growl, slinking in front of me protectively. A woman yells a moment later, causing the leaders to spin in the direction the voice came from. My hackles prickle, my whole body tensing at the sight of Paige waving her arms and running in the leaders' direction.

"Help! Someone help!" Paige yells. Shit. Did she have witches spell the community or something? Why else wouldn't the leaders know I've been found? Why would she be running like her life depends on it, too?

I don't get much more time to think about it. A roar answers my question, echoing through the forest behind her.

"Oh, shit," I whisper through my mind. I don't believe it.

"Lyric, run," Sagan says, shoving his big head into my chest, herding me back. "We have to go."

But I can't get my paws to work.

I stare in horror as a lycan plows into Paige, knocking her down. But it doesn't stop there. The beast roars and charges forward. It heads straight for the pack leaders, slashing its claws and snapping its frothy jowls.

I close my eyes as it launches into the group of women.

Several scream.

5

WEAKNESS

"SAGAN, GET LYRIC OUT OF here! This is a setup," Dax calls, his voice echoing through my mind. He barrels away from us, ready to tear into the lycans.

Sagan shoves his big wolf head into my side, trying to get me to move. It takes him biting the fur on my neck and dragging me a foot for my mind to focus. I just can't stop staring. I want to see what happens and figure out what the hell Paige is doing. Because she looks like a victim. Did the witches set her up, or is she setting us up for something? I wish I knew.

My heart beats wildly, watching Dax and Sterling dart through the trees toward the lycan. My muscles tense, my mind wanting me to chase after them, but my body remains frozen. Maybe because of the fact that I've faced lycans before or maybe because I don't want to face Paige again, but either way, I need to get my shit together. It's unlike me not to react. My dad would knock some sense into me if he were here.

Sagan whimpers and continues to push me in the opposite direction, far gentler than what I'm used to from growing up with my hard-ass, yet loving, dad. I resist Sagan's pleas, my mind shifting from worry to fury as one of the lycans tosses a competitor a dozen feet.

I growl and snap my teeth at Sagan. "I'm not going anywhere. This asshole can't get away with this."

How dare this creature come into my territory in an attempt to cause harm. I will not run and hide, waiting idly by while a monster goes after the leaders. I might not agree with how they run things, but I sure as shit don't want to see them die. And as for Paige? This was her. I know it. It's the only thing that makes sense. I can't let her actions against me hold me back. I need to face her straight on and show her that she's nothing compared to me.

"Lyric, please," Sagan pleads, shoving his snout under my belly, trying to throw me in the direction of our den without transforming back into a man. He jerks away from my teeth again, turning desperate with my lack of cooperation. "There are enough competitors to handle this. Dax thinks Paige set this up, and if that's true, they will come after you. I've already almost lost you once. I can't bear the thought of it happening again. Feeling your agony, your pain—it was the worst thing in my life. Please don't put me through this."

A whimper escapes my mouth as growls and snarls rip through the air. My heart thumps in erratic beats, my soul wanting to give in to Sagan, but the rest of me knows that if I give in and hide, I might end up hiding for the rest of my life. I've already told the guys how I want to do things, and I can't let them hold me back because of their need to protect me. I understand, because I want to protect them too, but that will get us nowhere. "This is my duty, Sagan. I can fight. You know this, and I need you to accept it. I have to help in any way I can. Look at the leaders. They're defenseless. I will not turn into them. This is our home and territory. The packs need us."

Sagan bares his fangs, his hackles rising. He slinks around me until he repositions himself by my side, flanking me. "Just so you know, it kills me to do this, yet you're so awe-inspiring. I know you're right. I know you can kick ass. But damn it. It's harder than I expected it to be, so I need you to stay close to me. I mean it."

"No, you stay close to me." I launch forward, bolting through the trees in the direction of the community, knowing that Sagan can keep up. He stays near my hindquarters, nudging me to keep me in position instead of trying to slow me down.

Sagan howls when we near the fight, alerting Dax and Sterling that we're coming. I push hard on my paws, letting my wolf have complete control of my movements. My focus narrows on the lycan as it swings its massive claws at Sterling to get him to back off. This beast is huge. Over eight feet, dark knotted fur with claws several inches in length. Its eyes flash green with its movement. If there is a human trapped inside the lycan curse, I can't see them. Their humanity is long gone, their beastly form swallowing them whole.

Snapping its foamy jowls, it searches for an opening in the circle the competitors create around the monster. Two wolves attack from opposite sides, but the lycan spins quickly to knock them away. The guttural, wet noises escaping its muzzle dig under my skin, and its shriek pierces my ears as it tries to barrel through the wolves only to have several competitors bite and tear at the beast's legs and back.

"Go to the leaders. Protect them," Dax commands, his voice snapping through me. I spot him among the group, barking out directions I can't hear. I don't know if the competitors purposely bow to Dax's control because his presence is a force to recognize or if it's because he's the son of Trista, but it's mesmerizing to see him in action. I want that. I want to stand beside him and help.

He breaks away from the circle and risks splitting his attention to peer in my direction, knowing where I head from.

"Please, Lyric. They need you more right now."

He's right. They do. I'll prove to them exactly how much they need me. Maybe then they'll stop the madness and just let me do my own damn thing. Getting almost killed by Paige proves that I can't just go with things. I need to figure out how to change things without making them think I'm trying to rise against them. Proving my worth and capabilities will hopefully do that.

Switching directions, I charge toward the cluster of women taking shelter near the side of the building. They huddle together, their fear palpable. I'm just relieved the younger she-wolves aren't around. I've only seen them once and know they remain separated through the territories, learning from the leaders until they reach maturity and can participate in the games. It's strange to think about, having to give up your daughter to the community to raise as a whole, but I understand the concern in this moment. It still sucks.

I snap out of my thoughts, my mind returning to the frightened leaders. I've never seen such a pathetic sight in my life. The women who came into my dad's fight gym were usually tough as nails or learning to be. They were the type who wouldn't wait idly by to be saved. They were strong and fierce and in control. I wish the younger she-wolves had women like that to look up to here. The thought pushes me forward. Because I'm here. I will be that someone.

Because this is utterly ridiculous. None of the leaders have transformed into their she-wolf forms. They don't try to run either. It's like their fear paralyzes them, and they have no idea what to do.

"They're too afraid to leave the packs," Sagan thinks to me, listening in on my thoughts. He runs so close that we move as one entity, our instincts and connection driving us forward. "They're never the ones to fight. It's always their warriors."

"That has to change," I think with a growl. Because even if they're never the ones fighting, they should know how to protect themselves. This is more clear than ever. The thought reminds me of something my dad always instilled in me. *There will be times in life where the only one you can depend on is yourself. It's up to you to make sure you're capable. Fight hard. Trust your gut. You're just as powerful as any one of these assholes here. Now prove it.* My dad's voice swirls through my mind, a memory of him preparing me for one of my first fights at his gym trickling to the front of my mind. Fuck, I will not let him down. I will prove he raised me into who the packs need despite the bullshit and the circumstances.

"Your dad was a smart man," Sagan says, his body flush against mine, the sensation keeping me focused even while losing myself to my thoughts.

"I miss him. I want to always prove he was right." I need my dad to know he did the best he could in the situation he was in. A part of me is angry that he kept everything a secret from me, but I can't blame him, not with what I know about the elders. If he had, I might have just run away and left the leaders to die. Deep down, I know he wouldn't want that. He didn't do everything he had because he was selfish. He wanted more for everyone. These aren't just women out to control every aspect of my life. They're the mothers of the men who stand beside me. They're just doing what they know, taught by those who came before them, and now I will fight to teach those who come after me. The pack leaders' weakness should end here. Today. I will show them.

Sagan leans into my side, re-directing me to run along the tree line instead of trying to rush through the fight. The wolves continue to close in on the lycan, surrounding it to wear it down. It takes everything in me to run past it and to the leaders. I want so badly to show everyone what I'm capable of.

"Trista," I call, sending my thoughts to Dax's mom, hoping she can be reasoned with enough to get everyone to listen to me. "You have to run. There could be more."

Trista, who stands on the outside of the cluster, turns her attention away from the fight. I barrel toward her and shove my head into her hip, pushing her. Grabbing onto my fur, she tries to force me back while releasing a yelp.

"Lyric, oh my fates, where did you come from?" she asks, her eyes widening. She pulls me closer and steadies herself on my back. "I'm so happy you came back."

I nudge her with my head. "I was kidnapped. I didn't just leave."

"What?" Trista's voice comes in only my mind as I allow her in.

I tip my head to look at her. "You know this. You sent the competitors after me and Antone was supposed to tell you I was found."

Confusion puckers her brows, twisting my stomach in knots. Dax was right. Something is incredibly wrong, and I think Paige might have done something to get into the leaders' heads. She did give everyone something to knock them out. She also had to come from somewhere with the lycans. "Lyric, I—"

"Did you say Lyric?" The breathy voice feels as if it smacks into my chest, knocking my heart free from my ribs to crash into my stomach. I didn't even notice the old woman, cowering within the circle like she belongs here.

Sagan releases a low, threatening growl as Paige peeks from her place sandwiched in the middle of the group of women. It pisses me off that she acts as if she's the one in need of protection from the lycan. I bare my fangs at her and snarl, wishing I could lunge and tear her innards out. I want her to know the lycan is the last of her worries. She's going to have hell to pay from me.

"There's no time to discuss this. Come on. We're getting you out of here." Sagan barks, getting the women's attention. "Head to the river."

"But—"

I nip at Bridgette, Bastien's mom, cutting off her protest. "Now. Sagan and I will ensure you're all safe. Trust us. We can't stay here."

I nudge Simone, Sagan and Sterling's mom next, getting her to move from her spot. Sagan rubs his head against her hip, showing her that he's here and will protect her. It's enough to get the rest of the leaders to follow me. We reach the edge of the forest, and the women undress and transform to follow me through the trees. I can't take my eyes off of Paige, her light coat similar to mine.

She eyes me, her blue gaze searching my wolf form like she's trying to get into my head, but I purposefully block her out. I hate that we're forced to take her with us when I just want to shove her to the lycan. I'll never give her even a crack to get into my head. I bare my fangs in warning, my threat darkening her expression, and wait for her to turn away before I bolt ahead, trusting Sagan to watch my back as he finishes the line, ensuring the leaders keep up.

I head toward the river, listening to Sagan's directions as he helps me navigate the forest. My paws thump against the cool dirt, and I focus on the world in front of me. The sound of rushing water perks my ears up, and I slow down to stop myself from diving in. I suck at swimming as a wolf, my mind and body always seeming to disconnect around water. It doesn't help that I don't know where Sagan plans to take us. I know it's not our den. Most likely to Night Forest, the territory he grew up in with his pack.

Stretching my paws out in front of me, I bow toward the

ground, pleading with my body to hurry up and transform into my human self. The ground shakes under my hands as I dig my fingers into the dirt, pushing through the spasms that steal my breath. It's hard to force my change in this moment. My guard remains up, my she-wolf instincts controlling me.

A loud crack snaps through the air. The ground quivers again, sending a shiver down my back. Sagan growls, hearing the same guttural noise that I do. Fuck. I knew it. I knew there would be more than one lycan.

"Run into the water! Hurry!" Emerson screams, her voice ripping through the air. She chose to follow my lead and transform into a human. Waving her arms, she points at the forest. "It's another cursed beast."

Only half the pack leaders make it into the river when a roar booms over the sound of the rushing water. A tree falls toward us, smashing against the ground a few feet away from me. River water shoots up from the make-shift dam to splash over my back. A lycan stomps through the forest, its heavy weight shaking the ground with its movements and fuck does it move fast. It snarls, bending forward to get on all fours to jump over low branches and scattered boulders in its path. Sagan launches forward, trying to cut the lycan off, but it rises on two legs again. It slices a huge branch from a tree, swinging it like a bat to knock him away.

I cringe and suck in a breath through my teeth. Sagan skids across the riverbank and hits the water, tumbling away from us.

The river washes him a few feet, leaving me without back up. Another roar snaps my attention from Sagan and to the beast.

The lycan drops onto his hands again, running at full speed in our direction. I tense and try to strategize my next move despite the fear coursing through me. This is a new level of pressure. I have no clothes, no weapons, and a bunch of people to protect.

The leaders scream and scatter, trying to get away. With a guttural howl, the lycan shoots upright and swings his arm, catching Svetlana, the leader of the Stargaze Hill pack, by the neck. She screeches and flails, her blood spattering across the pebbly bank as she tries to break free of the lycan.

"No!" Charging forward, I dodge around the massive beast and sweep my leg out to knock it off balance. Pain swells in my tender ankle, the move feeling as if I just tried to knock down a metal pole bolted to the ground. The beast doesn't even budge, but it's enough to jerk its attention to me. Craning its neck, it glances at me. I don't have to know what the beast thinks to know it considers me more of a threat than the weak woman he holds.

It roars and throws Svetlana a dozen feet into the air, sending her splashing into the river water. The lycan jerks its arm back, trying to slice me with its dagger claws as it spins around to face me. I drop and roll out of the way, his large, tall frame making it harder for him to get to me at a low level. A growl hums from the other side of the lycan, drawing its attention from me and to where Harlow snarls in her tri-colored wolf form. She fakes him out, lunging toward it but keeping out of its reach.

"Lyric, stay down," Sagan calls, jumping over me in a blur.

Colliding into the lycan's back, he knocks it onto its hands. The lycan scratches the ground, leaving huge claw marks. Sagan balances on the beast's back and sinks his teeth into the lycan's coarse fur, ripping a chunk of its flesh free. Sagan jumps to the ground as it straightens up to tower over everyone. Darting between the lycan's legs to skid right back around, he snaps at the monster's stomach, aiming to rip out its organs.

I take advantage of the lycan's distraction and make a running jump at its back. I dig my nails into the beast's hairy shoulders and squeeze its torso with my knees, clinging on as tightly as I can as it spins around. Sagan continues to attack, biting onto the lycan's leg. Swinging my arm around its throat, I use all my strength to cut off its airway. The beast jams its claws in my arms. I gasp and yell out in pain, but my body refuses to let go. If I let go, I'll land on my back. If that happens, the beast will surely tear out my insides.

"His eyes," Sagan says in my mind. He growls with the thought. "Blind that asshole. Whatever it takes."

Keeping one arm around the beast's thick neck to hang on, I use my other hand to claw at its face until my finger pokes one of the lycan's eyes. It roars and flails, pounding its hands into the ground and bucking its body like a bull to throw me off.

But I refuse to let go. I can't let this fucker hurt anyone else, nor can I risk it getting away. "Stop fighting and tell me who sent you, and I'll consider sparing your life," I yell, grinding my teeth through the pain of his claws swiping against my bare sides. I hate so much that I'm completely naked, feeling his hairy body in all the places I don't want it near.

The lycan growls. "I'm going to kill you, bitch."

I cringe at the rumbly, gurgle of the lycan's voice cutting through the air. I had forgotten how freaky it was that these half-men, half-beasts can talk. Or that they don't have any genitals because they spread the curse to humans who manage to survive an attack through their bites.

"Again, gorgeous. The other eye this time," Sagan commands, launching at the lycan's exposed stomach to sink his teeth into the soft, hairy flesh.

I do as he says and poke my finger into the lycan's other eye, feeling the warmth of blood trickling over my finger. I shudder at the sensation and the ear-piercing shriek escaping the lycan's mouth. His pain sets him off, making him fight harder, desperately. The lycan throws his body forward toward the river with me clinging to his back. I automatically let go of him, but I'm not quick enough. We splash in the water together, me landing within arm's reach. And fuck.

Green flashes across the lycan's gaze, and he snarls and launches at me. I try my best to swim away, but he's just as powerful in the water as he is out of it. Crashing into me, the lycan forces my head under, locking me in place. Panic squeezes my chest, my inability to breathe stealing all my fighting sense.

"Lyric, dive!" Sagan yells through my mind. "Dive and let the gateway take you both. I'm coming."

Opening my eyes underwater, I focus on the glowing light flickering around me. I've never gone through one of the magical gates that will take us to another territory in Lulupoterra alone. But I have to do something. I'll drown otherwise.

I throw my body forward, pulling the lycan down instead of trying to force my way up. A strange flash of blue light engulfs me, and a figure materializes in front of me underwater. I freeze at the blurry face of Flynn, his surprise arrival making me inhale a breath of the river. My lungs scream, and I thrash, the edges of my vision shadowing.

"Take my hand." Flynn's voice enters my mind, the sudden intrusion unexpectedly filling me with relief.

I stretch my arm through the water until Flynn laces his fingers through mine. Tugging me to him, he cups my cheeks and gets so close that he's all I see. His lavender eyes flicker with magic, impossibly lighting with electricity even underwater.

"I need to kiss you," he says, his voice growing softer in my mind. "Will you let me?"

My strength fades with my lack of oxygen, my mind whirling yet my body unable to do anything.

"Lyric, hey. Lyric, hold on." Flynn's voice swirls through my mind.

He leans in close, his lavender eyes lighting the river around us, the current freezing, keeping us in place as if the water turns to jelly. Leaning in, Flynn presses his mouth to mine, and a zing of electricity crackles to my very core. The shock makes me heave, and water expels from my lungs as if Flynn sucks it out of me. And then he chants something my mind can't grasp and a bubbles dance around us. Air fills my lungs, and I gasp a breath, startled, fear speeding my heartrate in a collection of discordant beats. This should be impossible. I shouldn't be able to breathe while being suspended in the river.

"Nothing is impossible," Flynn says into my mind. "Now grab the lycan and kick to the surface. Tell no one I was here, understand? You can't trust anyone."

The water shudders with Flynn's disappearance, sending me toward the surface without me even having to swim. I clutch onto the hairy body of the unmoving lycan, realizing that because I took him under with me, he drowned.

"There she is! Fuck, hurry Caz. She's floating your way." Sagan's voice echoes through the air.

Something splashes into the river, and warm arms encircle my waist from behind. "Shit, Lyric. Let the lycan go. Come on. I got you." Caz's voice hums in my ear, his warm breath tickling my skin.

When I'm not quick enough to release the beast, Caz pries my hands from it and spins me around to face him. Hooking one arm around my waist, he swims one-handed, kicking his strong legs to send us to shore. My legs refuse to work even when my feet touch the pebble bottom, and Caz lifts me in his arms like a blushing bride.

He combs his fingers through my hair to pull it out of my face. "Fuck, Lyric. Can you look at me?"

I blink my eyes, clearing the haze from my vision. Water drips down Caz's forehead, the strands of his hair plastering to his face. His brows furrow together as he searches my eyes, trying to figure out if I'm injured.

"It's going to be okay," Caz says, adjusting my icy body in his warm arms. "You're safe. The lycan is dead. You killed it, you badass. I'm so fucking proud of you. I knew since the moment I met you at Ripped Fitness that you would always put up one helluva fight."

I lick my lips, trying to replay what the hell happened in the river through my mind, but Caz's words draw my attention to him. I inhale a few small breaths, trying to get my shit together. Reaching up, I caress my fingers to Caz's mouth, his soft smile stealing all my attention. Dozens of voices hum through the air, at least ten guys say my name and ask how I am. But I can't bring myself to look around or to answer them. I can't do anything except stare at Caz's mouth. I'm afraid if I look away from his pouty lips, my mind will betray me and project something I haven't had time to think about.

"Please say something, Lyric," Caz murmurs, his nerves trickling through me. "Are you okay? You're blocking me out."

I swallow, my throat and lungs aching from inhaling the

river water only to have Flynn draw it out of me. And fuck. He saved my life again. How did he find me? What was he doing here? Why does he think I shouldn't tell anyone about him? The questions flit through my mind over and over again.

I just want them to stop. I want the commotion around me to quiet down. "I—I need—"

"Caz, my son. Please bring Lyric to the leader den," a woman says, her sultry voice familiar to my ears. It's Caz's mom Viviana, the pack leader of Meadow View. She leans into me, her striking red hair veiling the two of us as she plants a kiss to my forehead. "I'm so happy you're safe. I knew you wouldn't have abandoned my son like the others thought."

I purse my lips, trying to get my voice to work. "I was kidnapped, stabbed, and left to die."

Her eyes widen, and she looks at Caz. "Is that so?"

"You don't believe me?" I ask, anger swelling through me. It's like with Trista. Whatever Paige did or the lycans or whatever seems to have messed with their memory.

She presses her lips together without responding to me. "Please hurry, my son. It's imperative we don't keep the others waiting."

I open my mouth to yell at Viviana for flat-out ignoring my question, but she turns on her feet and struts away. A million thoughts swirl through my mind. I mean, what in the actual fuck? What do the leaders even want? I've been through complete hell and just want to return to my damn pink room in

Lunar Crest for a bubble bath, something hot to eat, and an extreme cuddle session. The last thing I want is to face the women who can't even take care of themselves while they twist some story about me and why I disappeared.

Caz groans in my ear, flipping me around to face him. I automatically wrap my legs around his waist, my heated flesh pressing into his abs. He flares his nostrils at the sensation, realizing what he's done without thinking about it first. He's been especially careful the last few weeks to make sure I'm comfortable around him as we both try to re-build the friendship we had in the Mortal World.

His Adam's apple bobs, and he tries to shift me, but my legs refuse to let go. And then I rest my head on his shoulder and breathe against his neck, inhaling a few breaths of his scent to help settle my nerves.

"Your thoughts are racing," he finally says, adjusting his arms carefully around me to hold me since I don't let him go. "Will you take a breath with me? I know you're on edge and the world is turning into a big-ass shitshow, but I want you to know that I have your back. I will not stand idly by and let them make up reasons why all of this happened. We will confront Paige."

I ease away from his shoulder to meet his soft brown eyes. "I'm going to kill her."

Caz's jaw twitches, his muscles flexing at my words. "We need to figure out what the hell she's doing here first."

I sigh and rest my forehead to his, surprising him with my

closeness. "Why do you have to be such a sensible bastard? Sterling would go charging in with me."

He chuckles, the vibration of his voice tickling my lips. "I guess I should prepare for a lifetime of getting both your asses out of trouble then."

I twist my lips and nod, making his smile widen. "I'm glad I can count on you."

A wave of heartfelt emotions wraps around me, flooding from Caz to me as his state of mind morphs from worry to happiness and relief, the sensation as if we snuggle under a warm blanket as bare as we are now, sharing a part of our souls. I can't help reaching out and running my fingers over his cheek. He tilts his head, getting me to sink my fingers harder to his skin like he loves just the weight of my touch.

I smile, finding my body leaning closer, something raw and real about this moment drawing me to Caz in a different way than ever before. His smile fades, his brown eyes darkening as he loses himself in my gaze, in the rising curiosity that has me remembering the one time we kissed and how much I've changed since that moment, how I'm no longer angry at him for things out of his control in the Mortal World or even his reasoning for putting his name down for a chance to win a spot on my pack.

Rubbing my lips together, I close the space, my sudden need to kiss him overwhelming me. His hands tighten around me, and he closes his eyes, puckering his lips, not meeting me halfway but waiting for me to do it on my own.

If only a howl didn't cut through the air before a hulking brown and white wolf pads its way from the forest. Caz groans and pulls away with a sigh, his annoyance mirroring mine. Caz struts forward, following the wolf's silent—at least to me—command.

The forest thins out into a quaint community completely surrounded by tall, dense trees that look similar to red cedars of the Mortal World. It takes my mind a second to realize we're no longer in Lunar Crest. I thought I was breaking the surface there, but this place is darker, the forest denser. Without having to ask Caz, I know it's Sagan and Sterling's childhood community.

Except it lacks the warmth and happiness I expect it to.

A strange somberness clings to everything, and I twist in Caz's arms to peer around, noticing dozens of wolves gathered, lying on the ground with their heads resting on the forest floor.

I spot Dax, Sterling, and Bastien among the wolves, and my heart sinks into my stomach. Sagan strolls from a structure carved within a massive tree trunk and heads in our direction, offering me a robe.

Caz sets me on my feet, and I dress and hug myself, unable to keep my gaze away from the wolves. There are far more here than those who compete in the She-Wolf Games.

"What is everyone doing?" I whisper, automatically reaching for both Caz and Sagan's hands.

Sagan squeezes my fingers, his sadness washing through me. "We're mourning the loss of Svetlana of Stargaze Hill. The injuries from the lycan were too great."

Oh, no. My chest clenches, the wave of sorrow permeating through the wolves stealing my breath. I thought I saved her. I thought I stopped the lycan in time.

"You fought harder than anyone I've ever seen," Sagan says, keeping his voice low. "Look at your arms and your own injuries, and you still managed to kill the lycan. Do not blame yourself."

"I can't help it. Paige...she did this. She did this because of me," I say, clenching my nails into my palms. Now that Sagan mentions the scratches on my arms, my body chooses this moment to complain.

"What do you mean?" Trista's voice draws my attention to her, waiting within a doorway carved into another gigantic tree.

I straighten my shoulders. "Paige is responsible for this bullshit. She's also responsible for kidnapping me and leaving me to die in the Mortal World."

Trista frowns. "Oh, Lyric. I think there's been a misunderstanding. Paige would never harm you. It was the witches of the Fire Mountain Clan. Now come join us. You need to hear everything for yourself."

6

CLEANSE

I LEAN MY BACK AGAINST Caz's chest as we sit on the floor of a circular room carved within a huge tree. The scent of wood, spices, and something more feral—warm musk, maybe—permeates the air. There is barely enough room for everyone. The nine remaining pack leaders, me along with Harlow and Emerson, one pack mate to accompany each of us, and then Paige.

It is so strange to be together with these women as they gather for what I imagine is a meeting that involves what the hell happened and what happens next. I wish Dax, Bastien, Sterling, and Sagan could be here to join us, but I guess it'll always only be one of my pack mates supporting me in these kinds of situations.

"If everyone agrees to the temporary shift in control of Stargaze Hill to Paige, we will notify Svetlana's pack mates," Simone says, leading the meeting because this is her territory. There are so many customs and politics involved in maintaining peace among the territories that I'm unsure if I'll ever fully grasp any of it.

My hand shoots up before my mind has a chance to process what the hell I'm doing. Everyone's eyes turn to me, and I grip onto Caz's legs to try to summon every ounce of his support.

"Please save your commentary until the vote is finalized," Bridgette says, keeping her voice even. "We will discuss your circumstances next. It is important that Stargaze Hill knows that they will not be abandoned in this heartbreaking time."

"But I don't agree," I say, the sharpness of my voice snapping through the room. "Paige is full of shit, and I demand you punish her for her crimes against me."

Several of the leaders gasp in surprise, and one of the younger ones from the last She-Wolf Games even growls. I straighten my back, not letting them intimidate me. They're like miniature poodles compared to the vicious beasts I've faced. It's nearly laughable that they think they're tough, considering I'm the one who helped save their asses.

"Crimes against *you*?" This comes from a hulking man standing against the wall behind Caz's mom. "It's your fault Svetlana is dead. You should've never led our she-wolves into danger like that."

My muscles tense at his words. "Are you fucking kidding me?"

"Son, get your damn mate under control before she embarrasses our bloodline," he snaps at Caz, ignoring me.

And oh-fucking-hell-no.

I launch from the floor, fisting my hands, preparing to get into Caz's dad's face. A collection of growls hum through the air, and another man grabs Caz's dad's arm, stopping him from closing the space to me at the same time Caz hooks his arm around my stomach. I jerk my elbow back and clock Caz in the stomach for intercepting me. He groans under his breath but doesn't let me go.

"You will not blame me for this bullshit!" My voice rises with my annoyance. "It was Paige who brought the damn lycans into my territory. She—"

"It's not your territory yet," another man says, stepping forward to try to intimidate me with his towering frame.

"If that's the fucking case, then screw you and your games." I struggle against Caz's grip on me. "I'm leaving. Try and stop me, asshole."

"Lyric, please. We will get this figured out," Caz says, speaking into my mind. He tries to fill me with calmness, but the tension in the room is too great. I'm too angry. Annoyed. In serious need of kicking a bunch of cocks.

"Get her in line, Caz!" the guy shouts.

Caz growls, his chest heaving against my spine. "Then back the fuck off and shut up. You're helping no one. This isn't your place. She's mine and I have her."

Stomping closer, the man ignores Caz's threat and tries to get in my face. "You obviously don't know how to tame your bitch."

Jerking my foot up, I kick him in his weak, flaccid cock as hard as I can. He drops to the ground and clutches his junk.

"Get in our faces again and your balls will end up inside you next," I threaten, my body buzzing with the adrenaline of knowing I put him in his damn place. "If you dare think my place is beneath the leader position I've been given, then your leader needs to get your ass in place, you fuckhead."

Caz groans. "Lyric, please. Please, just let it go. We will handle this together another way." His soft voice trickles into my mind again, and he pulls me back protectively as the man pushes up.

Caz's words do nothing for the wave of fury cresting over me. I don't even know why anyone here bothers with pretending the she-wolves are in charge, because obviously most of these hot-headed assholes think they have a right to speak on behalf of the supposed leaders.

I shake my head at Caz. "No, I will not stand here, be

blamed for the death of a leader instead of thanked for doing something these douches can't even accomplish. They allow this traitor woman to come waltzing in here with a bullshit story about escaping the witches who supposedly only temporarily killed her to steal her from this place. It's screwed up." The more I think about Paige's story, the angrier I get. "She drugged you all with wolfsbane and bloodroot, muzzled me and chained me like a prisoner, and then stabbed me with poison and left me to die in the Mortal World."

"I told you, my dear niece. It wasn't me. It must've been witchcraft. Someone messing with your head. A doppelganger disguised as me." Paige waves her hand up and down in my direction. "Show us your stomach and the wounds you claim I inflicted."

I tighten my mouth, glowering at her. This damn bitch.

"You can't, can you? Because it never happened," Paige says, remaining expressionless. Her eyes remain locked on mine as she dares me to argue with something I have absolutely no proof to show otherwise. "And I'm so sorry you struggle to grasp this. I know the Mortal World really ruined your ability to see things as they are, and it's okay. I will help you through this. We are all here for you now as it should've always been."

"Liar!" I scream, trying to break free of Caz. I don't care if I look or sound or act crazy. I won't let her manipulate me. "You won't get away with this!"

"Oh, Lyric," Viviana says, her face frowning with sympathy.

"Please, settle down."

I clench my body and scream. "You have to listen to me!"

I can't believe this is happening. I can't believe people actually believe her.

"Caz, get her out of here until she calms down. She's most likely experiencing residual effects of the magic used on her," Paige says, pouting her bottom lip while looking to the leaders. "I know what it's like to be spelled, and it will take time for her soul to mend."

"And have Bastien give her a thorough exam and cleanse. She needs to be ready for tomorrow's games." Trista gets to her feet and straightens out her robe. Glancing at Harlow and Emerson, she adds, "The same goes for you two. Rest up."

Bridgette touches Trista's arm. "Are you sure we should proceed so soon?"

Trista stares at me. "It's more imperative than ever. The games must go on."

"I don't need a cleanse or whatever the hell the leaders insisted on," I say, pacing around a glowing pool in the middle of a sauna-like room.

Steam fills the air, leaving my skin damp. It's hot as fuck, which doesn't exactly make me want to get into the warm pool. I don't care how pretty the water looks or how Sterling already sits on the seat, naked and glistening, his platinum hair sticking to his forehead. I'd prefer a dip in the icy river over this.

Dax scrubs his face, his expression remaining somber. He's not happy about any of this. Neither is Sagan. It probably doesn't help that they feel my horrendous mood much more intensely than the others, which makes me feel even worse.

Sagan snatches my hand, spins me toward him, and hoists me onto his shoulder, trapping my arms. I thrash in annoyance, his plan trickling through my mind before he even tosses me into the pool. He's far too fast about it. The only thing I can do is suck in a deep breath as the strangely thick liquid, which definitely isn't water, cocoons me, slowing down my movements.

Two arms slide under me and lift me to the surface. I gasp a breath and smack my hand against the jelly-like water, sending it pelting across Sagan. He flares his nostrils, narrowing his eyes at me. Sterling locks me in place from behind, silently resting his chin on my shoulder, his body sliding against mine as he struggles to keep me in place.

"A bit faster, bro," Sterling says, flexing his muscles. "She's fucking strong as hell when she's in a bad mood. Not to mention I'm about to bend her ass over, because damn. She feels so good, all slippery and warm. I bet this is exactly what her love tunnel feels like."

Sagan stands in front of me, his stomach touching mine, his mouth close enough to kiss, but he doesn't try. I'm the meat in this distractingly sexy man sandwich, and my body decides now to disobey me and relax.

"Get that dirty mind of yours in check, blondie," Sterling

murmurs, his cock hardening without any place to go except between my legs. "If you set Sagan off, there's going to be a sword battle for that tiny space between your thighs, and I can't promise not to accidentally go in. This pool is like straight lube."

Oh. My. Fuck.

I clench my legs together, trapping his cock in place. Sagan remains flush against me, testing my resolve while silently begging for my attention despite his brother. Licking his lips, Sagan clutches my face between his palms and rests his forehead to mine. No one speaks, but I listen to the soft footsteps of Dax, Bastien, and Caz joining us in the cleansing pool.

And then I'm surrounded.

The comforting silence engulfs the six of us, the room feeling as if it's the only place left in the entire universe. My heart thrums against Sagan's chest, his closeness filling my senses. I can't resist closing the space to his mouth and brush my lips to his, just savoring the sensation of our bodies buzzing.

"The cleansing pool isn't what it sounds like," Bastien says, breaking the silence. "This is a place of reflection, bonding, and healing. Somewhere only for the leaders and their mates. Like you, this is our first time here."

"And technically, only Caz should be here." Dax brushes his fingers along my bare shoulder. "But no one will check in on you."

Sagan searches my eyes. "What we make of it is up to you, but it's our job to ensure your spirit lightens. Your anger is intense and consuming."

"So take advantage of our sausage fest. I have a feeling shit's going to get harder around here, and not the good kind of hard. My mother asked if I'd volunteer as a guardian on the nights I have to be away from you, which means the she-wolves will be monitored even more." Sterling trails his fingers higher up my stomach like he can't resist exploring my body every chance I let him. "Which will be a huge fucking downer. I don't want to hear anyone but you and one of these assholes get it on if I can't spend the night wearing you down with my seduction."

I tip my head back to try to look at him upside down. "You better be joking."

"Getting off on even the sound of your pleasure is no joking matter, blondie." Sterling tries to bump his hips against my ass, testing whether or not I'll loosen my thigh's grip on his cock to let him tease me.

I do, but only to turn around. "That's not what I'm talking about."

Flattening my palms on his chest, I keep a few inches of space between us, knowing that he'll try to close it completely otherwise, his horny ass dying to tease me until I give in...which makes me just want to play hard to get even more. I've thought about banging him at lease a hundred times, but then I worry he'll flip from having fun to giving me his soul, and I'm already responsible for Dax and Sagan's. I just—I'm not ready.

Sterling lifts an eyebrow, and I realize he listens to my

thoughts because I'm too emotional to filter things. "Stop overthinking shit. We can still have fun without the soul-bonding if that's what you're hung up on. I don't need to claim you. What I need is to slip my hotdog into your delicious furless burger buns and satiate that burning curiosity of yours."

I laugh, unable to remain serious. Sterling knows which buttons to press to pull me out of a bad mood. "*My* curiosity?"

"Mmmhmm." He hums under his breath, ignoring the fact that we're not alone, despite the quietness of the others as they give us a bit of pretend-privacy.

It never fails to amaze me how they can all do it. They can always sense what and who I need in a situation. And Sterling's ridiculous comments always cure me from losing myself to the bullshit. It's hard to remain serious with his absurd playfulness.

"You want to know what it would be like if I stretched your leg up right now and pushed my cock in balls deep." Sterling grins with his words as they send electricity between my legs to shoot through the rest of me. And the cocky-ass bastard. I might not have been thinking about it before, but now I am. Damn.

"Damn is right," Sagan murmurs from behind me. He reaches over my shoulder and holds his fist out to Sterling. They bump them together. "Nice way to work her up for me, brother, considering it's my game to win."

"No more of that shit," I say, wondering how the hell I'm going to survive a future of high-fives, playful punches, and damn fist bumps when the two of them feel the need to celebrate their victories in regards to me.

"The two of us? Hah, no, blondie. You bet your tight little ass that we'll be chanting *teamwork makes her cream work* in no time." Sterling stretches his mouth into a grin, his smile seriously getting to me in the best way. It's brilliant, dazzling even. My vagina tingles at the fantasy he sneaks into my mind, and now I can't help but want to know exactly what pack mate love feels like. Because this brotherly love is so sweet and strangely hot.

Fuck. Me.

"My pleasure," Sterling teases, responding to my thoughts. "Bend your knee up a bit, and I'll do the rest."

With a groan, I sink lower until the bizarrely thick water of the pool engulfs me, silencing the world. It does nothing to cool me off, but it does help loosen my tense muscles. Prickles spark across every inch of my skin, and I hover beneath the surface, waiting for my racing heart to chill the hell out.

Ten hands each pick a part of my body and gently guide me until I lie horizontally and break through the surface. Goose-bumps sprinkle over my skin, and I float with my face and breasts out of the water as the five of them support me to ensure I don't sink under. My nipples tighten in both cold and excitement, and I savor the warmth their appreciation of my body brings. I feel incredibly sexy, even in goo, and I love every second of it.

Caz cradles my head, massaging his fingers into my temples and next to my ears, getting me to loosen my clenched jaw. I stare up at him, drinking in the sight of his chocolaty eyes as he stares at me, giving me all of his attention. Our moment from earlier flashes to the forefront of my mind, and I trail my gaze down to his lips, wondering if I'd feel the same incredible spark I feel when kissing the others now that our minds are open and my guard is down.

"I'd like to find out later, Lyric," Caz thinks to me, smiling. "Just you thinking about it makes me so incredibly happy."

I smile and bite my lip. "I'd like that."

"Yeah?" He's so cute, reminding me of how flirty our friendship used to be in the Mortal World.

"Mmmhmm. Just steal a moment alone with me. I don't want any cheering," I tease.

Dax taps his fingers to my wrist, drawing my attention to him. "You don't have to steal a moment alone with any of us ever. All you have to do it say something."

I blush, realizing that I was so caught up with Caz and comfortable that everyone heard our conversation.

"And it's taking everything in me not to comment. I mean, what if he needs our moral support?" Sterling asks, his voice trickling into my mind this time.

I stick my tongue out at him without comment and everyone continues to massage my body, igniting utter bliss through me. Dax and Sagan stand at my sides, stretching my arms out. Each of them works their hands over my muscles, kneading away the knots in my shoulders. Massaging my calves and feet, Bastien and Sterling complete the circle around me, and I close my eyes and savor the sensation of what it's like to have such support around me.

I know it's only been a few weeks since we've met, and part of that time I've spent fighting and resisting, but this moment suddenly feels significant. These men choose to stay at my side, lifting me up and treating me as if I'm the most important woman in the world to them. None of them has even mentioned my confrontation with the leaders, but without even having to ask, I know they understand and empathize with the situation. They validate my feelings instead of brushing them off.

"This is so much better now, isn't it, Ma Belle?" Bastien asks, keeping his voice low as to not disturb the tranquility filling my soul. "How do you feel?"

I lick my lips, tasting the strange glowing residue clinging to my skin. "Like I can win the games...like I *will* win the games."

"I'd love that," Sagan murmurs, bringing my hand up to nuzzle his cheek to it. "Being the mate of the first-ever she-wolf to win the games and award me with a day-claim...the competitors will be jealous as fuck."

Sterling works his hands up to my knee, gently stretching my leg out of the water to kiss my calf. "Ah, shit. I guess I have to convince you to pick me instead. Sagan can swap with me. He owes me a favor anyway."

"Hmm, maybe I'll just win the games myself and enjoy Ma

Belle a bit more. Today wasn't enough for me." Bastien smiles teasingly. "What do you say?"

I grin. "You can try, but don't be disappointed when I cross the finish line alone."

"Uh-oh, gorgeous. It sounds like you want to actually play for real. No rigging or cheating or rotating, huh?" Sagan pokes my bottom lip. "I'm game. What about the rest of you?"

"If that's what you all want," Dax says, smirking a cocky-bastard grin, loving the idea of a challenge. "The leaders waived the no-repeat day-claims this round because of the postpone-ment, so I'm happy to win."

I laugh and sit up, allowing them to surround me in a tight circle. Their naked bodies brush mine, sending excitement rush-ing through me. "I think we should add a little bit to the com-petition to make sure you all try your hardest. Because I won't go easy on you."

The five of them smirk at me, and Sterling says, "Winner gets to bang you?"

I laugh and wag my finger at him. "I was thinking some-thing along the lines of all you losers giving me a show."

Dax play-growls under his breath. "It's on. You're going to owe me one helluva show, Lyric. Lap dance, striptease, some self-love after, the works."

I laugh. "I guess we'll see, huh?"

Sagan captures me and lifts me onto his shoulder, flashing my ass to everyone. Dax takes advantage of Sagan holding me in place and spanks my ass cheek. Bastien kisses the same spot, and I laugh and crack up. Squirming, I nearly slip off and back into the water. I hate to admit it, but the cleansing pool did help my mood...but I'm sure the guys would've succeeded regardless.

The six of us rinse off in the showers, taking our time to enjoy our privacy from the outside world. If only the door didn't swing open. If only Paige didn't barge in, her soft, weathered features turning into a scowl at the sight of me.

I launch at her without thinking.

I attack.

7

WITCH DEBT

THE WORLD FREEZES AROUND ME, a bright blue light stealing my vision. I stare wide-eyed at Paige squeezing her eyes shut beneath me. My fist remains stuck a few inches from her face, and I try to pull it back, but something strange locks me in place. Panic rises through me, stealing my breath. What. The. Hell.

"Here, let me help you, she-wolf," Flynn says, his frame shifting to block out the light from the edge of my vision. He touches me on the shoulder, sending energy across my skin. The heavy invisible weight locking me in place eases off, and Flynn catches my wrist before I punch Paige in the nose.

With a tug, he pulls me to my feet. A towel materializes in his other hand, and he offers it to me. I glower at the warlock as I wrap my body in the soft fabric and peer around the room. Not only does Paige remain frozen on the ground where I knocked her off her feet, but the guys also stand stiff and unmoving behind me, all in various positions as if someone hit the pause button as they were rushing to my side.

I spin around and smack Flynn in the shoulder. "Let them go! You can't come in here and start throwing your damn magic around like this is your home."

Flynn tightens his jaw, his eyes roving over Dax, Sterling, Sagan, Bastien, and Caz like he intends to imprint them into his mind. "I think instead of yelling at me, perhaps you should thank me for stopping you from doing something you would regret."

"I would never—and I mean, fucking never—regret pummeling the psycho she-wolf who stabbed me. I don't know what the hell is going on, but she has the leaders convinced that I'm losing my mind because of something a witch did. If the leaders won't do anything, I will." I ball my hands into fists and inhale a few deep breaths.

Flynn shifts on his feet and stares at Paige for a long moment, not responding to my words. He runs his fingers through his hair, messing up the wild chestnut strands even more. His lavender eyes flash with a crackle of magic, and I wonder what I'd have to do to get him to release the guys. I don't like standing in this weird state, unsure of if time passes or not.

"So, this is the woman who tried to kill you?" Flynn asks, finally responding.

I groan and scrub my hands to my cheeks. "Why do you sound like you don't believe me?"

He flicks his gaze to me and purses his lips. "Oh, I believe you. I just—I don't believe this whole situation. She bears the mark of a witch debt, which means you need to stay away from her, understand? If you hurt her, there will be consequences, and I don't know you well enough to want to deal with them."

I furrow my brows in confusion. "Why are you even here? You know my mates are after you, right? I should fucking tackle you and hand you over."

"But you won't." He smirks as he says the words. "I overheard you plead with the wolves to spare me, even knowing the risk. It was awfully kind, coming from the woman who wanted to bite my face off. I wasn't sure such a gesture was possible."

"Now I'm not so sure that wasn't a mistake." I cross my arms and shuffle back a few steps, getting closer to Dax, who sure as hell would've been the first to reach me. I purposely bump into him, seeing if it'll break whatever the hell this spell is.

Flynn waves his hand at me, sending a bolt of purple

electricity at my hand. It shocks me, startling me, and I hop back and shake out my arm.

"Not so fast, she-wolf. You and I need to talk." Flynn steps closer, and he trains his gaze on mine, though I catch him checking me out in only the towel. His rugged, masculine features aren't so different than some of the men here, and I can't stop myself from thinking about how fit he looked without his shirt. How I wanted to trace the geometrical lines of his tattoos, ones I notice peek from his collar. I didn't notice the ones on the inside of his arms before, but now that I do, I want a better look at them too. I wonder where else he has them and if he'll show me...

What am I even thinking?

"The only thing I want to talk about is how the hell you got here and why you're here. Why did you help me in the river? What is it that you want?" Because he's mentioned magic costing a price—exactly what? I don't think I want to find out. I still can't get the vision of my dad getting hauled away out of my mind—the cost of the protection spell used on me being his freedom and basically his life.

"Would you believe me if I told you it was out of the goodness of my heart?" Flynn asks, inching even closer. His cautious bravado tempts me to react how he expects—wild and on guard, ready to pummel him, but his soft lavender eyes make me resist.

Instead, I scoff and get into my fighting stance, spreading my legs to give me better balance. "Do you think I'm stupid?"

"No, I think you're naïve," he replies, waving his arm at me. "A bit in over your head. Overly trusting. You call these guys your mates, but I only sense a soul link with two of them, and it's not as strong as I'd expect it to be coming from you. You're unsure of the whole thing, which I can't blame you. You did say you grew up in the Mortal World."

Annoyance rushes through me as he dissects my life like it's any of his business. I might not know everything, but I'm not naïve. "You act as if you know everything when you had no idea that the wolves of Lulupoterra were still around, so why don't you release my mates, take your know-it-all ass attitude out of here, and—"

Flynn's eyes widen, and he disappears from view in a flash of blinding light. The world shifts and shakes, and I watch in surprise as Paige disappears too. The world suddenly clicks back on, and I can't even brace myself before Dax crashes into me. Spinning midair, he takes the brunt of the fall onto his back, protectively holding me to him.

"What the fuck?" he mutters, squeezing me against his broad chest as I stare up at the sky outside the room. "What happened?"

"Tell him Paige has a witch debt." Flynn's voice trickles into my mind. "She used it to get away."

"How the hell would I know that?" I respond, realizing a little too late that I've said the words out loud.

"Shit. I think Paige has a debt to a witch," Sagan says,

holding his arms out to help me off Dax and to my feet. "It would explain her blinking out of existence."

"What does that even mean?" I shift on my feet, clutching my towel.

"It means she made some sort of bargain in exchange for something. If it's something costly, like freedom or some shit, the witch will protect their future investment, AKA Paige." Sterling comes up beside me and bunches the front of my towel in his hand. "But that's not as important as my question...where the hell did the towel come from?"

I blink a few times. "Uh—"

"You don't know," Flynn says, once again speaking into my mind.

I squeeze my eyes shut, trying to push his presence from my head. It freaks me the fuck out that he can do such a thing.

"The spell's a hit or miss. You're more receptive to me, probably because I saved your life, so you instinctively allow me in." Flynn responds to my thoughts, reminding me of the first few days here, and how everyone could hear exactly what was on my mind. It's annoying as hell.

"Bastien, give her another exam. Make sure she's not marked," Sagan says, nudging my shoulder. "She seems kind of out of it."

"Caz, Sterling, come with me. Let's search the area as discretely as possible. If the leaders didn't believe Lyric the first time, they might not now, but we can't take our chances.

Whatever the hell Paige is up to involves Lyric and now the rest of us." Dax stretches his muscular arms above his head, preparing to transform into his mahogany wolf form.

I jerk my hand out and grab his wrist. "Don't do anything that could get you in trouble. She's mine to handle, understand?"

Dax narrows his eyes and growls at me. "Your overprotectiveness is testing me, so you know."

I laugh in exasperation. "Get used to it. I take your safety seriously." I turn to look at each of them. "That goes for all of you. Now be careful out there, okay? I want you all to be in good shape for the games."

Leaning in, Dax kisses me softly, pulling my body to his by my lower back.

I nearly laugh as Sterling gets behind him, waiting his turn for a kiss. Sterling squeezes my ass and lifts me off my feet, spinning me around. And then the cocky bastard smacks my ass. He laughs and dodges out of the way, avoiding my retaliation. With a stretch, he transforms into a wolf and howls.

I roll my eyes and turn to Caz, realizing he's waiting for my attention before he goes. I curl my index finger at him with a smirk, motioning for him to come closer. Unlike the others, who've already grown used to showering me with affection, Caz still remains cautious. And I appreciate it. Having the leaders pick him out as my mate without my consent really got to me. He might've put his name in for the chance to be with me, but in the end, it was the leaders who were responsible.

I open my arms for Caz and hug him, tipping my head back to lock into his eyes. "Will you make sure they don't do anything stupid?"

He nods his head and kisses my cheek. "Behave yourself, too."

I laugh and pat his cheek before backing out of his arms. "I don't think that's possible."

"Doesn't seem like it." This comes from Flynn inside my head.

I try my best not to react, but this is getting ridiculous. He needs to leave me alone, and the only way I might be able to get him to stop is if I tell everyone. They need to know that the warlock is now stalking me.

"I'm hardly stalking you. Stalking implies I have ill intent and am obsessed. Consider me more like...a guardian angel." Is he for real?

"Lyric, hey. You okay? You're spacing out." Bastien touches the back of his hand to my forehead. "Why don't we get you out of here and grab you something to eat and drink?"

Sagan and Bastien stand together near the door, staring at me as if I'm having a mental breakdown. And maybe I am. Maybe the warlock stalker is a figment of my imagination. I'm exhausted from everything that's happened, my mind and body in serious need of rest, but I feel as if I can't. Not now. Not with Paige lurking around.

"Gorgeous?" Sagan asks this time, twisting his lips to the

side. "Come on. Let me carry you. You're trembling."

I inhale a deep breath and shake out my hands. "No, it's okay. Sorry. I just have a lot on my mind."

"Then let me carry you because I want to love up on you as much as I can. Please, let me be here for you. Your emotions are all over the place, and while I know you're fierce, powerful, brave, and can handle your shit...I need to help you in one of the only ways you'll let me." Sagan opens his arms, wiggling his fingers to see if I'll give in.

How could I not? I've been so used to being on my own and taking care of myself since my dad was taken from me that it's still hard to allow others to do so. I just don't want to seem weak or needy. I shouldn't let Paige's bullshit get to me. She tried and she failed to take me down, and she should be the one terrified.

If Sagan or Bastien hear my thoughts, they don't comment on them. Neither does Flynn, wherever the hell he is—which is hopefully somewhere else and not intruding on my life any longer. Why he is being so persistent and helpful? I don't know. The fucker must want something. I just need to figure out what exactly.

Sagan strolls toward me, closing the space when I'm not quick enough to do so. He's right about my emotions being all over the place. I can barely focus. If I can't focus, I'm going to lose the games. I'm so fucking tired of losing. It's time for me to prove to everyone, even the guys, that I can win on my own. I don't need them to rig the games or ask them to let me win. I'm going to beat them and enjoy the hell out of my reward.

"I'll ensure you do," Sagan says, lifting me into his arms. He nuzzles his nose to mine, his blue eyes crinkling in the corners with his smile. "Now, can I kiss you while Bastien does one more quick exam?"

I groan. "No more exams. I'm fine. Just give me all the kisses."

Bastien hugs me from behind, draping his arms over both mine and Sagan's shoulders. He kisses my shoulder while Sagan caresses his lips to mine, the sensation of both their mouths on me lighting every molecule on my body with sizzling electricity. I break away from Sagan's mouth and turn enough to meet Bastien's lips next. I savor their closeness, their devotion, and especially their loyalty.

We only make it a few dozen feet out of the building with the cleansing pool before howls erupt through the air. I had no idea wolves could sound so sad, but I can feel their sorrow deep in my soul, and I can't help feeling awful about Stargaze Hill's lost leader and everyone she left behind. I couldn't imagine such a fate. It makes me not only sad but also angry as hell.

Because Paige did this.

Lycans did this.

The pack leaders are so entangled in their own worlds that they just can't see beyond what is right in front of them.

"Shit, we're being called to gather for the games already," Bastien says, curling his fingers into fists.

"I thought we had time." I swivel my torso to peer behind me in the direction Bastien and Sagan stare, listening to the continuous howling.

"Who fucking knows what they're even thinking," Sagan says, adjusting me in his arms. "This should be a time to heal and mourn."

"You know they never let anything interfere with the games," Bastien says.

"Well, I'm tired of this. They're so far re—"

"If yer so damn tired, then why don't ya admit defeat and accept that the lass is only givin' ya attention because she hasn't had 'er chance with me. I have a good feeling about the games today, arsehole. I know my home territory unlike anyone, and I'll beat the lot of ya." The coppery red-headed man licks his lips and winks at me. "You're gonna love being my queen."

Sagan growls. "What are you talking about, Fergus?"

"Where ye been all day? The games have been moved to Eclipse Valley tonight. Stargaze Hill tomorrow. Storm Haven after. The leaders think the risk of attack in Lunar Crest is too damn high. I can't blame 'em." The man, Fergus, risks the safety of his limb to touch my shoulder.

I whack his hand hard enough that he shakes out his fingers with a chuckle. "No one told me."

He shrugs. "Now why would they? They think yer cursed. But don't worry, lass. Once I win yer day claim, I'll tell ya anything ya wanna know. Maybe ye won't fight me as hard."

Inhaling a deep breath, I close my eyes and shut down, not even giving him another ounce of my attention. I haven't been nervous about the games in at least a week, but now that the leaders pulled this bullshit, swapping locations just when I was starting to get used to my territory—well, it fucking blows.

Fergus hums under his breath and gently strokes his fingers against my loose tresses. I swing my arm and he hops out of the way of my fist before I clock him upside the head. Bastien growls, but a whistle cuts through the air, calling everyone once again.

Fergus twitches his fingers at me. "Wish me luck, lass. I'm sure the two of us will have a helluva time."

If Sagan didn't tighten his arms around me, I might've launched myself at the asshole. He struts away from us and purposefully drops his shorts to the ground, giving me a view of his naked ass. And damn my eyes. He spins around and flexes, grinning at the fact that he caught me looking, and winks one more time.

I imagine what it would be like to kick him in his balls hard enough to send them inside him. Because that's exactly what I'll do if he even thinks of trying to capture me. I'll make him regret ever fantasizing about it for a second.

Tipping his head back, he roars a laugh and shakes his hips, swinging his flaccid cock back and forth as if to tempt me. I grimace and bonk my head to Sagan's shoulder, choosing to stop any and all attention to Fergus, knowing he enjoys it no matter what. If my threat to kick his balls doesn't dissuade him, I don't think anything will. Some guys get off on the fight for dominance, and I'm not in the mood for that bullshit.

"Don't worry, Ma Belle. We won't let him get anywhere near you. Caz will help you navigate the new course if you want." Bastien stands behind Sagan to meet my gaze.

"I want to win on my own," I mutter.

"Fair enough." Bastien leans in even more. "Then let's get you there a bit early, so you have more time to prep."

I nod my head with a sigh.

I bet there is another reason the leaders chose to change things up. My outburst probably left them nervous, since I'm ready to stand against them to change the packs' way of life. I bet Paige already got in their heads, and they're also doing this to give other competitors an advantage, since no one can know every territory.

"You're going to do great," Sagan adds, hugging me tighter.

If only I didn't feel like I'm being set up to fail.

If only I didn't feel like I've lost the games already.

8

GAME CHANGER

I HUG MY ROBE TIGHTER around me, bouncing on the balls of my feet. Even though it hasn't been that long since the last competition, I feel already out of shape and in some serious need of extra training.

Emerson drops her robe to the ground and stretches her arms over her head. "This is so exciting. I haven't gotten to run here in a couple of years." Because the she-wolves are born pack-less, the leaders each take time to bond with them, raising them as a community, which means they only stay in a territory for a limited amount of time, spending their lives in rotation.

"I hope your endurance is good, Lyric," Harlow says, following Emerson's lead by stripping her robe off too. "There is a lot of sprawling hills and valleys without trees to hide behind."

Damn. Hiding is one of my specialties. I don't feel as much like prey if I can't exactly see that I'm being chased. My heart might not be able to handle this bullshit.

"Don't let Harlow freak you out. We have plenty of time to get ahead." Emerson bumps her shoulder to mine. "Just keep heading north until you reach the river. The forest turns dense and is harder for the men to navigate. We're smaller, so as long as you remain in your true form, it'll give you an advantage."

"It's also the perfect place to scope out who you want to catch you." Harlow bites her bottom lip. "I'm hoping for Ryland, tonight. He's a bit shy, and I can't wait to see if I can change that."

Emerson laughs and claps her hands. "He's going to just love you."

"Hopefully enough for him to give up on trying to catch you, Lyric." Harlow bumps my other shoulder, pursing her lips. I can tell she sometimes gets jealous by the attention I gather from the competitors, but there isn't much any of us can do. "He thinks he wants someone wild, but he's just going to end up losing since you're unwilling to give many a chance...which the leaders notice, by the way."

"Why would I? You know my feelings about the games. I want to be with men I choose, not have some asshole think I'm a fucking prize to have his way with." I stretch my legs into a lunge, groaning with the movement. My body still feels off since my injuries, the lycan scratches still tender despite being only pink lines now. The memory of getting stabbed by Paige doesn't help me either.

"How do you know you won't want to choose someone else?" Harlow grins at me, knowing she makes a point.

But I don't want to admit as much, so I shrug. "No one has given me a good reason."

My dad chose Dax, Sterling, Sagan, and Bastien with a purpose in mind. For us, these games aren't solely about starting a new pack and blending bloodlines. This is my chance to help further our future to leave the past and the old ways behind, especially now more than ever. Unlike with the current leaders, I will not stand by and grow weak. I won't allow the same for our future she-wolves either. Once the games are over and my pack mates are solidified, we can teach the maturing she-wolves how to really lead, instead of tailoring them for a future of re-population.

My thoughts pump me up, giving me the strength and confidence I need to get through tonight. I don't know if it's because I almost died or what, but I'm no longer feeling as bad about the games and the idea of a territory. Because with it will come what I need to ensure my future. I can save my dad. I can finally help pull the wolves out of hiding.

"Except for Caz," Emerson says, smiling at me. "You didn't think you'd want him, but I saw the look you gave him earlier. You guys are starting to bond."

"That's different. I knew Caz from the Mortal World," I retort.

"And you can know the other competitors now." Harlow swivels on her feet and points behind us. "I mean, look at them. You can't really go wrong with whoever you end up with. Mating season will be an amazing time. I can't wait."

I follow her line of sight to the gathering men, standing naked and ready for the whistles to sound off for the start of the games. I wish I'd kept my back away. In Lunar Crest, there were always dozens of trees in the way, and I could only hear the men. But now, I can see them, and they can see me, and a few of them I don't even know the names of catcall and flex, trying to get my attention.

Flicking my gaze over the crowd, I narrow my vision on Dax, Sagan, Bastien, and Sterling. They look as anxious as I feel. The change in location really screwed things up. The fact that we haven't even had much time here doesn't help. No one got the chance to explore, and I only had a few minutes to study the course instead of the usual day. The competitors don't get any time at all, because this is their time to prove their worth. And damn it. There are far better ways.

"I'd strip down now, if I were you," Harlow says, drawing

my attention away from all the cocks on full display. I wish my eyes could learn to control themselves. I know how much everyone loves even a second of my attention. "I see Trista getting ready to blow the whistle from the platform."

Bouncing on the balls of my feet, I gather my nerve to shrug out of my robe. Stripping down for a bunch of horny men doesn't get any easier no matter how often everyone around here is naked. It takes me inhaling a few deep breaths and concentrating on the world in front of me to get my nerves in control.

Emerson rubs her hands together. "I'll race you both to the top of the first hill."

"That could be interesting...sticking together," Harlow says. "What do you think?"

Hmm. She's right. It could be interesting. If we stayed together, every damn man around here will fight each other to get within reach of us. It will slow them down. If they do happen to break ahead of the crowd and catch up, all I'll have to do is run faster than both Harlow and Emerson. Not many of the guys will pass up the opportunity of winning a day claim, even if they originally had their eyes on someone else. The more they win, the better it is for their chances of snagging a spot on one of our packs.

"It would be safer until someone catches us. I am still a bit shook up over the lycan attacks." Emerson's mouth pouts with her memory.

"Among other things," I mutter, the words coming low to

keep them between the three of us.

Emerson and Harlow don't get the chance to respond. The whistle blows, sending the competitors into a frenzy as they howl and cheer and catcall in their human forms. We get a ten-minute head start, but damn it does it fly by way faster than I want. Harlow transforms first and circles us with an excited couple of barks.

Closing my eyes, I will my body to get itself together and embrace the shudder of my tensing muscles. Emerson playfully leaps on me the second I turn into a wolf, knocking me over. I skid across the dirt and play-growl at her excitement, launching myself from the dirt. Harlow darts away first, getting the two of us to focus and follow her until I allow my wolf complete control, giving in to my need to run.

Breaking into a sprint, I dart past Emerson and Harlow, taking the lead. Emerson's laughter trickles through my mind. Harlow nips at my back legs, trying to slow me down, and then she releases a howl, getting at least a dozen competitors to respond to her call.

"Pace yourself, Lyric," Emerson says into my mind, pushing hard on her paws to run next to me. "This is only the first hill. There are at least four more coming up. The competitors count on us wearing ourselves out early on."

"I don't mind making it easy on them," Harlow says, chiming in.

"You do that. I plan to win." With a bark, I dart ahead,

pushing my paws to carry me faster up the hill.

The world blurs around me, the sun disappearing into the horizon, leaving the clouds aglow in pinks and oranges. I bet when night comes, the stars shine like a million diamonds fastened to endless black satin to sparkle over the valleys and hills, being the reason this territory is named Eclipse Valley.

The second whistle rings through the air, declaring that the competitors can now run the course in search of us. A blip of fear clenches my chest, but I suppress it the best I can and focus my attention on the view of the magical-looking valley below. Thousands of rainbow flowers dance in the breeze, enjoying the final rays of sunlight before closing for the night. I've never seen anything like this, the beauty and color of the floral field breathtaking.

My attention on the landscape before me distracts me, and Emerson accidentally crashes into my ass. The two of us lose our balance, and my paws fall out from under me. I yelp as I skid forward, the steep terrain leading to the valley doing nothing to slow me down. Rolling at least two dozen feet, I crash to the ground on my back with Emerson on top of me. Harlow trots her way down the hillside and stops short of us before she barks.

"Fuck, you two okay?" she asks, slinking forward to nudge Emerson in the side with her snout.

Emerson scrambles off of me and gets to her feet, shaking off the dirt from her red and white coat. "I think so. What about you, Lyric? You okay?"

I push my paws into the ground and get up, twisting my middle back and forth to throw the dirt and flowers off my fur. "Barely. Shit, I'm sorry. I just—I've never seen anything like this."

Emerson nudges me with her body and licks the side of my face. It should be weirder than it is, but somehow, the gesture feels natural in this form. "You can enjoy it during your day claim tomorrow."

Several howls sound through the air, dragging my attention to the top of the hill. Harlow yips excitedly and shoves her head under my belly to help me to get moving. Charging forward, I bolt from my spot and rush toward the next hill. Emerson and Harlow come up beside me, their excitement flooding through me in a wave of laughing and taunting the wolves racing behind us.

"Nice ass, blondie. I can't wait to nip it." Sterling's voice hums over the rest of the men projecting their thoughts into my mind until I manage to shut them out.

"Don't you dare, Sterling," I call, trying not to let his teasing slow me down.

"Fine, then I'll kiss it instead." He chuckles at his own thought.

"Not in this form, you won't." I race up the hill in front of Harlow and Emerson, my body slowing at the extreme exertion.

Sterling howls. "So does that mean you'll let me as a man? I'm down for that. I'll kiss and lick and taste every inch of that sexy body of yours. You have no idea how good you smell. You're practically hypnotizing the—"

Another competitor must interrupt Sterling's thoughts, because his voice leaves my mind, and I hear his familiar growl echo through the air. Instead of checking on him, I push my paws to carry me faster. The wolves race closer, their determination to catch us so intense that it feels palpable. I can't tell if it's because their emotions run wild or mine do, but it's enough to push me faster, increasing the distance between me and Harlow and Emerson. I doubt they'll catch up with me before they're caught.

"Damn, look at the bitch go." This comes from Radek, his deep voice already getting on my nerves even though it's the first time it has managed to intrude my thoughts.

A deep howl cuts through the air. "Watch out. I'm catching her fine ass."

"Wanna fucking bet? She'll be too tired not to submit." Ugh. Radek has something awful coming to him if that's what he thinks.

Damn it. My plan might've backfired. I should've known better than to think that just because I'm ahead of Emerson and Harlow that it would dissuade the men from pursuing me. Fuck, it probably makes them more determined to stop me, so I don't cross the finish line.

The noise of heavy paws thumping into the dirt sounds from behind me. My heart races at the thuds of another set and then another. The world dims as clouds cover the sliver of remaining sun, sending the hillside into shadows. I can't see the wolves coming up on me, but I can hear and smell them on the wind pushing me forward.

"One more hill, Lyric. Keep up your pace," Dax says, his comforting voice pushing out all the other noise. "Once we hit the forest, we'll cut them off."

"You guys can cut them off. I'm getting her. That day claim is mine." Sagan's voice comes with a growl.

"Yeah-fucking-right. I'm too damn close to wearing her down. Once she lets me kiss every inch of her, she will crave more." Sterling's fantasy sends a wave of desire crashing through me.

"Damn, she likes the sound of that," Bastien says.

"Better push those sexy little thoughts away, Lyric. You're making it easier to track your scent." Dax's words come out breathy, totally hot, in my mind.

And now I can't stop thinking about his mouth all over me. Or his cock inside me. Damn it. I'm horny. It feels like forever since the last time I had sex with him, and my body totally wants the reminder of what his massive boner feels like between my legs.

"Fucking damn it. I'm coming for ya, lass. I need to bang that thought from yer mind." Fergus's voice penetrates my thoughts in a way I don't enjoy.

Two wolves growl behind me.

"Lyric, duck!" At the sound of Bastien's warning, I skid to

a halt and drop to my belly.

A huge red wolf flies over me and lands on his paws. Fergus charges at me, not giving me a chance to dodge out of the way. I brace for the weight of his impact and the pain that will ensue with his attempt to pin me.

My nerves trigger my human transformation, my body wanting to be in what I feel is my strongest form. My muscles spasm, and I gasp, my mind and body tense enough to shoot a deep ache through me.

A guttural growl prickles over my body, erupting goose-bumps across my skin. Dax's huge, mahogany body launches over me and crashes into Fergus. The two wolves roll and snarl, fighting each other.

"Come on, gorgeous. Fifty feet to the trees," Sagan says, bonking his cool nose into my side, trying to get me to move.

I groan and press my hands into the ground to push up. Sagan nudges his head into the small of my back like if he doesn't help me, I'll crash back to the dirt. And maybe I will. Because now that I'm not running or in my wolf form, my body screams that I might've reached my limitations.

"That's it. You can do this." Sagan pokes his nose to the back of my leg, making me jump.

Reaching behind me, I link my fingers through his light fur and tug him, so he doesn't try to nose me anywhere else. If he were Sterling, he'd definitely try. Instead of saying anything else, I jog forward, the steep hill testing my balance. Sagan remains by my side, rubbing his furry body to my leg.

The dense forest ahead reminds me of Harlow and Emerson's warning. If I head into it in my human form, I might not get far. I need to use my agility and smaller frame as a she-wolf to navigate the wild terrain.

But I'm afraid to stop out here. The other wolves are far too close for comfort. If I pause to transform, someone else will catch up and test Sagan. Some of the assholes would pick a fight and try to hurt him. All I want to do is protect him, especially after everything. All bets are off during the games when it comes to fighting. Injuries happen. It would be excused.

Sagan noses me in the ass, and I startle and swat my hand at his snout. He dramatically whimpers, though he chuckles into my mind. The gesture is something I'd expect from Sterling or Bastien, and now I wonder if I need to separate them before they start rubbing off on each other too much.

"Maybe if you hadn't transformed, I wouldn't have to nudge you like this. Would you prefer I use my teeth?" Sagan asks, his voice light and teasing. "If a love bite would get you to keep running, it'll be worth another swat. But maybe wait until I'm a man. You can spank my ass if it'll make you feel better."

The idea of doing such a thing excites me more than it should. He's totally prodding at the dominant side of me that loves to test everyone. He hasn't admitted it yet—not like Dax has—but I know a part of him loves the idea of being in control on occasion. All of the wolves competing do. Getting a spot on a she-wolf pack guarantees control over a territory and also the chance to pass on their genes. If they don't make it, they're stuck under their pack leaders. That's why the games are so important.

"But don't think the gesture would go unreciprocated," he adds, pushing me again. "I want nothing more than to see you on your back under me. If you hurry, we can evade the others and take advantage of the tree cover."

"Or we could just hurry and finish," I say, slowing as I reach the tree line, the dense forest too dark to see much of as a human. "Take a hot shower. Roll around in the blankets. Maybe let me give you a belly rub."

He chuckles. "Tease."

"You have no idea what that is, but if you'd like to find out—"

Sagan releases a deep growl, cutting off my thoughts to him. I duck behind a tree in time to see Fergus in his wolf form catching up. He has at least fifty feet, but it's still too close. He's far more determined now that I've given him an ounce of attention. He'll do what it takes to get more.

"Hurry, transform," Sagan calls with a howl. "Keep heading north. I'll catch up."

I do as he says and crouch on my hands and knees, concentrating on unleashing my she-wolf. My muscles tighten and spasm, and I breathe through the quick transformation. The forest lights up in a spectrum of rainbow colors, the world illuminating with my enhanced vision.

A collection of howls sound through the air, more competitors heading in my direction. I take off and weave in and out of the trees, some of the passageways so narrow that I worry I might get stuck. If I were any bigger, I would. There is no easy way for anyone to get through this part of the course, so it'll end up being the most agile, strong, and fiercest men of the group to catch up or even make it through. I slink under a twisted trunk, having to drag my body forward by sinking my claws into the ground. And fuck. I'm not even sure I can make it.

"Damn right, you can't. It's time to let me show you what you've been missing out on." Teeth sink into my tail with enough pressure to make me yelp. Radek drags me to him and locks his mouth to the back of my neck to overpower me and flip me onto my back.

I growl and snarl at him, thrashing as hard as I can to break free. It's been a couple games since he's bothered me—or that he could even get close to me—and now that he has, it reminds me exactly how much I dislike this dickhead.

"You don't have to like me to have some fun, baby," he says, listening to my thoughts. And damn it. My nerves have me all over the place. It's a struggle to keep things to myself. "Hate sex is fun. Passionate."

"Fuck off, Radek." I snap my teeth, trying to bite his chest. If he didn't pin me down with his heavy paws, I could.

"Mmm, I love hearing you say my name. I can't wait to find out how hot it is when you give into me and scream it."

This fucker. I think he loves just screwing with me and seeing how far he can push me. We both know that I'd bite his cock off before I ever let him even dream about trying to sleep with me.

Giving up struggling in my wolf form, I sink harder into the ground, faking submission. We've been in this position before, and Radek obviously remembers it as much as I do, because he still doesn't get off me.

So I do the only thing I can.

Closing my eyes, I transform into my human self. Radek huffs a breath through his nose, thrown off by me now lying underneath him in my naked human form. I grab onto the thick fur of his neck and lean up, surprising the hell out of him by kissing his cool wolf nose. If he were a man, I wouldn't, but it's easier to pretend he's a cute pet instead of a perverted beast.

It's enough to get him to transform into a man, his instincts driving him to take on the form he knows I prefer. I try not to react to his warm naked body resting against mine, my hands now linking through his hair as I cradle his head in my hands. A smirk softens his features, especially when I don't fight him or shove him off. I distract him by holding him in my gaze until I feel his desire harden his body against my leg.

He hums under his breath. "I've imagined what this moment would be like since I first laid eyes on you."

I shift beneath him. "Is that so?"

"Will you let me carry you over the finish line? I want to

prove to you that I'm worthy. You smell so incredible. Your skin is so smooth and soft." Oh, boy. It's like my fake submission knocked the asshole out of him. Harlow was right about some of the men needing to feel like they're the gods of the universe.

I smirk at how easy it is to distract this fucker. "Not as soft as your balls." Jerking my leg up, I knee him in his pelvis in an attempt to smash his nuts. It startles him, turning his smirk into a scowl, his features reminding me how fake his nicety is and how he will only use it to try to get between my legs. And damn it. I can't believe I missed his balls. So I try again.

Hollering at the force of my knee squishing his hard cock, Radek rolls off me, his fury consuming his pain instead of letting it weaken him. He rushes to grab my leg to capture me, and I swing my whole body, using my weight to strengthen the force of my kick. My foot clocks him in the side hard enough to send him sprawling to the ground. Scrambling to my feet, I dart away, putting as much space between us as I can. The dense trees, with branches tangling together, stop me from getting as far as I'd like in my human form.

"You're just going to make this sweeter for me, baby. There is no fucking way you're making it to the finish line without me." Radek growls and then howls with his transformation into a wolf.

Fuck. I had forgotten he was from Eclipse Valley.

"Come on, gorgeous. Prove his ass wrong." Sagan lunges at Radek, dragging him back by his tail to give me a chance to transform.

Teeth flash with their snarls and tufts of fur litter the ground. The guttural noises echoing through the air from them ignite a blip of fear in my heart, my human rationale reminding me how deadly it can be to get caught in the middle of two powerful wolves. I bolt away, despite my worry about Sagan fighting with Radek. I don't want him to get hurt because my dumbass couldn't move fast enough to get ahead of everyone.

"Don't worry, blondie. I got his back," Sterling says, his growl trickling through the forest as he approaches from somewhere I can't see. A few more howls cut through the air. "Maybe you'll pity fuck me later since I'm giving up my chance to carry your sexy ass over the finish line to protect my brother. Maybe you will kiss my booboos or let me lick your taco to distract myself."

"She won't have time to baby you, because she's going to spend the day with me," Dax says, his hulking mahogany wolf bounding through the twisted branches of a tree, busting right through them instead of going under. "I plan to ravish her for hours."

Lust crashes over me at his comment, my body loving the idea of whatever he has in store. My mind wanders to the weight of Dax's body on top of mine and how maybe he'll bend me over and mount me like a sexy beast. I wonder how intense his cock would feel inside me and if I'd feel it in my stomach.

Several groans intrude my mind, and Dax chuckles. Heat

floods my face. I don't know what is up with me, but I struggle to keep my fantasies to myself. Dax jumps over some twisted roots and lands on his paws beside me. The cocky bastard licks the side of my face, from my chin to my temple, showing me his affection.

"Time to change, so I can satiate your curiosity," he says into my mind. "No inviting the others to hang out, either. I want my alone time with you."

I want that too. I didn't realize how much so until now.

I don't know if it's because of the change in location or the fact that I know I can handle a lycan if another one manages to break through the protective shield around Lulupoterra, but I want to start spending more alone time with each of the guys to bond since I feel as if the relationship between the six of us together has strengthened since Paige tried to kill me.

Dax whimpers and nudges his big wolf head to mine. "Now I really want you to hurry, so we can finish this. I'm desperate to give you everything you want from me."

"I want that too—"

Fergus surprises the two of us, launching from a high branch of a tree. He collides into Dax, pinning him to the ground. Sinking his fangs into Dax's coat, Fergus tries to injure him to steal me away. I swing my fist out and punch him in the snout. He yelps and snarls, turning his sharp teeth to me. I flinch and throw myself back, afraid he'll bite me. Dax takes advantage of the opportunity and grabs onto Fergus's neck, flipping him off.

"Run, Lyric," Dax commands. "Transform as soon as you can."

Without hesitating, I rush to my feet and maneuver my way between two trees, scratching my ass and boobs against the rough trunk. I tighten my jaw at the pain but proceed to navigate through another tight space.

The cacophonous array of fighting noises continues on, and I try to push away my need to back up Dax. I know he can handle himself. I'm sort of certain that they'll stop as soon as one of them submits. But it's hard to trust the circumstances. It wouldn't be the first time things escalated between the competitors.

A bright flash of light ignites the forest around me, and I freeze in my spot instead of transforming. Flynn's fresh, minty scent trickles to me a second before he materializes within the light, and the world darkens as it disappears. I cover my boobs, knowing that he will automatically check me out as he's obviously not used to seeing women naked. And I get it. My dumb eyes still can't control themselves and look at the various dicks seemingly always on display and pointing at me everywhere I turn.

Grabbing the back of his shirt, he tugs it over his head and offers it to me. "How about we compromise? You cover up, and I'll give you a peek of me now. It's fairer if we're both half-naked since it seems no one ever wears clothing around here. I have to ease into your lifestyle, she-wolf."

I take his shirt and pull it over my head, the scent of his skin flooding over me. I hate how good he smells or how I can't stop myself from checking out his body. His tattoos seemingly dance with his movement, keeping my attention on every one of his muscles. I don't know if it's in my head or what, but he looks even more attractive to me. His lavender eyes drift to my body, now covered in his shirt, and I swear I hear his heartbeat pick up. I realize it's because the rest of the world falls quiet.

I shift on my feet, gathering my thoughts. "No, you don't," I finally manage to say after an awkward moment. "Getting used to this lifestyle means you plan on staying a while, and I think it's best if you go. I don't like you stalking me around. Did you freeze the whole place again? Because that's fucked up. We're not yours to mess with."

Flynn's lavender eyes flash with sparks of power. "No, I won't do that again unless I feel as if I need to intervene."

"But why? Why are you here? Are you now spying on us for your coven or something?" I twine my fingers together, the thought getting to me.

He sighs. "No, and...I honestly don't know. Perhaps for the same reason you haven't told anyone that I'm here."

I frown. I don't know the reason why I haven't told Dax, Sterling, Bastien, Sagan, or Caz. I should've. I know I should've. But a part of me fears how they'll react, especially knowing that I didn't tell them right away.

"Because you're unsure of them," Flynn says, stepping

closer. He shoves his hands into his pockets like he has no idea what to do with them.

I crinkle my nose. "They're the only ones I am sure of."

"Then why do they continue to insist you play this barbaric game? Why do they continuously tease you that you're something to be won?"

"Like you said, they're only teasing," I argue.

"You didn't answer my first question." Flynn tilts his head, studying me so intently that the weight of his stare prickles over my body, the sensation as palpable as his soft shirt caressing my skin.

I place my hands on my hips. "I don't have to. You obviously don't understand anything."

"Neither do you, she-wolf. This place is filled with powerful magic, and magic like this has consequences. Magic of this nature doesn't last forever, not without some sort of price." Flynn waves his hand around the forest. "There has to be a greater reason for these games. It's unnatural."

"It's none of your business," I snap. "I'm handling it. I'm changing things around here. I just need to get through these first. My future pack mates will ensure it. We're rigging the games."

"Come on, she-wolf. Do you think it's that simple? Do you plan to live happily ever after with men who could be messing with you? Using you? What happens if things don't work out as you want them? I overheard the leaders discussing an arrangement involving men who can supposedly get you in your place." His muscles flex with his words. "The bastards want to rig the games themselves. One of the guys even suggested revoking your ability to win altogether."

I blink a few times in confusion. "Guys? The leaders are women."

He lifts his eyebrow. "Wanna bet?"

Without getting a chance to respond, Flynn grabs my hand and pulls me into him. Our bodies practically melt together, my skin sizzling with a strange, explosive sensation that makes me gasp.

"Don't let go, she-wolf," Flynn commands.

Light consumes us.

9

Alpha-Mates

I DON'T BELIEVE WHAT I'M seeing. Flynn was right. Ten men sit around a bonfire, eating some sort of mystery food when they should be watching the games. I catch sight of Caz's dad, who was the one to confront me in the meeting with the women.

And then Caz appears, shocking the hell out of me. So do the two other men who have officially won a spot on Harlow and Emerson's packs. Killian and Gunner take their seats beside men who I think might be their fathers. Anger rushes through me, along with hurt and betrayal. I trusted Caz. He swore his loyalty to me.

A gentle hand touches my shoulder, stopping me from stomping toward the circle to drag Caz back. Flynn brings his index finger to his lips and motions for me to be quiet. Several howls trickle through the air, sounding over the crackling fire, but wherever we are is far enough from the competition that I doubt any of the competitors could find these assholes.

"What is the status of the competition?" Caz's dad asks, offering Caz the meaty bone he's been gnawing on.

"Harlow and Emerson are nearing the finish line now. Ryland's plan worked as expected to gain Harlow's interest," Killian answers.

"Good job, Killian," the man next to Harlow's mate says. He smacks his leg. "You already know your mate so well."

Killian grins. "She desires to serve us, but especially when we act as if we don't need her."

What. The. Fuck.

"Emerson is a bit more difficult," Gunner adds, speaking up. "She has been asking a lot about learning to defend herself lately, and even more so with the attacks."

"It's the Lunar Crest bitch's influence," another man says, punching his fist into the ground. "She will ruin our she-wolves."

"I still say we should throw her to the witches. The strength of her bloodline isn't worth it. She got my mate killed,"

Svetlana's mate, and I guess true leader of Stargaze Hill, says.

"Axel, settle down." This comes from Trista's mate, a man Dax never talks about.

"She deserved better," Killian adds, releasing a soft growl.

Caz's dad reaches over and touches Killian's knee. "You will get justice. One of our allies will get Lyric's claim tomorrow. He will ensure it." His justice? Why does he need justice? I thought he was on the Eclipse Valley pack before joining Harlow and Moonlight Canyon.

"Good, because if he doesn't, I will follow in my father's footsteps and claim more than just Harlow. I will take care of Lyric myself." Killian glowers at his hands. What the hell? Does this mean that the alpha-mates have been breaking their bonds? I don't understand.

I don't get the chance to think about it. I'm too engrossed in the conversation unfolding.

"You better be right about that, Calhoun. I had expected your son to have her in her place by now." This comes from Trista's mate as he speaks to Caz's dad. "Dax still hasn't let up in his decision to pursue her, and Trista refuses to be anything less than supportive. You know how she is since—"

A whistle rings through the air, cutting the man off. One of the competitors must've crossed the line with either Harlow or Emerson.

Calhoun stands. "We'll finish this discussion later." Turning to Caz, he adds, "Get your mate in line or you'll face far worse things. Her outbursts need to stop. Do you understand?"

Caz nods. "Yes."

"Radek or Fergus will ensure it," Killian says. "They will handle her well."

A whistle rings through the air again, declaring another she-wolf and competitor crosses the finish line. It takes Flynn locking me in a bear hug to stop me from confronting these assholes. Usually in this position, I'd strike his knee and try to kick him where it counts. But Flynn's too quick to gather magic, transporting us just within the line of trees near the river. He spins me and presses my back to the tree, covering my mouth with his hand.

"You need to calm down, she-wolf," he murmurs, leaning close enough that I feel his breath caressing my cheek.

"I need to neuter Caz, is what I need. He played me," I say, my voice deepening with a growl. "I knew I shouldn't have trusted him. And to think I started to like him."

Infuriating tears burn my eyes, my heart aching as everything sinks in. I wasn't just starting to like Caz. I like him more than I even want to admit. And it's worse than just my feelings. Sagan, Dax, Sterling, and Bastien have accepted him as a pack mate. This is so fucked up.

Flynn surprises the hell out of me by swiping his finger across my cheeks, smearing away my tears. His face softens, his lavender eyes wrinkling in the corners with his frown. "I'm sorry, she-wolf. This must be so much to handle."

The warlock engulfs me in a hug, his muscular arms sliding around my back as he squeezes me against him. I stand frozen in shock, my mind fully aware of how my breasts push against his pecs and how my bottom lip caresses the bare skin of his shoulder with my deep breaths. I love the feeling way too much, hesitating to pull away.

"What are you doing?" I ask, my hands sneaking up to clutch onto his sides. "Most men end up clutching their cocks for surprising me with un-asked for affection."

He jerks back, releasing me. "I'm sorry. I just—I thought you needed a hug. That's what people do in my coven when your heart breaks. But considering this fucked up situation...I should've asked."

His apology strokes at my wild she-wolf inside me, chilling my need to punch him down. Why didn't I react like I always do? Shit. Am I growing soft? Too trusting? What the hell would my dad say if he knew that I was thinking about how much I might want another one from Flynn? How would the guys feel?

"Please don't cry. It's going to be okay." Flynn sounds so certain that it's hard not to believe his ridiculous attempt to make me feel better with words he couldn't possibly know to be true. Words that I'm certain will never be true.

Because nothing about my life is okay.

First, my dad gets stolen from me.

Then my mortal life.

And now? My plans for my future slip through my fingers,

and I'm afraid to catch them before they shatter.

"I will do my best to help you, but I need you to do the one thing I'm not so certain you can manage after witnessing the truth about the pack leaders." Flynn grabs my hand and brings it to his chest. His melodic thrumming heart pounds against the back of my hand, the sensation keeping my attention off my rising despair.

"Which is what?" I ask, studying the bolts of electric power igniting his lavender irises. If I stare at them long enough, maybe I can discover more about him. Maybe I can figure out his motives and what he truly wants.

"I want you to trust me," he says, lowering his voice, keeping his gaze steady.

I inhale a sharp breath. "Trust you? *Trust* you? Why should I?"

"Because I saved your life." Flynn sucks his bottom lip into his mouth as he thinks of what might be an incredibly long list of the reasons he knows I need. "Because I had no idea that the wolves of Magaelorum were still around. I want to help you, because you need it. I don't have any better reason, Lyric. I know you're not used to it, but not everyone has to have a motive to be a good person."

"I don't think you have a motive, but I know that there is more to this than what you're saying. So stop bullshitting me. You can't expect me to just accept that you want nothing in return. You wouldn't be stalking me and interrupting my life if that were true. You'd accept that I've denied your help and move on to someone who wants it." I snag my hand from his and cross my arms protectively around myself. "I know that witches and warlocks have hunted us to near extinction for our magic. Is that your reason? You want whatever power you can get from me?"

"I—" Flynn snaps his mouth shut, swiveling to look at the trees behind him. "I have to go. I'll explain more later. Just— just go along with whatever the leaders have planned."

I scoff and shake my head. "No fucking way. I plan to win tonight's games."

Flynn rubs his hands together. "I can't allow that. Not tonight."

With a flash of light, the world shifts, and I fall into the icy river. Flynn's shirt vanishes off me with his disappearance, his actions more cautious as he erases evidence of his intrusion, including his scent. I screech underwater, my body tightening with the cold. I'm going to kill that warlock. I swear, I will. He's going to—

"Gotcha, baby." Two hot hands snatch me under my arms and hoist me from the river before I can orient myself.

I gasp and tremble, my teeth chattering from the freezing ice bath. My mind whirls with a dozen thoughts. Howls echo through the air, followed by the familiar growls of Sagan and Sterling. Radek adjusts his hold on me, tossing me on his shoulder. My arms smash against his hard muscles, locking me in place.

"Lyric, fight," Dax says, his voice trickling into my mind. "I'm coming."

His voice snaps me from my confusion, and I tense, preparing to buck my body. There is no way in hell I'm losing the games to Radek. I don't care what Flynn said. I will not just go along with things. I will fight.

Radek bolts forward, breaking into a sprint. I twist my body and jerk one of my arms free. Swinging it as hard as I can, I punch him in the middle of his back. He growls and tosses me off his shoulder. The world spins, and I brace for impact, tucking my head in protectively. A whistle rings through the air at the same time the breath abandons my lungs, shading the edges of my vision.

"Congratulations, Radek of Stargaze Hill. You've won the day claim of Lyric of Lunar Crest. Please take her to the podium and receive your victory cheer." Trista covers me with a robe, leaving me in shock on the ground.

I kick out my leg, knocking Radek off his feet before he can snatch me from the ground. He releases a guttural noise from his throat, and I growl right back at him, catapulting to my feet. This is unbelievable. I'm going to murder Flynn. I'm going to burn this whole world down and punch every damn man who tries to stop me in the cock.

"Get over here and stop acting like you don't want this," Radek says, strutting toward me.

I prepare to fight him, but someone locks me in a bear hug

from behind until the douche restrains me to him, holding me off the ground, facing out, and pinned to his chest.

"Lyric, settle down. It is one day claim. Do not act like a child. You have no idea whether or not you will enjoy his company unless you give him a chance. Radek is a worthy competitor and a fierce warrior. You don't want to make enemies with my pack now, do you? It will not go over well." A woman, who I am sure is Radek's mother, meets me with narrowed eyes.

"Try me!" I snap.

"If you don't comply, we will have no choice but to cage you. Is that what you really want?" She flicks her gaze to the asshole I caught conspiring against me.

He subtly nods his head, the gesture enough to cool my fury.

"No," I finally spit out. "I do not want the cage. Just—fuck. Let's get this over with."

I expect Radek to set me on my feet to let me walk to the podium, but he flips me around and cradles me like a damn blushing bride. I refuse to look at the crowd of competitors gathering around the three Eclipse Valley winners. I'd think people would be suspicious by the dominating territory win, but if anyone is, they don't mention it.

I remain limp and expressionless, hoping my annoyance and misery show everyone just how much I hate this situation. Each of the female pack leaders takes a moment to congratulate Radek, Ryland, and Fergus. I stiffen at Paige's presence, her scent triggering a flurry of hot emotions through me. Had she not brought the vicious lycans here, I might not be in this position.

"How well-deserved, Radek," she says, touching him on the shoulder. "Lyric looks wonderful in your arms. A strong man to care for such a precious being."

Gag me. I flinch and shift at the soft brush of her fingers through my hair. It takes everything in me not to punch her in her infuriating face.

"Congratulations, Radek," Caz says, his voice snapping my attention from the back of Paige's head. "Lyric. Enjoy your time together."

My chest clenches at his words, the lack of emotion in his voice filling me with everything he holds back. Tears burn my eyes, and I squeeze them shut, not wanting to look at him. I don't want to feel him in my mind either.

"Ma Belle, take a breath. I'm right here," Bastien says, his voice trickling into my mind.

"We're not leaving your side," Dax adds, his emotions teetering between shock and outrage. Disbelief.

"We're going to figure out how this happened. Something isn't right." Sagan's voice wraps around me, his strength helping to calm the panic storming through my soul.

Sterling growls softly from somewhere nearby. "And I'll murder that asshole if he so much as tries to sniff your hair. Just hold on. I'll get you."

I press my lips together, pushing away the sound of the

cheers ringing through the air. "No, Sterling. I don't want you getting in trouble."

"Caz will be on guard, all right. He'll ensure you're okay," Dax says. "I know you're in shock, but you're unintentionally blocking him out."

I stiffen. "Tell him I can take care of my damn self."

"But—"

"It's an order." My voice snaps through my mind, my heated thought surely stinging Dax.

He responds with silence, his emotions strong enough to alert me of his confusion. I don't even know how I'll tell him, Sterling, Sagan, and Bastien. But I need to. I need to tell them everything. It eats me up, tearing at my soul. Flynn fucked up by putting me in this position. I'm no longer curious about his motives, because no matter what he's done, or how he's helped me, he was never doing it for me. This proves it.

Radek jumps from the podium, not waiting a moment more than he has to. His anticipation to get me away from the crowd courses through me. My stomach twists at the excitement in his steps. We reach a cluster of buildings, and he tips his head back and releases a howl, his voice humming through the air. Several wolves respond to his human call, and he chuckles and kicks the door to his room open.

He tosses me onto the bed and slams the door, his smile disappearing with one look at me. I clutch the blankets in my hands, my whole body turning rigid. I half expect him to rush me. I prepare to disembowel him.

"Relax, baby. I'm not going to fight with you. I like my balls intact." Radek smirks at me and discards his robe on the floor. "You cold? You can join me in the shower if you want."

I lift an eyebrow. "No thanks. I'd like to keep your wet dog smell as far from me as possible."

"You know you like it. It's making you pant right now. I bet it's taking everything in you not to roll around my bed." He brushes his fingers through his hair, combing out dirt and leaves from the forest. "If you give in to your desire, you wouldn't be such a bitch. Are those assholes who are rigging the games not satisfying you enough?"

My blood cools at his words. "Fuck off. I don't know what you're talking about."

He laughs, his voice lowering. "You can't play stupid with me. I see what's going on."

Stepping closer, he curls his fingers into fists, his body rippling with his muscles. I scoot toward the edge of the bed and eye the door, calculating if I could beat him to it or if I'm going to have to fight.

I lift my chin, not letting him intimidate me. "So do I. The only ones trying to rig the games are the asshole alpha-mates of the leaders. I'm not stupid. Your pack would have never won three day claims without it."

He doesn't respond. He neither admits nor denies my accusations.

"Do the leaders know?" I ask.

His mouth curves into a scowl. "You don't know what you're talking about."

"I do. I know more than you think. I know that I won't let you all get away with this. I know that whatever the hell price you're supposed to pay for the continuous protection from the witches will catch up to you. You guys can't even protect your territories. You will—"

Radek snarls and transforms into a wolf, set off by my words. I scramble to my feet and grab a chair, getting ready to swing it at him.

"I'm done playing games with you, Lyric. There is an order around here, and it must be maintained. You're going to fucking submit to me or—"

A bolt of purple electricity zings across the room, striking Radek. His wolf body crashes to the floor, but he doesn't stay down long, baring his teeth, his hackles rising. Flynn grabs my shoulders, trying to pull me away. But I'm so over this. I need to take care of Radek now.

"Get out of here, she-wolf. I will handle it." Flynn summons more power into his hands with a soft chanting of foreign words.

"A fucking warlock!" Radek howls, the loud noise surely able to be heard through the territory. "Let go of her. She's mine."

Radek's words set me off, and I lunge forward, pushing Flynn out of the way. I crash into Radek's huge body, tackling him to the floor. He snaps his teeth in warning, the sound of his guttural growl reverberating through my bones.

"I am not yours!" I yell, grabbing onto his neck to squeeze his airway closed.

Radek transforms into a man, freeing his arms in the process. But I'm too fast. Too determined.

"I'm not yours," I repeat, punching him in the face. "If you're going to be anything to me, you're going to be mine. Now fucking bow down to me."

Because this ends now.

I will not let him even try to claim me.

10

ACCIDENTAL CLAIM

HOLY SHIT.

Holy fucking shit.

I stare at my bloody knuckles as Radek squeezes my hand, kneeling before me. I can't move or think, and I purposely hold my breath, afraid that the universe will come crashing down around me.

"What have you done?" Flynn whispers from beside me like if he keeps his voice low enough, Radek won't notice his presence.

I wiggle my fingers, easing them out of Radek's grasp. He bows down completely before me, and I stare in shock at his naked ass as he rests his forehead to the floor between my feet.

"I don't know," I murmur, shaking out my aching hand. "Clobbered some sense into him? I've seen it happen before. You can make them submit if you try hard enough." Because that's how Dax handled Antone's annoying ass. I just—shit. I never believed Radek would literally bow before me, and a part of me soaks in the satisfaction of seeing this dickhead on his knees.

"No, she-wolf. You just claimed him and the fates listened." Flynn cranes his neck to stare at the side of my face, remaining in his spot at my side.

I meet his gaze, grimacing. "You better not mean what I think you mean."

"You truly are naïve, aren't you? Your species, and many others for that matter, bond themselves by their souls. This used to be something natural, where mates would find each other on their own, but unrest in Magaelorum shifted things. The wars between your species' territories devastated things. Distrust prevented packs from creating alliances, and some powerful covens took advantage of it. Their need for your magic was thought to wipe the wolves out."

A part of me burns with anger that I'm just learning this now. Sagan had mentioned the past and the wars, but he never got into detail. And the others? Dax's grief over his father's death stopped me from prying. But if he claims I'm his mate, if they all want to be on my pack, they need to start opening up to me. They seem to know everything about my life...fuck. I need to find them. Now.

I spin away from Radek and dodge past Flynn, heading for the door. Flynn grabs the back of my robe, tugging me into him. A deep, threatening growl hums through the air, and damn it. I don't have time for this bullshit.

"Down, boy," I snap at Radek. "You have no right to act as if I belong to you or whatever the fuck this is."

"He touched you. You didn't like it." Radek narrows his eyes.

"I didn't like you grabbing me either, so fucking growl and smack yourself." I throw my robe off, surprising Flynn. I don't have time for this. He's interrupted enough of my night, even if I appreciated it a bit. Turning to him, I wave my hand. "You stay here and figure out what the hell happened and how to reverse this weird-ass situation. I don't want him thinking he can do shit on my behalf. I already chose my pack mates."

"Why should I?" Flynn asks, crossing his arms.

"Because you put me in this godforsaken position by handing me to this bastard. You want me to trust you? Earn it. Prove to me that you are on my side from the kindness of your heart." I twist the door handle and fling it open. "I'll be back by morning."

"At least tell me where you're going," Flynn says, standing

in the doorway, risking turning his back on Radek to face me. His muscular arms ripple as he clenches his fingers, his annoyance as clear as mine.

"To find my pack mates," I say.

Flynn groans. "Is that a good idea? I felt your pain over Caz. What if they're no different?"

"I guess I'll find out then." I stretch my arms over my head and prepare for my transformation. "And don't follow me. I'm leaving you in charge here. I meant what I said. Figure this shit out. Maybe teach him some damn manners. That asshole is yours to deal with for now since you insisted on forcing a day claim on me. Have fun."

"Lyric," Flynn calls.

I peek at him from over my shoulder. "Careful, warlock. You don't want me to claim you too."

Turning around, I focus on transforming into my wolf self in hopes of tracking down Dax, Sterling, Sagan, and Bastien. Flynn groans and closes the door to Radek's place, and a flash of magic lights the trees in front of me from the window. I pad my way around the building, silently hoping no one else is around. Most of the competitors should be knocked out from exhaustion. And the pack leaders? They'd have gone to their territories by now.

Bringing my nose to the ground, I inhale a breath through my nostrils. I feel weird as hell doing it, especially because I have no experience in scent tracking, but the competitors make it look so easy…and I'm pretty certain I'm familiar enough with each of my guys' scents to find them.

The quiet world keeps me on guard, and I use all my senses to pay attention to the area surrounding me. Stars shine brilliantly overhead, seeming impossibly brighter than in Lunar Crest. I follow the clearing between the trees to guide me away from what I think is where the Eclipse Valley pack resides and to the outskirts where the visitors would stay.

The soft thumps of heavy paws on the compacted dirt sound from behind me. I startle and bolt toward the trees, wondering if I could manage to hide long enough from my stalker to plan a counter-attack.

I race between two trees, my paws thudding in perfect sync with my racing heart. I thought getting chased during the games was bad, but being out here alone, knowing how many enemies lie in wait to take me down…I hate it. I hate having to constantly be on guard in a place that's supposed to protect me and cherish my existence because I have a damn vagina.

A gigantic wolf surprise attacks me from my right, knocking my paws out from under me. I snarl as I skid across the ground with the wolf on top of me. Thrashing my body, I knock the bastard off and plow my paws into his chest, baring my teeth.

Dax licks my snout, releasing a playful growl. "Now why the hell didn't you fight like this earlier?"

I flop on top of him, my heart speeding a billion beats per minute. Dax shifts into a man beneath me and engulfs me in a hug, scratching his fingers into my fur, knowing how much it drives me crazy. I wiggle, trying to escape, but he works his hands down my back, chuckling when I give up and flatten against him still in my wolf form. I know I'm the same to him regardless of the form I take, but I still find it weird as hell yet slightly enjoyable to get a rub down like this. His touch is full of adoration and amazement and not desire. Not like if we were both in the same form.

I lick the side of his face, making him laugh, and summon my transformation until I find myself straddling his naked body. Lust darkens his eyes at the sight of my bare breasts in his face and the heat of my skin on his stomach, my hands pressing the ground on each side of his head. I push my weight back and slide down his body, exciting myself in the process until his raging hard-on thumps against my lower back.

"I want to ask if you killed Radek, but I also want so badly to kiss you and apologize for my shortcomings," Dax murmurs, propping himself on his hands to sit up and face me. Easing me up a foot by my hips, he brings his cock out from under me to rest it right on my pelvis.

The sensation of his arousal so close to mine sends a dozen dirty thoughts racing through my mind. I don't let him decide which he should do and lean forward, crashing my lips to his. Our raw desires entangle, awakening the burning passion we share. I clutch his face and slip my tongue into his mouth, my soul craving him on a level that'll leave my body zinging and content, my lungs breathless, my body as dirty as the sexy thoughts filling my mind.

Dax moans against my mouth, tightening his fingers around my hips, pulling me so close that all he'd have to do is lift me up to slide in. I scratch my nails into his shoulder, my voice an incredibly embarrassing whimper of a plea.

"I want you," I say, running my fingers into his dark hair. "My body is desperate for you. Tonight has been rough."

Dax breaks from my mouth and kisses my throat, sending tingles down my chest. Lifting me higher, he flicks his tongue to my nipple and sucks it into his mouth. His fingers dig into my ass cheeks as he teases me with his shaft, rubbing my slickness across him without pushing inside.

And it drives me crazy.

I try to align my body to his, taking initiative to get what I want, but Dax hums deep in his throat and pushes to his feet with one hand. I cling onto him, arching my back as he explores and tastes my breasts, sucking hard enough to drag a moan from my lips. I squirm in his hold, my lust and need turning all-consuming. I can't even remember what brought me to him in the first place. My mind can't focus on anything until the fantasies playing in my head turn into reality.

"I missed you," Dax whispers in my ear before kissing my lobe. "You're all I ever think about."

I shiver at the sensation of his lips and bend my neck, silently begging him to continue his way down to my shoulder.

He strides toward one of the small cabins at the bottom of a hill, his quiet footsteps muffled by the soft-looking grass. Moonlight illuminates the world in a silver glow. I ease away to meet Dax's golden eyes, his skin bathed in the cool light from above. I touch my hand to his cheek, wanting to imprint the way he looks at me in this moment. His gaze embodies his unconditional, irrevocable feelings for me, searing my soul. I open my mouth to tell him, but he kisses me, silencing my words.

"We have to be as quiet as possible," he thinks into my mind, adjusting me in his arms to ease open the door to the cabin.

The quaint studio setup gives me an entire view of the place, from the massive bed to a small kitchenette with a tiny table and two chairs. The rooms in Lunar Crest are far more elaborate and strangely inviting compared to this bare-bones place.

Dax carries me across the room, kissing me deeper, tasting my mouth with his soft tongue. He glides it over mine in even, sensual strokes, awakening my body more. Dax blindly makes his way to the bed and tosses me onto it. My back hits the soft blankets, and I bite my lip and drink him in as he stands at the end, his muscles rippling, his desire so prominent that I'm sure if I stretched forward completely, I could pull him to me.

He releases a soft growl at my thought and reaches for my ankles, dragging me to the edge of the bed. I release a soft breath, my whole body singing in anticipation as he kneels before me and licks his lips like I'm all he craves. Sliding his big hands under my ass, he lifts me to his face and watches me watch him as he kisses my thigh. My breathing quickens in anticipation. He draws out the moment, slowly gliding his tongue toward the apex of my thighs, his low voice vibrating with his hum of desire.

Unable to stand his teasing any longer, I reach up and comb my hands into his hair, pulling him to me. He digs his fingers into my ass cheeks and smiles a second before drawing his tongue along my body and flicking it over my sensitive skin. A moan escapes my mouth, and I cover my lips with my hand, trying to muffle the noise.

I twist the blankets in my fingers, holding on as tightly as I can through the wave of pleasure crashing over me. Dax's thoughts trickle into my mind as he thinks about how amazing I taste and smell to him, how he wants me every second of every day for the rest of his life. And damn it, do I want that too. His mouth sets my body ablaze in ecstasy, and I arch my back as his tongue brings me to my peak. I bite my lip through the intense hurricane of tingles tightening my muscles, feeling as if they'll sweep me away from this crazy-ass world. A part of me hopes they do.

Dax's face lines with his desire, his gaze drinking me in as I lie exposed before him, blush blossoming over my heaving chest, my skin warm and craving more of what he has to offer. He pulls me upright and kisses me passionately, ensuring my breath will never even out again. I lace my fingers around his hard-on and stroke him a few times, loving the sensation of it flexing under my touch. I try to align my body to his, but he shakes his head.

"Not like this. I'm going to give you what you've been thinking about all day." Dax releases another deep hum from his throat, the noise so incredibly sexy that my vagina clenches in excitement. His thoughts of what he plans to do next trickle to me a moment before he acts on them.

Dax flips me over onto my stomach and adjusts my knees under me, giving my body another few inches of height. He rubs his hands from the backs of my legs and up my back, massaging me as he savors the sight of me from behind.

"That spankable ass," he murmurs, tapping my ass cheek with his hard cock. "You have no idea how much I love it. So sexy."

Dragging his hands back down, he spreads me a bit wider and thunks his erection against my sensitive skin. I stretch to look at him, his dark eyes smoldering over mine, and he graces me with a teasing smile as he rubs his tip over me and uses my excitement to stroke himself.

"If you don't stop teasing me, you're going to be the one to get spanked," I say, arching my back to reach for him.

He hums his disagreement and bends down, sliding his hand across my clavicle to hold me up while he kisses the side of my mouth, his hard body hot against mine, his boner so close to where I want it that the anticipation drives me a bit wild.

"Good," he murmurs, responding to my thought out loud. "Maybe you'll learn your lesson. Because those thoughts of yours…mmm. They're enough for me to risk everything to experience exactly what's on your mind."

Running his fingers away from my clavicle, he releases me only to link his fingers through my hair. He tugs my long strands to pull them away from my shoulder and aligns his body to mine from behind. I pant and squirm, squeezing my thighs together, wanting to feel his thick girth and length in all its sexy, mind-blowing intensity sink into me in a way that I can hopefully experience the pleasure in every nerve ending possible.

Dax grazes his mouth to my neck, teasing me with his tip, his fingers twisting my hair as he sucks my neck hard enough to leave a hickey behind, his way of marking me as he awakens the beast inside me. I want more. I want to experience the feral side of him, the powerful warrior I know he is. I need his strength and desperation, his ferocity and roughness. I want to know him as my future pack mate and the man who will back me up.

He moans at my thoughts and yanks my hair in one hand while bracing my shoulder with the other. Thrusting inside me, Dax releases the sexiest growl in existence, his hot desire crashing into me with his strength.

I moan so fucking loud at the sensation of his deep penetration. His body stretching mine in a way that sends tingles exploding through me. If I didn't know any better, I'd think his cock was deep enough to be felt inside my stomach. A husky, throaty noise escapes his lips at my thoughts, and he rocks his body to mine, determined to fuck me senseless so that I only think about the pleasure cascading between us, how good he feels, giving me the roughness I want after an intense night. I don't need to be coddled and drenched in affection. What I need is to find out for certain that I handle this hulking man. That I'm strong enough, wild enough, that I can truly give him whatever the hell he needs when he needs it and that he can do the same for me.

"You're the most powerful and fierce woman I've ever met, Lyric," he says, continuing to tug my hair and hold me in place to feel every throbbing inch of him. "You're mine."

"I'm yours," I say, my breath gasping.

He hums his satisfaction at my words. Dax's mind wanders to how hot he thinks I look in this position, how mind-blowing the warm wetness of my body feels, and how perfect I am. How I'm his forever and how he won't let those unworthy of me get in the way.

And then he thinks about how he wants to hear me scream his name, feel my body clench his, how much he enjoys the raw feelings of getting me off. Releasing my hair, he moves his hand around my hip, his fingers searching for the spot he knows will help fulfill his desires. I gasp and press my face into the blankets, his fingers rubbing between my legs in a quick, rhythmic motion that matches his powerful, fast thrusts. The whole bed rocks with his movements, thudding against the wall. My body explodes with sizzling ecstasy that leaves me squeezing my legs together, my orgasm so intense I can feel it rolling through every inch of my body.

Dax grunts and says my name with his release. I lie placid on the bed, my knees aching from the position, and I'm sure I couldn't stand up properly even if I tried. Dax eases out of me and rolls me over only to sink on top of me. He meets me for another kiss like he missed my mouth against his during our passion, and I hug him, feeling the thumps of his heartbeat racing against mine.

"I will do whatever it takes to fill every night with whatever you desire," he murmurs, flopping next to me to hold me close. He twines his fingers through mine and brings our hands to his chest, keeping me as close as he can. "This was the last time I'll ever allow someone else outside our pack to win your day claim."

His words trigger a rush of memories through my mind. I don't know if he can hear my spinning thoughts, but he stiffens at my intense reaction toward his words. I lick my lips and rub them together, gathering my nerve to tell him everything. About Flynn. About the pack leaders' mates. About Radek bowing down to me...about Caz.

My silence steals the light from his expression, his brows now furrowing, leaving a crease on his forehead. His brown gaze flickers with gold, and he waits for me to speak what's on my mind out loud.

"You did kill Radek, didn't you?" he quietly asks when I'm not quick enough to say anything. "Did he hurt yo—you have to make it clear that he hurt you. You can't let anyone else know otherwise."

A blip of fear flows from him to me, sending goosebumps over my skin. I don't know how to feel about his words and how he thinks I murdered Radek. I mean, yeah, I totally could and I would've killed him had he tried anything vile, but what the hell?

"If the leaders think you purposely killed him, they will award a claim to Eclipse Valley," Dax adds. "The consequence is supposed to deter competitors from manipulating the she-wolves into getting rid of their competition. If they suspect you're rigging the games—"

I cover his mouth with my hand, stopping him from continuing, sensing the rising panic inside him as he figures out what he needs to do. "Radek is alive."

Dax blows a breath out. "So you just kicked his ass and ran? He might be able to convince the leaders to give him another ch—"

I sit up and crawl on top of him, using my naked body to push thoughts of Radek from his mind. He flares his nostrils and inhales a breath of my scent like he needs it to calm his nerves. My distraction is enough to snuff out his assumptions and get him to focus on me. I draw my finger across his taut chest, busying myself until I know for certain that Dax will let me speak without interruption.

"I don't want you to panic," I start, grabbing his hands in mine. "But I have something important to tell you, Sterling, Bastien, and Sagan." I purposefully leave Caz's name out, which doesn't go unnoticed.

"I'm not so sure I can wait for them to hear what you have to say, Lyric," Dax admits, sitting upright with me on his lap. "What is this about? I can feel your hesitation. You can tell me anything, you know."

I suck in a deep breath and puff the air through my lips. "I know...I just..."

I need to spit it out. My bunching nerves are making it worse.

"Lyric, please." Dax brings his hands to my face and cups my cheeks, searching my eyes like he can untangle my racing thoughts to decipher what's on my mind. "Whatever it is, I want to help you. I won't judge you. I won't—"

"You can't know that for sure," I say softly.

He strokes his fingers over my cheeks, combing away the hair trying to veil my face. "But I do."

"Dax, I—"

Howls outside the door draw my attention away from Dax. He stiffens and slides me off his lap, grabbing the blanket to tug around my shoulders. We fall silent and listen to the rising commotion. A man yells out, but it's not fear. It's anger.

"Where are Radek and Lyric?" a deep, threatening voice asks. "Has anyone seen either of them?"

Dax growls under his breath and motions for me to head toward the bathroom door. He struts toward the window and cracks the curtain to peek outside.

"She's come through here," another man says, his voice humming right outside the door.

"Caz, you were on guard. Where are they?" The familiar voice of Calhoun stabs at my heart, sending it dropping into my stomach.

Dax's muscles ripple with his annoyance.

"I don't know. They were fighting, but I chose to let Radek handle her without intervening. Was I not supposed to? I thought you—"

A loud slap echoes through the air, the sound of flesh against flesh twisting my insides. Caz growls but shuts up. A ripple of pain radiates across my cheek as if Calhoun slapped me too, and I do my best to shove Caz from my mind. I still struggle to keep my guard up with him, a part of me praying to the universe that this is a misunderstanding.

"You worthless, piece of—"

"That's enough, Calhoun," Sterling says, his voice cutting through the low murmurs of what I can only assume belongs to the onlookers.

Calhoun growls. "Is she with you? What have the two of you done with Radek? My mate was informed that Lyric had planned on killing the competition to ensure she got whoever she wanted. I sent someone to investigate, and they found blood. Radek's blood. Now someone tell me where the hell she went."

"Lyric isn't a killer," Sagan says, his deep, velvety voice wrapping around me as he stands up for me.

"Yeah, she might've handed him his balls, but Blondie wouldn't murder even that asshole. You know she hated that the leaders sentenced Hendrix to death. Whoever the fuck you heard that warning from was full of shit." Sterling's familiar footsteps draw closer to Dax's door.

"What about you?" Calhoun asks. "You two spend a lot of time with her."

"Are you fucking kidding me?" Sterling asks, his voice rising in annoyance. "I wouldn't jeopardize my chance at winning the games."

"You should ask the Storm Haven competitors," an unfamiliar man says. "The bitch can't ever take her mind off Dax. Fuck, I don't know about you, but I think I can smell her nearby."

"Dax is on guard with Bastien," Sagan says, speaking up. "You probably picked up her scent from Caz."

"They're lying." The sound of Paige's voice cools my blood. "I suspected my niece was up to something. She's here. I know it."

A howl sounds through the air, and something crashes to the door. I startle and duck into the bathroom. Dax snarls as someone flings his door open. Calhoun rams into Dax's chest, sending him sliding across the room. I rush into the shower and try to hide the best I can.

"Lyric! Get your ass out here," Calhoun hollers.

The air buzzes around me, crackling with static. I brace to

fight like hell. I prepare to confront this bastard and everyone else. Paige is a dead woman for trying to stir shit up.

"Lyric!" Footsteps clomp toward the bathroom.

Flynn materializes next to me and wraps me in his arms. "Time to go, she-wolf."

The world falls out from under me, and I heave a breath, my mind spinning like crazy. I catch the feral, musky scent of Radek before my mind has a chance to process that Flynn transported me into the forest. Radek lifts me off my feet and spins me around, pressing my back to the rough bark.

"Moan for me," he whispers into my ear, making me shiver.

I nearly sucker punch him, but some tree branches rustle nearby.

"Do it, Lyric," he commands, his voice growling.

I cringe at even the thought but open my mouth and fake the loudest, most obnoxious moan in existence. Radek groans deep in his throat, getting turned on by the sound of my voice. I dig my fingers into his shoulders and glower at him.

"Get that thing any closer to me and you'll lose it," I warn.

"Shhh, they're coming," he whispers.

Releasing a growl, he threatens whoever closes in on us. A howl sounds through the air, drawing my attention away. I spot Calhoun and two of the other she-wolf mates hovering in the trees.

I scowl. "What the fuck, you creeps? Are you spying on us?"

"Everything all right?" Calhoun asks, keeping his face

expressionless. "Someone heard fighting and smelled your blood, Radek."

Radek bares his teeth. "What they heard is my helluva good time with this sexy, feisty as hell babe."

I try not to grimace, but then more people gather, spying on us through the trees. Sterling swears, and Sagan growls. Dax stares at me in confusion, knowing I was in his bathroom. Bastien turns away and links his fingers through his hair.

I open and close my mouth, trying to get my voice to work. I'm so angry at Flynn for this. At Paige for putting me in this position and fucking Calhoun for all the other bullshit.

"Now get out of here, you fuckheads," Radek snaps. "This sweet, sexy thing is mine."

11

BETRAYED

SUNSHINE WARMS MY FUR AS I sleep curled up in the dirt in my wolf form. I couldn't face a walk of shame through the community despite having nothing to be ashamed about, and I also couldn't go after Bastien, Sagan, or Sterling. I could sense Dax hovering nearby, but he kept his distance because of the confrontation. There was also no way I was spending the night in a room with Radek, letting the competitors minds fantasize about trying to win my next day claim, so I transformed into a wolf, commanded Radek leave me the hell alone, and slept by myself for the first time since coming to Lulupoterra.

Except I'm not as alone as I thought.

A warm body molds to mine with a heavy head resting on my back. I snap my eyes open and stiffen, my mind a jumbled mess from awakening to a dozen scents that waft through the air from last night. It takes me a second to realize Caz sleeps ultra-close, his big wolf body flush against mine.

I release a low growl. "Get the hell off of me," I say, the thought burning through me with the reminder of Caz's betrayal.

A blip of confusion and sorrow whips through my head, Caz's mind open for me. "It's me," he thinks, his soft voice prodding at the part of me that can't help caring about him. "You're okay. Safe."

I growl at his words and jerk my head around, snapping my teeth into his thick coat. He kicks his big paws into my back, shoving space between us as I try to bite him again. I lunge from the ground at him, attempting to pin him to the dirt, but he rolls and tosses me off.

"You better run like hell, Caz," I snap, unable to control my anger. "If I catch you, I will bite your fucking balls off."

He takes my threat seriously and launches away from me, skidding his paws across the ground. Snarling, I chase after him and try to bite his back end. He weaves through the trees like a scared little animal, fleeing as fast as he can. My instinct to catch him drives me wild, and I lose myself to my wolf.

"Caz!" I yell in my mind along with a howl through the forest. "You can't run forever. Your balls are mine, you asshole. You betrayed me. I trusted you."

Caz doesn't respond, focusing on his escape. The trees grow denser, slowing him down. I snap my jaws, barking and growling, yipping, and yowling, my wild nature ready to bite this fucking bastard.

He tucks his tail between his legs protectively, and I manage to grab the appendage in my teeth and yank him to me. Growling, he flips around and pounces on me, shoving my body to the ground. Fury unleashes inside me, and I jerk my head up, trying to rip out his throat.

Baring his fangs, he meets my anger with his own and nips me hard enough on the ear to drag a yelp from my muzzle. I submit under him, whimpering like he just chewed my ear off. I know I sound like a wounded animal, and I flop back completely and expose my belly to him. He flares his nostrils, distracted by my position. He'd never admit it to me, but he loves this. I can feel his excitement in finally managing to get me to lie docile beneath him no matter how much he's told me he enjoys my wild side.

"Lyric, fuck," he says, his voice trickling to my mind. "What the hell ha—"

I stretch my body and transform into my human self, cutting off his thought. His surprise over my shift slows him down, and I ram my palms into his chest. He might be huge and agile in this form, but I'm determined as hell to show him exactly what happens to the men who betray me. I tackle him to the ground and dig my fingers into the thick fur of his neck. He tries to fight me off, but my fury turns me seemingly unstoppable.

"You're dead, Caz. I trusted you as my pack mate and you broke my fucking heart," I say, tightening my hands around his neck.

He growls with his shift back into a man. Grabbing my wrists, he tries to break free of my hold, so I let go of his throat with one hand and swing my fist behind me, punching him hard in the junk.

He hollers at the same time a heavy wolf body collides into me, knocking me off of him. I screech and flail, unable to get a good hold on my attacker as the beast drags me away from Caz by my long blond hair. Caz turns on his side, cupping his junk, but manages to get his shit together to rush in the opposite direction.

"You coward!" I scream. "Go ahead! Let another asshole fight your fucking battles! I'll bite his damn cock off too."

"It's a good thing I have my tongue as back up, blondie." Sterling's voice sounds through my mind as he releases his hold on my hair. "I'll lick your pleasure port even if you gobble my pussy pounder."

I swing my hand up and grab the front of his chest fur. Flipping him onto his back, I climb on top of him and flatten against him in a hug. His familiar scent washes over me, and I totally bury my face in his fur. His big wolf body wiggles beneath me until his warm arms wrap around my back with his embrace.

"Fuck, Sterling," I murmur. "I wasn't sure if you'd want to see me today after last night."

He groans and sits up, pulling me with him. "It's like you don't even know me. I not only want to see you, I want to hold you, kiss you, lick you, spank you, tease you, please you, and hump the hell out of you right here, right now...but first, what the fuck is going on? Why did I have to risk those sharp fangs of yours on my cock to save the mopey bastard's balls? I feel as if I'm missing something."

I bonk my head to his shoulder a couple of times, trying to calm my still racing heart. "You shouldn't have intervened. He's a dead man."

Sterling gently pinches my chin, guiding my head up to look at him. "You're serious."

"Of course I'm fucking serious. He—he—" I'm so angry that I can barely spit the words out.

Pulling me higher, Sterling silences my squeaky voice with a kiss, stroking his hand down the length of my back. He doesn't do it to purposefully interrupt me but to stop me from saying something out loud. Soft voices muffle nearby, probably some asshole guardians sweeping the area for threats.

"Transform, blondie. I want you to follow me somewhere." Sterling's voice enters my mind as he continues to kiss me sweetly, just savoring the sensation of my lips against his.

His tranquil emotions snuff out my burning anger. For what feels like the first time, he doesn't try to cool me off with his dirty humor or sexual suggestions. He simply snuggles with me in silence until I gather myself and transform right in his arms.

"Such a good girl," he teases, ruffling his fingers through the fur between my ears. "That's better, right. Where's your spot? I need to give it a little scratch for good luck." Reaching toward my belly, he teases me with a ridiculous belly rub that makes me scramble off him.

"You're going to get it, Sterling," I warn, releasing a low growl.

"Am I now?" he responds, his pouty mouth stretching into a smile.

"Damn straight." I drag my tongue across his face, making him laugh.

He tries to block me with his arm, but I nip his skin and proceed to lick his face again. And I keep licking him, slobbering all over his hair and face. He might tease that he enjoys whatever form I take, but it's totally driving him crazy that he's at the mercy of my tongue and not in the form or in the way he desires.

"You got five seconds to control yourself, blondie," Sterling says, wriggling beneath my heavy paws, trying to block my wolfy affection.

"What exactly do you think you're going to do?" I ask,

slurping my tongue across his neck.

He jerks and laughs, no longer trying to resist knocking me off of him. "I call mercy, blondie. That fucking tickles."

His words only make me want to continue to push him until he can't stand it. I've never had the honor of tickling someone, and his laughter is worth risking him retaliating. He hears my thoughts and growls at me, the noise half-assed in his man form. He tries to protect his face from my slobbery tongue with his arms, and I yip and bark in excitement at the opening he leaves at his sides. If I were human and thinking clearly, it might gross me out to lick his underarm, but I'm beyond caring. I just want his musical laughter and pleas to fill me up in a way that makes me feel as if I'll float away.

"Don't you fucking do it, blondie. This won't end well for you," he threatens, his body tensing under my tongue that drags the best laughter I've heard in a while. "Fuck! Fuck! Mercy! Mercy!"

"Not until I'm ready," I think to him, poking my cold nose into his side.

"You're going to make me piss, damn it," he says, his voice turning rumbly, his fingers digging into my coat.

"That's one way to keep the assholes away," I retort, shocking the hell out of him.

Sterling growls and flails, finally managing to knock me off him. He tries to tackle me, but I lunge away and dart between two trees. His soft howl hums through the air with his transformation, and a wave of his determination crashes into me.

"You're in so much trouble, blondie." Sterling barks, darting behind me. "You just wait."

My laughter sounds through my mind, and I rush forward, letting my wolf take complete control over my movements. I have no clue where I'm heading, but I don't want to stop running. Something about the playfulness of this moment rouses a peace inside me I had no idea was still possible. It's enough to make me slow down to let Sterling catch up. He rubs his body along mine, guiding me deeper into the forest. The trees block out the sunlight above, and a strange quiet falls around us.

Sterling runs past me to lead the way, weaving through trees and ducking under low branches until we have to crawl through a tangled mess of overgrowth on our bellies. Sterling breaks through some gnarled branches acting like a wall, and sunlight blinds me. A sweet floral fragrance permeates through the air, but when I wiggle out of the forest, a cave greets us.

"Almost there, Lyric," Sterling says, prancing closer, his excitement wrapping around me through our mind link. "Just gotta go through the tunnel."

I dodge past him and race toward the narrow opening in the hillside. He growls and tries to beat me to it, but I ram into his side, throwing him off course. Darting inside, I slow down, waiting for my eyes to adjust. Glittering stones glow from within the walls, guiding my way through the darkness.

"You better move that sexy ass of yours. Your teasing makes

me want to hump the hell out of you," Sterling says, shoving his head between my back legs to sneak under me to get ahead.

I release a playful growl and let him exit the tunnel first. I plop on my stomach at the mouth and rest my head on my paws. "You better transform first, or I'm not coming out."

"Because you know you're in trouble, blondie. But don't worry. You can come out. I'd prefer to get you back when you least expect it." To prove his point, he stretches his long body and transforms back into a man. Raising his arms, he stretches his muscular back and flexes his muscles, tipping his head up to soak in the sunshine.

He grins, his cocky-bastard expression goading me to sneak my way from the tunnel. He licks his lips and turns around, strolling a few feet forward, giving me a view of his ass. And now I want to nip it.

I stride forward, my paws thumping the ground. Sterling expects my attack and spins around. He catches me and lifts me up, wrapping his arms around my middle. He snuggles his face to my chest, inhaling a breath. I growl and thrash away from him. He narrows his eyes at me and opens his arms, preparing to try to grab me again.

I bark and race around him. He spins on the balls of his feet but I surprise him by weaving through his legs. Jumping up, I pounce against his back. Instead of knocking him down, he stiffens, bracing against my strength. He knows if I knock him down, I'll lick the hell out of him again.

So instead, I hook my paws around his waist and hump him.

Tipping his head back, he laughs louder than I've ever heard him before. He tries to break away from my hold, but I hop on my hind legs, keeping with him.

"That's it, blondie. I can't stand this anymore." Snatching me from the ground, he flips me onto my back.

He straddles me, scratching my stomach, trying to pet my entire body. I squirm and thrash, his strength too much for me in this position. Closing my eyes, I shift into the form I feel most powerful. Sterling's fingers tangle in my blond hair, his smile fading as his naked body rests between my legs, his chest pressing into my boobs. His cock hardens and thumps against my sensitive flesh.

I intake a small breath, my whole body humming with desire. Bowing closer, Sterling kisses me tenderly, grazing his lips to mine, testing me to see how I'll react to his closeness. And fuck do I react. I slide my hands around his neck and tease him with my tongue, gliding it over his until his hands travel down my back and he squeezes my ass.

I moan and reach between us, stroking my hand along his raging hard-on. His mind opens for mine, and my vagina clenches in excitement at how hot he is for me. How much he craves me. And I yearn for him too. It would be so easy to align his body to mine and guide him in. The thought of the good pressure that will come with his thrusts sizzles through my mind.

"You're so beautiful, Lyric," he murmurs, breaking from my mouth to kiss my jaw, his hand reciprocating my gesture by rubbing between my legs. "I can't get enough of you. I want—"

I groan and grab his hair, yanking him from my throat before crashing my lips back to his. Slipping my tongue into his mouth, I ensure no more sweet words come spilling from him. I might enjoy them, but I've learned my lesson with Dax and Sagan. Sweet words come before the claim doom.

He hums deep in his throat. "I already told you. I will not claim you. I don't want to be sweet with you," he thinks, using our mental link to continue his thoughts. "I want to be dirty. Filthy. I want to pin you down and punish you for that naughty tongue of yours. You smell so damn good that all I can think about is sinking my tuna torpedo into your fish biscuit until you drench me in your love juice."

I laugh against his mouth at his ridiculous thought. Hooking my arms around him, I roll him off to get on top. He pinches my hips and slides me over his hard length, his gray eyes heavy-lidded with his desire.

I lean down and kiss him again, savoring the sensation of rolling my hips to rub against his body, knowing that all it will take is one little adjustment, and I can ride him the way I want, pinning him down instead and hearing him say my name, feeling his fingers pinch my ass cheeks as he guides my body hard and fast and deep on him. The thought builds so much excitement inside me that I feel as if I won't survive another second longer until I can satiate my desire and live out my fantasy.

Sterling moans at my thoughts, at my slippery lust rubbing over him until I align our bodies, not even caring if we're outside without the cover of the trees. I don't care what the hell is going on in the world around us or the position I've been put in.

All I can think about is how much I want to sink onto Sterling and bounce my body hard and fast until I make myself scream, and then I want him to flip on top of me and stretch my legs over my head, leave my muscles burning and hot, my breath gasping.

Because he's mine. He's all mine.

With my thought, I align my body with Sterling's and gasp in pleasure as he guides his throbbing cock inside me. He releases a sexy, deep moan that vibrates against my mouth, and I bite his bottom lip and stretch it with my teeth before kissing him harder, tasting his tongue, memorizing the sensations of our passion as we give in to our raw, natural desires.

Rolling my hips, I bounce up and down on his cock, my moans coming in quick bursts as I ride him desperately, losing myself to the ecstasy zinging between my legs, sparking across every cell in my body. He reaches one hand up and massages my boob, flicking his thumb over my tight nipple to intensify my pleasure. Breaking from his mouth, I sit up and lean back, clutching his legs as I rock back and forth over and over, his cock hitting me in just the right spot that an orgasm is within my reach.

Sterling rubs his thumb over my clit, helping me reach my peak faster, and my whole body tenses as I swear to the universe that I feel the pleasure and intensity of my release even in my toes, my strands of long hair, my fucking brain. Grabbing my ass, Sterling doesn't let me catch my breath and fulfills the fantasy running through my mind. He sits between my legs and hooks his fingers to my hips, pulling me onto him while guiding me into a backbend, stretching my muscles in a way that makes me moan so loudly when he pushes inside me.

The sun above haloes him in pale light, his platinum hair sparkling while the shadows on his face turn him even more handsome. He rocks his body to mine, watching me with his pouty mouth panting for breath. I grip the grass between my fingers without taking my gaze from him as he pleasures me even more, the position exposing my clit to him, giving him access to make me scream in ecstasy.

My second orgasm sets Sterling off, and he grunts, his face scrunching as he cums. Slowing down, he pulls me back up and hugs me to him, our bodies still connected with our embrace. He nuzzles his face into my hair and inhales a few deep breaths like the scent of my skin, of our passion, will imprint this moment in his mind forever.

I kiss him again, my heart light and so full of something indescribable I feel as if I might float away. "You exceeded my expectations. I mean, damn."

He chuckles and plays with my hair, leaning in to kiss the

base of my throat like he can't get enough. "You didn't even let me finish my foreplay."

Heat burns across my heaving chest, my heart thumping wildly at just the thought of going at it again and again. "I just—I don't know. Something came over me. I've never wanted anything so much in my life as I wanted to be with you in this moment. You know exactly what to do to pull me from my bad moods. You make me happy. I want you to know that."

Something indecipherable flickers in his eyes at my words, and he wraps his arms around me and holds me close, resting his forehead to mine.

"I had no idea how fucking incredible your claim on me would be," he says, kissing me again.

I stiffen in his arms and pull back. "What are you talking about?"

"You claimed me—your soul called mine. You said I was yours and—"

"Fuck," I breathe, my heart refusing to slow down. "Fu-u-u-u-ck. I didn't mean to do that. I—"

Sterling's brows pucker together, the light that was shining in his eyes now darkening with my words. His emotions shift, and I swear I can feel his heartache as if it's my own.

"Please don't say what I think you might. I don't want you to regret something out of your control. Our souls know what is in the fates. I know you feel what I do." Sterling caresses his fingers to my cheek. "But I also know you're afraid of your feelings.

Of mine. I swore to you that I wouldn't try to claim you as mine, and I won't unless you're a hundred percent sure, but this—" He presses his fingers over my heart. "This beautiful, fierce, incomparable heart and soul of yours can't be denied. I couldn't deny you. I'm yours, Lyric."

His words touch me so deeply, his raw honesty bare like he wears his heart pinned across his chest. I knew Sterling had a side to him I hadn't seen, and to see him and to feel him in such an intimate way where he's not hiding his feelings with his humor, trying to constantly make light of this situation, digs deeply to my soul. He's everything I could want—loyal, devoted, protective, funny—but a part of me fears that even if he's everything I want, I might not deserve it. He might deserve better than this life that is out to get me. What if things don't turn out as my dad planned, and this claim I accidentally laid on Sterling dooms him?

Cupping my face, Sterling searches my eyes. "Hey, whoa, blondie. I already told you I wanted to be doomed by you. I'll go down with a bang or a hundred. Your snake bait is luring me to you again already."

I groan and bonk my head to his shoulder. "Sterling."

"Not even a little laugh?" he asks, stroking his hands down my back.

I sigh.

Nuzzling his nose to mine, he tries to get me to smile. "We'll get through this. What you're feeling—what you've been through—it's fucked up. You don't deserve all this bullshit. You deserve to create the life you want, and I'm here to help you. Always. Especially if you plan to surprise hump me from now on."

I smirk, unable to remain serious.

"You know there's going to be payback for that, right?" he adds.

Pushing him back, I rock against him, surprising the hell out of him. "You can try."

"You bet—"

A loud whistle cuts through the air, drawing our attention toward the hillside covered in thousands of colorful flowers. I frown, listening to several howls follow suit, a strange eeriness to their calls.

"Brother? Lyric? You two here?" Sagan's voice whispers through my mind.

Sterling tilts his head. "Yeah, what's up?"

"Lyric has been summoned by the leaders, and the guardians want to know where you are." Sagan's voice rings through the air as he stretches outside the tunnel. "Caz is covering for you, brother. The leaders still think Lyric is with Radek, and no one has seen him. Dax didn't think they were together."

"We weren't—aren't," I say, answering him. "Last night, I—"

"You don't have to explain anything, gorgeous," Sagan says, cutting me off.

I grimace. "Yeah, I do. It wasn't what it looked like. I—"

Flynn materializes a few feet away with a burst of light like the sun just fell to the earth. Sterling grabs me protectively, and Sagan transforms into a wolf, releasing a warning growl at the warlock.

Flynn ignores both of them and extends his hand to me. "She-wolf, we have to go. Now."

"Go?" I ask, grimacing. "Go where?"

"To the Mortal World. I found out what's different about you. It's best if we leave." Flynn waves his hand to me again. "Come on. I'll explain everything."

"I—I can't leave." I flick my attention to Sagan as he stalks his way closer. I hold my finger up to him, getting him to stop in his tracks.

"You must," Flynn argues, his lavender eyes flashing with magic. Desperation lines his pleading voice. "Please."

Flynn jerks out his hand to grab me, but he doesn't get the chance. Bastien launches from the tall grass, his white fur blurring with his jump. He collides into Flynn and knocks him away. Dax darts toward him next. Lurching closer, Sagan growls. They surround the warlock, baring their teeth, ready to rip him apart.

"Don't hurt him," I say, my voice rising in worry. I extend my arms out like my gesture will get them to chill out. "Please. Flynn's been helping me. He saved me from the lycans. Helped me when Paige walked in on us in the cleansing pool. He doesn't want to hurt me."

"What?" Sterling asks, his body tensing. A sharp pain explodes in my heart, his emotions leaving me breathless.

I knew he'd be upset. I knew all of them would be. I had hoped to tell them when we had a chance to breathe, but the universe hates me. It wants me to suffer. My betrayal, my withholding this from them, could very well ruin things. We're a pack. We're not supposed to have secrets. But damn it. I think we all do.

The thought drenches me in annoyance and hurt. I want to defend myself and throw it in their faces that they haven't told me everything either, but my heart wins. I will not excuse my behavior by throwing theirs out in the open. I just—I just want to fix this.

My throat burns with my words. "Please, Sterling. I'll explain everything. I—"

A howl cuts through the air from the tunnel, and I tense at the sight of Caz. Flynn disappears, taking advantage of the distraction. Anger rushes through me at the sight of Caz and his true betrayal to all of us. He has a lot of nerve to show up here.

"You guys, we have to hurry," he says, barking as his words whip through my mind.

"I'm not going anywhere with you," I snap. I inhale a few deep breaths, trying to suppress Sterling's wild emotions, far more out of control than the others. It must be the claim, leaving his bond to me powerful and overwhelming. "You're a bastard traitor. I know everything."

"What are you talking about, Lyric," Dax asks, his voice trickling just to me.

"What do you mean?" Caz scrubs his hands over his face. A wave of confusion and grief washes from him to me. "I'm not a traitor. I'm trying to help. Everything is going to shit. My dad is dead. He's been murdered."

I dig my fingers into my palms. The hot emotions from everyone send me bowing. "What? Who? How?" A dozen questions flit through my mind.

Caz's hackles rise on his back, and he narrows his eyes, looking past me. "I don't know, but Meadow View is accusing you."

"*Me?*" Surprise heightens the pitch of my voice.

He shakes his head and motions behind me. I hadn't realized Dax lingers close. "No, Dax. He's to stand trial immediately. If they find him guilty, he'll be sentenced to death."

"THIS IS YOUR FAULT!" I scream, rushing toward Caz. "You're a traitor! You're probably setting us all up. I knew it was a mistake to let my guard down for you after you fucked with me in the Mortal World. You're a bastard, Caz! A fucking asshole!"

I race toward him, expecting him to run away like the coward he is, but he straightens his back and prepares for my attack. Two warm hands latch to my sides and yank me off my feet. I smack into Bastien's chest, his strong hug locking me against his muscular body. I bend forward, throwing off his center of gravity enough to flip him onto his back.

I don't make it far.

Snagging my ankle, Bastien trips me, sending me sprawling on top of him. He huffs a breath at the force of my fall but manages to drag me back as I attempt to launch toward Caz again. My knees hit the ground on the sides of his head, and I sit on his face, surprising him enough to loosen his hold. The scent of my passion with Sterling probably still clings to my body, throwing his senses into mating mode or whatever. At least it's one advantage to the nearing of my season.

If only Sagan didn't snatch me away before I throw myself at Caz and punch his fucking cock.

"Stop intervening!" I yell, bucking my body. "That's a command. I don't want to hurt you."

"Don't let her go," Dax says to Sagan, his voice rumbling with a growl. "Same for you, Bastien. Keep Sterling back. The both of them are still coming down from her claim. They won't be thinking straight."

It's now that I realize Bastien pins Sterling to the ground. He must've been trying to help me get to Caz, feeling the hot emotions coursing through me. I know they affect Dax and Sagan more intently, but they've had a chance to learn to handle them in the last few weeks. Sterling hasn't.

"Caz, tell us what the fuck is going on," Dax adds, strolling around me to block my view of Caz. His muscular body ripples with his flexing muscles, his tall form towering over Caz and his bastardly pouty face like I'm the one who wronged him.

"He's a traitor, is what happened," I say, trying to keep my body from attacking Sagan in the process. I'm furious but not at him. "I saw him during the last game. He was with the pack leaders' mates, and they were strategizing rigging the games. He's been playing us. He was instructed to get me in line."

Caz's serious expression softens with his wide eyes. He takes an automatic step back at my accusation, looking scared as hell and ready to flee like the coward he is. He was afraid to face me upon my arrival, and he's terrified to face me now. And he should be.

Bastien releases a low growl. "You better explain yourself, Caz. What is she talking about?"

Caz clenches his fingers into his palms. "It's not what she thinks. Please, I'll explain everything, but we have to go. They're coming."

"I saw you! I heard everything! I know the truth about how the damn leaders' pack mates are manipulating things behind their backs and how the she-wolves are being hindered and purposely kept weak because of them. I know they fear me. I know they will do whatever it takes, so I end up with men who they think can control me, so they can continue with their fucking asshole ways, treating us as things to get their dicks wet and pass on their genes." I struggle in Sagan's arms, wishing he'd let me go. "And you're a part of it. You almost fooled me with your bullshit promises. Your fake loyalty."

"Lyric, I swear. I didn't know the alpha-mates were meeting. I had no idea until you went missing and my dad told me. They don't initiate alphas until after the games to ensure they pick the ones they think are worthy to rule the territories." Caz locks his gaze to mine, his desperation for me to believe him crashing through me. "I was planning to tell you—"

"When?" I snap, cutting him off. "When you were certain you claimed me? Made me fall madly in love with you, so you could use my heart against me? Fucking bullshit!"

Ah, hell. Fuck. Don't cry. Don't fucking cry. My eyes burn and I blink them like crazy, so pissed off that I do actually care about him. I opened my mind and soul and was starting to bond. I had accepted that he would be on my pack and was able to push away the bullshit surrounding my arrival to remind myself that Caz was my friend before all this. But now?

Sterling yells from Bastien's arms, jerking himself free of his hold. He's too fast for Dax to catch and collides into Caz, knocking him off his feet. Pinning him down, Sterling shoves his hands into Caz's chest, making him gasp.

"I don't believe you, you asshole! I'm going to kill you for this. You fucking broke her heart! I can feel it! I knew this shit was a setup when the leaders picked you to bring Lyric here." Sterling punches Caz in the face, splitting his lip. "My mother said it was because the Meadow View pack was neutral in regards to Lyric's parents, but I knew it was something else."

"But I'm not neutral!" Caz yells, blocking his face with his arms. "You damn well know that I believe in Levi's teachings. My uncle—"

Several howls hum from the tunnel, cutting Caz's words off. Silence falls between everyone, and Caz shoves Sterling hard, knocking him off. He scrambles away, transforming into a wolf so quickly that no one has a chance to grab him as he bolts from us. I tense at the soft thuds of paws growing louder and louder at the pace of my speeding heart.

"Fuck. Bastien, take Lyric to the river. We'll hold them off," Dax says, his muscles rippling. "Get her back to Lunar Crest. We can't risk them trying to take her from us."

Fear clenches my chest. "What? No. I'm not leaving you."

Dax growls with his transformation. "You have to. If what Caz said is true, they—"

A giant red wolf launches from the mouth of the tunnel, crashing into Sterling. Another and another beast blurs with speed as they dart towards us. Bastien scoops me into his arms and makes a run for it as Dax and Sagan block the wolves from chasing us.

But we don't get far.

Paige materializes out of nowhere and transforms into a blond wolf with fur a bit darker than mine. She launches at Bastien with a snarl. He spins and she sinks her teeth into his side, ripping at his middle.

"Traitors must die," she says, her voice shocking me as it erupts in my mind. "Your parents will regret their alliance with the Fire Mountain Clan. The Nightstar Coven will ensure it."

Neither Bastien nor I have a chance to fight or run. A huge black form knocks me away from Bastien, and Antone pins his brother to the ground. Paige locks her teeth into my hair and drags me a few feet.

"Get the cage ready," she snaps, yanking my hair. "I have her. She is now yours."

They're dead. They're all fucking dead. If the leaders or their mates even dare mess up a single hair on Dax, Sterling, Sagan, or Bastien's heads, I will skin them all and give their pelts to the witches. I'll—

"You are scary as hell when you're angry." Flynn taps his knuckles to the top of the cage in the middle of an empty room. It's more like a cell, if anything, without even a window. Only one door leads in or out, and it's guarded by an unfamiliar wolf, who is a part of the Stargaze Hill pack.

"Get out of my head," I mutter, sticking my hand through the slots in the bars. I grab Flynn's wrist and yank him down until his chest presses into the top of this humiliating cage. No one even offered me clothing or anything, but I can't seem to summon my wolf self. It's bad enough I'm locked in here. I'd be far too anxious trapped in my true form.

"I can't help it. I'm sorry. You're just so open to me." Flynn wiggles his fingers, trying to loosen my death grip.

Tipping my head back, I meet his lavender eyes. "Well, you're about to be open to me if you don't get me the fuck out of here. I need to get to my pack mates. They're being set up. They wouldn't kill anyone."

His jaw twitches and he gives up trying to pull away and instead rests his forehead to the bars, closing the space so much so that I can feel his soft breath caressing my lips. "Are you sure? They seemed pretty hell-bent on killing me and the she-wolf indebted to the witch. I'm nearly certain they would kill anyone on your behalf, but especially if they felt you were threatened. Last I checked, you were, and by your mate's father no less."

"Caz is not my fucking mate. He's dead to me. You will be too if you don't stop wasting time and use your damn magic to get me out of here." I grip my fingers to the front of his shirt and release his hand, still managing to keep him in place.

But right now, I don't think he'll move. His eyes challenge mine in a staring contest. Something magical flickers across his lavender irises the longer we battle with each other, trying to make the other break first. My heart picks up speed, thumping like a discordant melody.

"Lyric," Flynn whispers, my name sounding so terribly sad coming from his pouty mouth that I feel bad for him. How is that even possible? Maybe because it's one of the few times he's ever used my name or maybe because I feel a bit guilty that he's on the outside of my cage, pitying me, when he knows he could be fucking helping me.

"Please," I say, my voice just as low and pleading, my heart hurting the longer the heavy silence of our racing thoughts drags between us. "I—I know you won't understand, but I can't lose them. I don't deserve to be in this damn cage. You were so adamant about helping me before. Why won't you help me now? What do you want in return? That's how this works, right? We make an unfair deal that leaves me at your mercy. I don't even care anymore. I understand why my father did it. Help me, Flynn. Please."

My lip uncontrollably quivers, and I suck it into my mouth, trying not to let him see that my strength diminishes with every passing second.

My dad taught me a lot in my life. He taught me to be smart and brave and how to defend myself. He taught me not to take bullshit from anyone. But the one thing he never taught me is that there is more to life than me and protecting myself. He never warned me that there will be times that I so fiercely want to protect others that I'd be willing to sacrifice myself to do so.

"Please, Flynn," I repeat, twisting the fabric of his shirt in my fingers. "What is it you want?"

He opens and closes his mouth, his eyes flicking back and forth across my face as he studies me, gathering his thoughts. "I—I don't want anything from you, Lyric."

I release my breath, my heart sliding into my stomach. "There surely must be something. Wolves have magic witches want, don't they? Can't I give you that or something? I just need to get out of here to save my pack mates. I—I—they're mine. It's my job as their leader."

Flynn breaks our stare, closing his eyes so I can no longer plead with him with my gaze. His mouth purses, his jaw tightening, and he whispers something under his breath. I loosen my fingers on his shirt and drop my hand to my side. Disappointment rushes over me in an icy wave that makes me shiver. Before he can even open his mouth, I know his answer. He won't help me. I know he won't.

"Lyric, I'm sorry. I'm so sorry," he murmurs, easing himself off the cage to stand upright. "This cage—it's been spelled. This place is so full of powerful magic that what I can do here is limited. If I could break you out, I would. I would transport you to your pack mates and help you leave Lulupoterra. I'd put a stop to those fighting against the fairness of the games and taking advantage of the she-wolves. I'd fight the witches involved."

"What do you mean?" I ask, knowing he speaks the truth. Paige had mentioned a coven when she captured me. "Is this about Fire Mountain and Nightstar? Paige said—"

"Nightstar? Fire Mountain? Are you sure?" Flynn combs his fingers through his hair.

I nod my head. "The coven of the Fire Mountain Clan has my father. Paige said something about him regretting working with them against Nightstar."

"Shit." Flynn glances around the room. "They're the ones

responsible for all of this." It's not a question.

"I was told there were five witches who came together to help the pack leaders," I say, shifting on my knees. "I don't know much else."

"Then I guess we better find out, which means you need to win the games tonight." Flynn paces around my cage. "If multiple covens are involved, there is more to the games than population re-growth."

"I would've won the games last time had you not been such an ass," I snap. "None of this would've happened if it wasn't for you. Radek—" I shut my mouth and turn to look at Flynn. "Where the hell is Radek, anyway? What did you do with him?"

"You asked me to help, so that's what I'm doing." Flynn rubs his hands together, sending purple power sparking across his palms.

"What does that even mean?" I scrub my face with a groan. The longer I sit here with Flynn, the more questions I have. It's even worse with him than with everyone else. He seems to know far more stuff, especially about the covens.

"There's no time to explain. They're coming for you." Flynn moves toward the door and presses his ear to it. "Remember what I said. You have to win the games. I want you to pick the Stargaze Hill alpha-mate. You should be able to since the death of his mate."

"But Paige—"

"She can't claim him. She's too far spelled. But you can,

Lyric. You can pick him and—"

Something thuds on the door.

Flynn gathers magic between his palms. "Just win the games, okay? Win the games, and I'll handle the rest."

I don't get a chance to ask him what the hell is running through his mind. The door to the room opens, and Killian and Gunner, Harlow and Emerson's mates, strut in. Caz slowly enters the room behind them, and it takes everything in me not to lose my shit.

"Stay focused, she-wolf," Flynn says into my mind. "They're not the ones we're after."

The hell they're not.

"Mmm-mmm," Killian says, standing before me in only a pair of shorts. He rests his palms on the top of the cage and leers at me, drinking in the sight of my naked body as I sit exposed and defenseless under his scrutiny. "You're a lucky man, Caz."

I reach through the bars and try to punch his crotch, but Killian moves before I can. "Fuck off, asshole. How would Harlow feel if she knew what a douche canoe you were?"

"She would be even more desperate," he says, his cocky grin stretching across his face. "She'd never get off her knees."

This. Fucker.

Caz releases a warning growl. "Enough."

Tipping his head back, Killian laughs. "Oh, shut it. I don't know why you're standing up for a bitch who refuses to even screw you. If I had her claim—"

Charging Killian, Caz shoves him, sending him crashing into the wall. Gunner tries to intercept Caz, but I reach out and trip him. These fuckers are so hot-headed and self-absorbed that they'll take care of each other for me.

"Enough!" a feminine voice snaps, drawing my attention from Caz as he gets in a punch to Killian's nose. Viviana stands in the doorway without looking at me, her back erect and her mouth seemingly in a permanent frown. "We don't have time for this. There is a murderous traitor that needs to be dealt with, and I cannot fathom giving him even one more night."

My heart stalls at her words, and she finally flicks her gaze to mine. Her reddened eyes shine glossy with tears, her grief palpable.

"I'm sorry, Viviana. I'm sorry for your loss, but you are mistaken. It wasn't Dax. He wouldn't kill anyone," I say.

Viviana flares her nostrils and stomps forward to stand next to my cage to peer down at me. "He had the motive. His scent was everywhere that it shouldn't have been. He's one of the few that knows how to access every portal gate. I know you like him, and I'm sure it has something to do with both of your fathers' bond, but all of the evidence of my poor Calhoun's tragic death points to him. We don't take these things lightly, considering we think I was his target."

She's out of her fucking mind.

I glare at Caz. "Does she know, Caz?" I ask, glaring at him, silently referring to the fact that Calhoun was manipulating

Viviana to do his bidding.

Caz averts his eyes and stares at the floor.

"Caz, you fucking coward. Look at me. Answer me. Does she know?" I repeat, clenching my fingers around the bars.

A whistle trickles through the room, the familiar call for the start of the games drawing everyone's attention away from me.

Viviana motions her hand toward my cage without asking Caz what it is I'm talking about. "Get her to the starting line. Let's get these games over with. Make sure to inform the competitors that the winner of her claim will get the honors of choosing three others to help him proceed with Dax's death sentence.

"You can't do this!" I yell, trying to break the damn cage open.

Viviana turns her back on me. "Five minutes. The games are about to begin."

13

DEATH SENTENCE

HARLOW AND EMERSON STAND QUIETLY on either side of my cage. Neither of them looks at me, but I can tell they feel bad about the situation. I was disallowed from looking over the course that will take me to the finish line, and since I've never been to Stargaze Hill, I have no idea how I'm going to manage this. I'm nearly certain every competitor here will fight to capture me. From what I know, Sagan, Bastien, and Sterling were all disqualified tonight, pending whatever the hell investigation the leaders are doing to ensure Dax acted alone.

I've never been so angry in my life.

So scared.

Even when my dad was hauled off, I managed to keep myself together enough to get out of town and put into action everything he taught me. I had an apartment the next day with the cash my dad had ready and a job at Ripped Fitness the day after that. But this? I have no idea how to handle this. Even if I manage to win the games, how the hell will I stop the leaders from issuing Dax's death sentence? How will I take down so many competitors if I'm weaponless? I'm barely a match now.

"When the gate opens, head north until you reach the cliffs. You will see the river below. Follow it south until it ends at the lake. Swim across instead of going around. It's the easiest way and forces competitors to change into humans. Some of them aren't as great at swimming as they are at running." Harlow's voice trickles to my mind though she still remains staring forward.

"Watch out for the guardians. I overheard Gunner talking to his uncle about setting a couple of traps," Emerson adds, curling her fingers around one of the bars that enclose the top of my cage.

I groan under my breath. "Why are you two helping me?" Because I have to know. They could be setting me up. They could be working with the leaders to ensure I don't fuck up these twisted games, now more barbaric than ever.

"We know Dax wouldn't kill anyone. Not that he isn't capable but because we know how madly in love with you he already is. He would never jeopardize doing something that would break your heart." Harlow grips her fingers to the other side of my cage, silently supporting me without making it obvious. The guardians lurk just out of sight, watching and waiting.

"We also know something is going on that shouldn't be. You've taught me a lot, Lyric. It wasn't until your arrival that I realized how little some of the competitors think of us. It's grown worse the last couple days. They don't think we hear them or watch them, and because of this, I've seen some rather strange things." Emerson drops her robe next to me, preparing for the upcoming whistle for the start of the game.

"Like what?" I ask, focusing on only allowing her and Harlow to hear my thoughts. At this point, I can't even trust myself. If I accidentally project my thoughts or my plan, I'm screwed.

"The leaders have been including their pack mates in meetings. They said that it's only temporary until the games are over, but the mates have been speaking out more. Making suggestions. This was never the way. The leaders used to never allow anyone to speak up and share opinions. Their mates should trust them completely to do what is right for their territories, and something is off. I can't explain what exactly. But it worries me." Harlow shrugs out of her robe next and crouches on her knees beside me, preparing to transform. "I've also been denied the request to work with the warriors to learn to fight. It doesn't sit right with me. The men usually give us whatever the hell we want."

My mind whirls with a dozen thoughts. Of course the men wouldn't want to teach the she-wolves to fight. They claim to like how fierce I am and how much fight I put up, but I know it's only because some of them think they're more powerful than me. They're starting to see that they're not, and it hurts their fragile need for dominance. It scares them, because I'm sure they realize that I will not bow down. I'm not here to follow their customs, nor am I here to help with their cause. I'm here to claim what my mother was forced to abandon and what my dad gave up his freedom to ensure. I'm here to change the rules of the games. They're afraid because I'm not a damn prize. This isn't about population growth. It's about me picking only the best of the best to be my pack mates. It's no longer the She-Wolf Games. It's the damn Wolf-Mate Trials.

The starting whistle rips through the air, ringing in my ears. I close my eyes and will my transformation to take hold, praying that the shift into my wolf in the tight space pushes my body to work harder than ever. Emerson and Harlow drop the gate, and I bolt from the cage and run as fast as I can in the direction Harlow told me to.

My paws pound into the compacted dirt, and I sniff the air, trying to familiarize myself with the scent of my surroundings. I pick up a spicy, nearly overwhelming fragrance. I growl, my body trembling at the gross smell as I realize what the hell it is. One of the guardians must have pissed out here. I never paid much attention before, but now that I do, I realize something I had yet to figure out.

I can follow the rancid smell and use it to guide my way. Because the guardians run the course beforehand. Because this is a new location, they would've had to have done it recently, and I bet these fuckers find pleasure in pissing all over another pack's territory. I know in Lunar Crest, it wasn't allowed within my community, but everywhere else was fair game.

A part of my humanity dies with my plan. I can't believe I'm now purposefully sniffing out piss.

Blowing a breath through my nostrils, I charge forward and run through the overgrowth of the terrain. Stargaze Hill sits on the edge of a canyon with a vast view of an endless valley that goes on for seemingly forever.

The second whistle blows through the air, and my heartbeat stalls, nearly causing me to stumble over a tree root. I skid on my paws, catching myself. Another whiff of wolf piss assaults my senses, and I hate that I recognize it as Fergus's. He'd be on guard since he won a day claim yesterday. And the fucker is gross as hell.

Pushing myself to get moving, I head north and weave through the trees, heading up an incline that will eventually lead to the cliffs Harlow told me about. A few howls echo around me, and I can't tell who they belong to. They could be guardians or competitors. Or maybe it's the guardians telling the competitors that they see me. And fucking shit. I want so bad to open my mind a bit to see if I can hear anything, but if I open a connection, it could also allow one of the dickheads into my mind.

"We'll throw them off as best as we can," Harlow calls, her voice sounding through my head. "Just keep going. Don't look behind you."

A loud screech steals my hearing for a second. Surprise washes over me at the sound of Harlow crying out in her wolf form. If I didn't know any better, I'd think the agonizing calls for help were real.

Howls respond to her calls, and hope rises within me. I never in a million years expected Harlow to ever help me in this way, but I won't let it go to waste. I'm going to win these damn games even if it's the last thing I ever do. And it might be. Because I will not let anyone hurt Dax, Sterling, Sagan, or Bastien. I will not let my pack down.

A figure materializes in the edge of my vision as a wolf catapults from the trees in my direction. The black and white wolf growls and snaps at my back leg, trying to pull my paws out from under me. I guess not every competitor cares about the safety of the she-wolves. This guy probably didn't even consider stopping the hunt for me to check on Harlow.

"Might as well give up, Lyric," a masculine voice says, managing to sneak into my head. "Even if you reach the finish line first, nothing will change. Don't prolong Dax's fate. He doesn't deserve even an ounce of mercy."

"Fuck you," I say, pushing my body harder, faster. My

muscles burn under the exertion, but I think about his words, knowing what's at stake, and it pushes me to keep going.

"You will later. I can't wait to hear my name on your lips, so start practicing it now. It's Dre," he says, growling with his name.

"The only time I'll ever say that shit is when someone asks me about the severed dick I'll leave the leaders as a present when I'm through with you," I snap, playing out the possibility in my mind. And usually, I'm not so sadistic, but I love the thought of handing him his balls.

He yips a bark. "It's a good thing there are muzzles around here. Chains. I'll make you into a damn good girl when the leaders realize you can't be tamed."

I slow just a bit and shove my body against his, trying to knock him into a nearby tree. He uses his front paws to push off of it and lands a few feet behind me.

The black and white wolf attempts to snatch my leg again. "Just give up, Lyric. You can't beat me."

I skid to a stop and race in the other direction to throw Dre off. He's trying to distract me with his comments, but I'm not going to let him get to me. His mind games and attempt to manipulate me into fighting him won't work tonight. I have far more important things than slowing myself down to put this asshat in his rightful place, face first in the damn piss puddle that grabs my attention, ensuring I weave back on course.

Dre howls, alerting whoever the hell is around to my

location, choosing to invite another competitor to team up against me. If they can stop me and make me submit, they'll then turn against each other for the chance at the claim.

Fury pours through me, burning over my body, narrowing my focus on the world in front of me. I don't let the collection of howls ringing through the air steal even an ounce of my focus, continuing to push my paws to work. I know I'm nearing the cliff by the thinning of the forest. How I'll actually get down it? I have no idea. There is bound to be a competitor who doesn't waste their time on the chase and will surely block my way.

I slow down, knowing that some cliffs in Lulupoterra will sneak up on you without warning. Some of the territory's terrains don't like to register with my human rationale. It's still hard to think that I'm within another realm completely, magic keeping the land away from Magaelorum and the Mortal World.

Howls sound from behind me, and I spin around to peer into the forest. I can't see any of the wolves yet and hope that maybe they're busy trying to slow each other down, underestimating my abilities for the bazillionth time. I know in previous games, it was customary for she-wolves to get help down cliffs or across the river that connects the territories but screw that. I can do this. I know I can.

Turning back around, I face the canyon that separates the river from the vast valley beyond it. The moon hangs overhead, the bright crescent illuminating enough light to see the trail that winds down the cliff wall just narrow enough for a wolf.

Studying my surroundings for a moment longer, I find the access point to the trail to take me down. But something doesn't feel right. Silence fills the air as the competitors go quiet. I can't even hear anyone nearing me within the trees.

I pad my way closer, trying to suppress my rising panic. Fuck. If I'm afraid as a wolf, something is definitely wrong.

Closing my eyes, I transform into my human self and jog toward the tree line to take cover. I snap off a thick branch, using my body weight to do so, and cringe at the noise echoing through the air.

"My dear great-niece. It's a shame it has come to this." Paige's voice trickles through the air as she's unable to intrude on my thoughts. "I'd like to make a bargain with you. I'm sure you would prefer that your mate doesn't pay for your shortcomings."

I clench my fingers into fists, searching the forest. I knew she had something to do with this bullshit. I knew she'd resort to something unthinkable. I mean, she tried to kill me after all and accused my mother of being responsible for so many deaths among the packs. A part of me had hoped that she'd back off. I know it was wishful thinking, but she can obviously see that the last thing I want is for more people to die. I'm determined to change everything so that they can live.

"Show yourself," I say, adjusting the branch in my arms.

Paige hums in her throat as she emerges from the trees. Surprise washes over me at her flowing dress. It would mean she didn't chase me down as a wolf.

And fuck.

I hear the crackle of static zing from behind me. Without thinking, I drop into a crouch and twist my body, performing a low sweep. My move surprises the witch behind me, sending her burst of power across the dirt. A sulfur-smelling cloud of dust permeates the air, consuming my senses.

I don't wait for the witch to attack again.

Propelling myself forward, I tackle the woman and lock my fingers around her wrists. Her soft chant ignites agony through my middle, and I automatically release her. Red light flickers in her eyes, her lips curling into a snarl. She doesn't try to speak to me or anything, continuing to chant words I can't understand.

Another wave of pain snaps through me, seizing my muscles. My eyes widen at the witch trying to force me to transform into a wolf. Paige shuffles closer and pulls out a metal contraption from a bag at her hip. I recognize the spelled muzzle, the memory of how much it hurt, how helpless I felt, rushing through me.

A whimper escapes my mouth as fur shoots through my skin, the witch drawing nearer, holding her hands up. I try to scramble away to put some space between us, but my muscles freeze, not allowing me to move.

"Help!" I scream, opening my mind completely to the competitors that will surely be nearby. I had not expected Paige's arrival with a witch, and I'd rather face all the assholes than try my luck against magic I can't understand. Magic I'm defenseless toward. "Someone help me!"

The witch waves her hand, sending red energy in my direction. I can't get my body to move fast enough, and a shockwave explodes through me, stealing my breath. Something snaps inside me, a strange energy capturing my wild nature and suppressing my wolf.

"Lotera fianigra bollossa cantania!" The witch shouts the words, flicking her hands toward the sky. My skin buzzes, but nothing happens. Her magic fails to work on me. "Hippol cuf lul—"

"Freyeter baliso et rivola!" Flynn materializes next to the witch and shoves her with a blast of lavender light.

My muscles relax at the interruption of the witch's spell. With a growl, Paige grabs the back of my hair and drags me a few feet before I can get my shit together and fight. She attempts to place the muzzle on me, but the second I feel the burning of my flesh, my body kicks into action. I jerk my arms up and back, punching her in the vagina with enough force that she falls on her ass. The muzzle clatters from her gloved hands, and I launch at it, screaming as I lock my fingers around the collar. But I don't let go. I push through the pain and slam it on her head, flicking the buckle into place.

Paige drops to the ground, her body convulsing at the magic stealing her ability to speak or do anything without agonizing pain.

"Lyric, run!" Flynn yells, sending a shower of sparks through the air. The ground rumbles beneath my feet, the earth suddenly splitting open under the magical fight. Flynn doesn't stop and continues to face the witch, the two of them using enough magic that I think the whole territory might collapse.

If it does, I'm taking Paige's evil ass with me.

Kicking Paige in the side, I send her rolling a few feet toward the edge of the cliff, hoping it'll crumble. If the dirt didn't crack beneath my feet, sending me clambering away, I'd push her off. Scrambling back, I race the magic pulverizing the ground and run toward the entrance to the path leading to the river.

Fear slows me down. I can't bolt my way along the winding ledge like I could if I was a wolf, but a part of me hesitates to transform. The witch was trying to force the change on me, and I don't know why. So human-me it is.

A bright flash of light pops through the air, setting the cliff aglow. Flynn and the witch suddenly disappear. Dirt and small rocks pelt my head and shoulders, the cliff still crumbling, no longer stable with the attack of magic. Howls echo through the air, drawing my attention to the forest behind me. It's like the witch's departure kicks the world back into motion. And fucking fuck. I can't catch a damn break.

"Lyric, stop!" Caz's voice cuts through the air, trying to steal my attention from my unsteady rush down the narrow ledge of the pathway. "There was a land quake. Please, you have to stop. The cliffs might collapse at any moment."

I don't stop. I can't.

"Lyric!" Caz yells my name again, and I spot him above me at the cliff's edge in his wolf form. He barks before releasing a loud howl. The ground disintegrates beneath his paws, forcing him back.

I avert my attention away from him and to the path and keep going. This crazy-ass interruption by Paige and the witch might have worked to my advantage. If the wolves can't travel the pathway to the bottom, they'll have no choice but to go around.

A growl, followed by a yelp, comes from above me. I tense at the noise closing in on me. I don't even have time to react before Dre lands on the path and snarls, blocking my way. And holy shit. I can't believe he did that. Winning my day claim is so important to him that he risked falling off the cliff.

I fist my hands and rush him, trying to knock him over the edge, my mind and body in full-on defense mode. I don't care how badly injured he'd get—or even if he dies—I just need him out of my way. He'd deserve his damn fate for testing me.

Dre dodges my move, slamming his body against mine, forcing me into the rock wall. I gasp as the breath escapes my lungs. My vision shadows at the burst of pain, and the wolf sinks his teeth into my shin, trying to disable me.

I jerk my leg and kick him away from me, sending him scrambling along the edge to keep his balance. A baseball-sized rock collides into the side of his head, disorienting him, and I tense as Dre falls over the edge.

"Lyric, hurry!" Caz yells from above me, and I realize it was he who threw the rock. "Make your way down. I'll meet you at the river."

"Do you think stopping Dre suddenly makes up for your bullshit? Don't bother. I don't have time." I stand on the ledge of the path and peer down, expecting to see Dre's body on the riverbank below, but I can't see it. I don't know if it's because the shadows of the night obscure it, but it leaves me on edge.

I close my eyes and transform into my wolf, willing to risk the witch finding me to hurry my ass down to the river. Knowing it's so close within my reach gives me the strength I need to push through the pain of the bite on my leg and to keep going.

The glowing river water sparkles under the pale moonlight, rushing its way toward the lake. The sound of the water consumes my hearing, suppressing the noisy wolves above to help keep my focus on making it to the finish line.

I jump down the steep incline to land on the ground instead of seeing the path all the way through. My heart rams against my ribcage, my breath panting and erratic, my whole body on the verge of falling ill to the exhaustion and fear threatening my every movement. Glancing up, I stare at the side of the cliff. Annoyance explodes through me at the sight of several wolves risking their wellbeing to continue the chase. And damn it. I need to win. I don't know exactly what to do once I claim the alpha-mate of Stargaze Hill, but Flynn seems to have a plan. I don't trust him, but I also don't trust the wolves more.

I break into a sprint, letting my instincts take over to carry me in the direction I need to go. The river glows beside me, reminding me of the dozens of times I jumped in with Dax, Sterling, Bastien, and Sagan. A blip of sadness squeezes my heart. What if I can't fight hard enough? What if the leaders decide to keep me caged for the rest of my life, only allowing me out to breed during mating season? The thought sickens me, making my head spin. I'd rather die. I'd rather fight until I can no longer do so than bow down to their rules.

Something crashes into my side, knocking me off my feet and into the river. The ice water engulfs me, and I swallow a mouthful. My lungs scream in pain, my body automatically transforming as I cough and spit, trying to suck in air. A muscular arm snakes around my body and lifts me from the shallow riverbank. Pain explodes across my back as Dre tosses me onto the pebbly ground.

My stomach rolls at the sight of his broken arm, bent the wrong direction. It doesn't slow him down though. He rushes me and grabs my hair with his other hand and hoists me off my feet. My body stiffens with the chill of the night, and I can barely get enough power into my kick to try to break free of his hold.

"You bitch," he says, throwing me toward the ground again. "Tearing Dax apart piece by piece as you watch will be the most satisfying thing until I have the chance to claim you. You're fucking mine."

I lace my fingers around a smooth rock and chuck it at Dre, surprising the hell out of him. It bashes into the center of his forehead. He hollers and clutches his head. Blood streams down his face, the force of me chucking the rock injuring him even more.

Dre's eyes darken, his face lining with a look that penetrates me to my core. Balling his fists, he charges at me, baring his teeth. His wolf peeks through his skin as he starts to transform, his hunger shocking through me as he sneaks into my mind.

I brace for his impact. For his sharp fangs to sink into my flesh. I brace for the fight of my life, because he looks ready to murder me.

His focus narrows on me, his eyes flickering with a blip of red light, not unlike the eyes of the doppelgangers that weakened the barrier to allow in the lycans. I startle at his features morphing. He reminds me of Hendrix when he attacked me. That fucker warned me that I don't stand a chance. He warned me that someone would finish where he left off. And now, I believe he meant Dre. There are traitors and enemies among all the packs.

A huge black wolf collides into Dre, knocking him onto his side. Antone snarls and bites onto Dre's neck, only half transformed into his wolf. My breath heaves, my whole body tensing at the sight of the attack.

"Lyric, go! You're almost there. Hurry!" Antone's voice rushes into my mind, kicking my ass into motion.

I try not to think about his interception and help. He confuses the hell out of me, constantly a dickwad but also always helping me. He saved my ass during the first lycan attack, yet he also didn't do anything when they came for Dax. I know he's Bastien's twin, but it seems like those types of relationships are severed for the games. Everyone is a competitor against each other.

Pushing the thoughts away, I run as fast as I can along the river to at least protect one side of me, so I can focus on the threats that could come from the other. Howls continue to cut through the air, the wolves calling out to each other, to me, to who else the hell knows. I can no longer treat this course as just a game. This is a run for my life, to save Dax's, to find the rest of my pack mates so that we can stand together and face this treacherous world that was supposed to feel like home.

Hope rises within me at the sight of the lake up ahead, the water glowing turquoise with the magic that protects this world. Pounding my bare feet to the pebbly riverbank, I charge forward, focusing on my heavy breathing, my heart crashing around my chest, how it feels as if the world around me pulls me closer and closer to a part of me I feel as if is missing.

Dax told me that his claim was a bonding of our souls and how he gave me a part of himself, but I know I also gave him a part of myself too. I gave all of them a piece of me the second I decided to agree to their plan and to follow down my dad's path, no matter how dark, dangerous, or deadly it may be.

Icy water engulfs my feet as I reach the lake without slowing. I disturb the tranquil surface, sending ripples across the top to blur the crystal-clear reflection of the crescent moon on the water. More howls and growls and snarls echo from behind me, the wolves fighting each other in an attempt to overpower anyone who might get in their way of claiming me.

Stroking my arms and kicking my legs, I swim toward the middle of the lake, trying my best not to let my mind wander to the dark depths of pitch-blackness below me. The water might glow on the surface, but the light fades into nothing, and with how the rivers and water work as a portal through Lulupoterra and gateway to the Mortal World, I wouldn't be surprised if something lurks in the depths in wait. A witch? Some other creature? I have no idea. I don't plan to find out.

The only thing I plan on is winning this game tonight and tearing this place down.

There is no other option. I can no longer trust anyone here when enemies lie in wait everywhere.

My chest heaves as my knees hit the shallows of the lake, and I crawl my way toward the gathering crowd of onlookers from the different packs and territories. Pain stiffens every molecule on my body, and it takes listening to the splashing behind me to get my ass off the ground. I have fifty feet until the finish line. Fifty feet to keep ahead of the wolves.

"Go, Lyric!" a high, childish voice calls through the air. "Go, go!"

My heart lightens at the sound of one of Bastien's little brothers cheering me on as the rest of the crowd falls silent. I spot Youssef standing near Bridgette, the rest of her young sons surrounding her.

"Whoa! A she-wolf is winning!" another boy says, stepping away from Trista. Without having to ask, I know it's one of Dax's little brothers. I know all of the guys have them, but it's weird and alarming to see them here.

"Don't slow down!" Youssef yells. "They're coming!"

Summoning my last ounce of strength, I dash toward the finish line, my emotions swirling out of whack as I spot Dax in the middle of the circle created by the onlookers. A muzzle covers his wolf head, singeing the mahogany fur of his neck. Four men hold onto chains, restraining him in place.

"Dax!" I scream, bolting forward. "Dax!"

A huge man, even bigger than Dax, tackles me, forcing my face into the ground. My chest clenches, my heart breaking. Tears blur my vision as I lie on the ground ten feet within reach of Dax.

A whistle cuts through the air, and the man hauls me to my feet. Everything happens so fast, my mind struggles to keep up. I lost. How the hell could I have fucking lost?

Trista saunters forward, a serious expression stealing the beauty from her face. She grabs my hand and hoists it into the air. "What an astounding win. Congratulations to Lyric of Lunar Crest, the first she-wolf to have ever won the games. Please go to the podium and announce who you've picked to give your day claim to."

I blink a few times in confusion. "Wait, I won?"

It's now that I realize that the man wasn't capturing me as a prize. He was stopping me from getting to Dax.

"Lyric," Trista says, her voice softening. "Why did you fight so hard to win today?" She keeps the words between us.

I lick my lips. "I had to."

"You know what this means, right?" Tears leak from her eyes to drip down her cheeks.

I don't answer. I can't.

"You must pick Dax's executioner," she says.

I swallow the burning in my throat. No matter what, I can't win. In these horrifying She-Wolf Games, I will always lose.

14

WINNER

"AS THE WINNER OF THESE fucking games, I demand you give me five minutes with Dax," I say, holding my head high. I will not break down. I won't do it. No one here will see me cry, even though my soul weeps, drowning in my despair.

"Absolutely not," the alpha-mate of Svetlana says, crossing his arms. "You cannot make these types of demands. You won by default. The cliff—"

I lose my shit and rush him, preparing to rip his head off. A man snags me by the waist and lifts me off my feet. Spinning around, he sets me down and stands between me and the asshole. It takes everything in me not to tackle this guy next.

"Axel, give the girl a break. You know as well as I do that she won fairly." It takes me a moment, but I recognize the man. It's Felix, one of Svetlana's other mates and the father of Hendrix. Because of Hendrix's treason, Felix ended up taking my side and saved me from having to seek justice. And now, here he is, once again stepping up to stand beside me, even if it means arguing with his pack mate.

"Shut the fuck up. Calhoun is dead. It could've been one of us," Axel says, growling with his words.

Felix balls his hands into fists. "Svetlana would never deny such a request. It is not your decision to make. Just because she is gone doesn't give you the right to try to fulfill her place. You could never."

Oh, shit.

Trista steps forward and touches Felix's shoulder. "Thank you, Felix." Turning to Axel, she says, "Mind your place. If you would like to sway the leaders' decision, please call upon Paige."

"Who is where?" Bridgette asks, coming up beside Trista. "She should be here, considering she built the evidence against one of Lulupoterra's strongest, most loyal wolves."

My heart pounds at her words. The two of them sound as if they have doubts. And why wouldn't they? Dax is Trista's son and Bridgette's sons' best friend. They believe that Caz also shares some sort of bond with them, so why would Dax kill Calhoun?

Several other people murmur their quiet thoughts to each other. I stare at the pack leaders, focusing my gaze on Viviana, silently pleading with her to give me this. I know Calhoun was her mate. I know she might want to see Dax pay for some crime she thinks he committed. But I also know that she might feel for me, knowing that I have grown a connection with Dax the last couple weeks. Everyone recognizes it. They might assume it's purely sexual, as my mind loves to wander to my fascination and lust, but they should recognize it's more than that in this moment.

"Please," I whisper, drooping my shoulders. "Five minutes. The other she-wolves aren't even here yet."

All the pack leaders turn to Viviana to leave the decision in her hands. I say a silent prayer to the universe that she gives me this. Five minutes will give me time to strategize and think things through. Five minutes is enough time for me to change the course of everything. Five minutes might not seem like much time, but it's all I need. I will not stand here and allow them to put this on Dax. I won't.

Viviana finally nods her head, her eyes glistening with tears. "Under our supervision."

I suppress my urge to argue that it's not like we're going anywhere, but instead I take her small mercy and close the space to her, grabbing her hand. A low, threatening growl escapes

Axel's mouth, but Felix whacks him, getting him back in line. It's enough to pique my curiosity. I thought perhaps all the leaders' mates might be manipulating the leaders, but it seems only those who think themselves as alphas do.

No wonder the alliances around here are so fragile and the she-wolves don't like to budge much in their ways. I'm the first female with five spots available on her pack, and it was only to keep the peace. But maybe I need to shake things up. Be the cause for outcry. Maybe I need to truly test the bonds within these packs, created from the She-Wolf Games to see where everyone around here falls.

Clearing my throat, I say, "Thank you. This means a lot to me, and I'm relieved you understand considering we've already claimed each other."

Silence falls through the crowd at my words. My heartbeat thumps with my nerves, and I know the weight of my revelation might set off explosives within all of the packs. Because to claim a she-wolf before the final packs are chosen—that's unheard of. The wolves have evolved, and the she-wolves accept multiple claims, but the men only give their loyalty and love, their soul, to just one.

"What do you mean?" Trista asks, her voice shaking with her words.

I lick my lips and peer around at the crowd, confusion lining everyone's faces. "It kind of just happened. I know things aren't official until the games are over, but I know Dax is my intended. He would've won my official claim."

"Impossible," Axel snaps, releasing a growl. "It requires a wit—"

Trista's alpha-mate grabs Axel's shoulder, silencing him with a growl. I stiffen at the look they share, their thoughts indecipherable but so incredibly obvious that they know something that everyone else doesn't.

"It requires the approval of the leaders," the alpha-mate from Eclipse Valley says, straightening his back, filling his form out in an attempt to intimidate me. "Which you clearly do not have. Do not take such words lightly, she-wolf. You two have not bonded in soul as you think. Now, please. Make your peace, so we can get on with this and kill the bastard. Justice must be served."

"Don't be so crass, Kai," Felix snaps. "What if it were you?"

Axel growls. "Fuck off, Felix. It wouldn't be. Let's finish this. Now."

With Axel's words, my heart sinks into my stomach. It didn't work. I can't believe they brushed off my admission, not believing it to be true. And I don't comprehend it. I feel it in the depths of my soul, with every emotion that courses from Dax to me, how Sagan knows exactly what I need before I need it. Even with Sterling and my claim on him. If it weren't true, then why are things as they are? Why does Bastien wait anxiously nearby, his need to prove he's mine and I'm his as palpable as his emotions filling me up with the strength I need to face Dax again.

To shuffle my way closer. To look him in his golden eyes and take the pain he feels in the moment onto myself.

I remain stiff in posture, trying to keep my body from trembling under the weight of everyone's stares. Dax whimpers the closer I near him, resting his head on his paws in defeat. I want to smack him upside the head for it. He'd expect me to fight, and I expect for him to do the same. So do Sagan, Bastien, and Sterling.

My dad did not pick these men to be my intendeds because he wanted a say in my life. He picked them out because he knows me best, because he sensed the truth that grows in my soul. They are my pack mates and will ensure Lunar Crest thrives outside the bullshit of the alpha-mates and leaders. Outside the witches and magic. We will rise from the tragedy our parents left behind because it is our fate. I know it. It's more clear than ever.

Silence turns the world around me heavy, yet it feels as if it stops to give me a moment to catch my breath. I can push away the sensation of everyone's burning stares on my back and focus my sole attention on Dax.

I kneel in front of him and meet his golden gaze. The four men clutching his chains lay them on the ground and step away to give us a bit more privacy, like it even makes a difference under everyone's scrutiny.

I reach out and glide my fingers above the muzzle, careful not to touch it. Agony steals my breath, sending pain coursing through every inch of my body. Seeing him bound and gagged, trapped in the same binds that witches used to use on wolves long ago to control us, burrows deep inside me. I can't stand it. Dax doesn't deserve this. No one does.

Locking my fingers to the collar, I burn myself on the spelled silver but don't flinch away. Before anyone can react, I flip the buckle open and yank the muzzle off. Dax transforms into a man. Growls reverberate through the air, the guardians reacting to my defiance. I could get to my feet and dare them to test me. I could chuck the muzzle and hope it hits one of the assholes posing a huge threat against us. But instead, I crash my mouth to Dax's and kiss him, sending a wave of warmth, of hope, of determination and strength from my soul to his.

Some might mistake this as a goodbye kiss as no one moves to intervene. They might mistake it as my final gift to the man who I believe is my intended. But the truth of my kiss will come as wild and unstoppable as I feel in this moment. I'm the first she-wolf to win the games, and this kiss is my promise to all of the packs that it will not be the last time. The games are changing. Tonight proved as much as Harlow and Emerson stood beside me, united in our desire to make the best of our futures.

This kiss, this promise that I feel so deeply in my soul, seals my vow to not only myself but also to my dad. To the future she-wolves and leaders. I will not bow to anyone. I will stand tall and fierce and challenge anyone who gets in my way.

And along with this kiss comes a promise from Dax. From Sterling, Sagan, and Bastien as they remain open to me in this moment. They will stand beside me. Fight with me. Change the world with me.

Starting now.

Breaking my mouth from Dax's, I unfasten one of the chains from his wrist. My skin tingles at the heat of the spell clinging to the bindings, but the chains themselves do not react to my touch. I whisper a silent thanks to the universe and wrap part of the chain around my hand. I don't have much experience with alternative forms of weapons, but I know how to kick ass, and I will knock every last asshole who stands against me to the ground and make the fucker bow.

"Lyric, please. Don't do this," Trista says, extending her arms to keep the men away, trying to reason with me with her words instead of using force.

I twist my lips, narrowing my eyes. "Don't do what? Save your son? Protect my future? Show you all what a huge fucking mistake you've made with these false accusations? Because Dax was set up. We were set up. Dax didn't kill Calhoun. He couldn't have. He was protecting me from the intrusion of your pack mates." I motion to Axel and Kai before pointing at the other alpha-mates. "They accused me of some bullshit involving Radek."

Trista turns and glances at the leaders. "Did you know about this?"

"Paige gave us approval," Axel says, straightening his shoulders. "She understands what needs to be done around here to ensure the safety of our territories."

Wow. "Are you fucking kidding me?"

"Shut up, she-wolf. This is not your place. Now, step away from the murderer before I show you exactly where you belong." This comes from a man I only recognize from the gathering of these assholes behind the pack leaders' backs.

Fury rushes through me, tensing my muscles. Several growls sound from the crowd, and I know they belong to Sterling, Sagan, and Bastien. Antone and some unfamiliar competitors. And Caz.

Shit.

Trista raises her hands, trying to settle everyone down. "Enough! I'd like to hear Lyric out."

"Of course you do," a man snaps. "You probably told your son to do it."

A fight breaks out within the crowd as one of Trista's pack mates tackles the man to the ground. The alpha-mate from Eclipse Valley takes advantage of the distraction and rushes me. Swinging out the chain, I whip him across the chest. He stumbles back in surprise, the metal marking his skin.

Dax transforms into a wolf and bares his teeth, preparing to attack anyone else who comes closer.

I inhale a few short breaths, trying my best to keep my attention every which way to ensure no one can surprise attack me. Sterling launches over two men rolling on the ground to join my side while Bastien, Sagan, and Antone move as many of the young kids out of the way.

A whistle screeches through the air, startling me with the high-pitched intensity. Bright light illuminates the world in a lavender glow. But no one reacts. No one even notices the figure emerge from within the light.

As quickly as it comes, it disappears, and I blink in surprise at the sight of Radek. He meets my gaze, a strange look puckering his brows. Nerves shudder over my body, and I reach out and grab Dax for support. He changes back into a man to hold me. A couple of wolves dart around us, dripping water across the ground.

Another whistle blows.

"Enough!" Simone says, speaking up for the first time within the protection of her pack mates. "Everyone stop or you will leave us no choice but to postpone the games until next season."

Who knew such a small threat could settle down so many men so quickly.

"I think it's in our best interest to call a meeting," Simone says, raising her voice. "I command everyone to return to their proper territories with exception to the she-wolves. They will be moving on to the next location with those who've won their day claims."

It's now that I realize that in the fray of things, both Harlow and Emerson have arrived in the arms of two men. My mind refuses to remind me which packs they are from and instead focus on everything else going on.

"What about Lyric?" one of the competitors asks, shaking water from his long hair.

The leaders turn their attention to me.

I throw my hands up. "I pick myself. I'm not choosing anyone tonight, especially because of what it could possibly mean. I will not spend the damn day with someone who could very well be instructed to hurt my mate come tomorrow's games."

"She must pick!" a man yells.

"Pick for her," another adds.

"Everyone shut the fuck up!" Radek's deep voice hollers through the air, drawing everyone's attention to him.

He clenches and unclenches his fingers, his muscles rippling over his skin. Silence falls through the crowd at his call for attention, and I notice confusion on Killian and Axel's faces. Because Radek is from their pack. He was supposed to be working on their plan to force me to submit, so they could rig the games. But what they don't realize is that their plan failed. Radek didn't get me to give in to him. He bowed to me.

"Dax didn't kill Calhoun," Radek says, turning his gaze from mine. He steps closer, remaining expressionless as everyone gives him their undivided attention. "He wouldn't risk losing Lyric and forcing her to share the same agony as him through the bond of their claim."

The she-wolves all turn to each other in silent conversation.

"What the hell are you talking about, Radek?" Killian's dad

asks.

"The bond they share is real. I know it. I've felt it. She has put a claim on me," he says, flicking his gaze to mine once more.

Dax squeezes my hand. I'm sure a dozen thoughts swirl through his mind. The same goes for Sagan and Bastien. But not Sterling. He knows what I'm capable of as I claimed him too without his reciprocation. I was able to do so without him affirming it. And now I have so many damn questions.

"It's why I lost my cool with Calhoun. I overheard him talking with Luke about rigging the next She-Wolf Games...just like they did before with me, Fergus, and Ryland." Radek bares his teeth at Luke, the man who I know is a part of Trista's pack. "They only want compliant males to win the competition, and no heirs belonging to those lost in the Great Sacrifice."

The what?

Luke transforms into a wolf and launches toward Radek, colliding into him. The second Luke's teeth rip into Radek, I scream out, searing pain digging into my skin as if his fangs sink into me as well. I wobble on my legs, my knees turning into jelly. The edges of my vision darken, and I can't focus on anything but the sight before me.

Radek hollers and growls, his wolf practically bursting through his skin to fight back against Luke. Fur flies and other wolves transform. The leaders try to call order to prevent anyone else from joining the fight.

"Ma Belle, shit. Dax, Sterling. Break them up. Now!"

Bastien yells, dropping to my side.

I blink and stare up at him. When did I hit the ground? How much time have I lost? The questions flit through my mind. I struggle not to succumb to the pain burning through me. It tears at my flesh, ripping me apart piece by piece, a deep-seated part of me experiencing everything Radek does on a level I never wanted to be on with him.

"What's wrong with her?" Bridgette asks, kneeling next to Bastien.

My cheek presses into the dirt, my focus unable to shift away from Radek and Luke biting and rolling and growling, shredding each other apart while Dax and Sterling attempt to get an opening.

"She's in pain. I know you question the truth of the claim unrecognized by the pack leaders, but it's very much real, *Maman*. And I think she somehow linked herself to Radek. I don't know. I have no experience with this." Bastien combs my hair from my face, trying to tilt my head up to look at him.

"I don't understand any of this," Bridgette squeezes my hand, leaning in close. "What has Levi done to you?"

Agony explodes through me, and I convulse and buck my body, the ability to breathe escaping me. I jerk my hands up and clutch my throat, trying to rip away the invisible rope tightening around my neck.

"Fuck! Dax, stop!" Bastien yells. "She's experiencing every-thing Radek does."

The invisible hold on my throat releases, and I gasp a breath. Jerking upright, I snap my attention to Dax clutching Radek and Sterling and Sagan struggling to restrain Luke as he continues to fight to break free.

And then he does.

No one has a chance to stop Luke from charging Radek. Bastien yells again. Several competitors join the fight, trying to intercept this unnaturally powerful wolf, now hell-bent on taking Radek down. Wolves howl and bark, some screech as they're bitten and tossed away. Dax drops Radek and shifts into his wolf. But Luke plows right into him, knocking him off his paws.

Landing on Radek, Luke smashes his heavy paws to Radek's chest, pinning Radek down. Luke sinks his teeth into Radek's throat, and I screech in unbearable pain. Fire burns my esophagus, my voice cutting off completely.

Something breaks inside me, and I feel as close to death as I did in the forest, bleeding out and poisoned. I wonder if this is what Dax and Sagan felt or if this is some curse created just for me. I wonder if this is how I die. I never considered my death to be anything like this, even after discovering who I am.

But death can't be sweet. It's agonizing and lonely. Terrifying.

The world shifts as strong arms wrap around me and lift me up. Bastien calls out to Dax, Sterling, and Sagan. I can barely see the world through my hazy vision, but they are moving me.

And then the pain suddenly stops.

My soul screams with Radek's last breath.

Light consumes my vision, stealing my senses away.

"Give her here. Now!" It's Flynn.

Everything disappears.

15

Storm Haven

I SIT ON THE EDGE of a bed in a room I've never seen before. But the familiarity of Dax's scent clinging to everything helps stifle the panic threatening to combust my heart. It was unsettling waking up alone and in this cave-like room, lit only by candlelight with no windows. A gleaming metal door remains closed in front of me, but I haven't moved from this spot. I'm afraid if I move, the world with burn down around me. I have so many questions. So many fears. I have no idea what the hell is going on in my life or what any of this means.

My heart aches with every thump as a reminder that I felt what death was like through Radek. A part of me wonders if it's my fault. He wouldn't have ever done what he did if it wasn't for my unexpected claim on him. I know it. But what's worse is that I don't feel bad. Just anxious and hurt, wallowing in my own self-pity that I had to go through that bullshit. Does that make me an awful person? Maybe. Yet, here I am, still not giving any fucks for the asshole who thought he could treat me as someone beneath him.

The metal door to the room creaks before whining as it opens. I expect to see Dax, knowing this is his room, but Bastien enters with a bag tucked under one of his arms. His gaze darts to me on the bed, and he offers me an unexpected smile. How can he? I don't know. I know they know about Flynn. He appeared twice last night—or whenever the hell the last games were, because right now I have no fucking clue even what year it is—and I haven't had the chance to explain myself and why I haven't told anyone that the warlock has been hanging around.

"I brought you some things," Bastien says, crossing the room, his gaze never wavering nor does his smile fade. "Are you hungry? In pain?"

I hang my head and glance at my bare feet. "Both."

"It'll be a few more hours until you feel a hundred percent yourself. What you went through...I'm so sorry, Ma Belle. We had no idea."

Because I didn't tell them. I had intended to, but things just kept getting shittier and shittier.

I release a long sigh through my nose and tilt my head to meet his beautiful brown eyes. Bastien reaches for my hand and laces our fingers together. I accept his affection and pull his hand to my chest, wanting to feel the weight of his skin as close as possible to my heart. I want my heart to chill out with its aching to realize that I'm okay. I'm alive.

"You shouldn't be the one apologizing," I finally manage to say after a long moment of just savoring Bastien's comforting warmth against the icy chill clinging to my bones. "I fucked up."

"How so?" he asks, scooting a bit closer until his leg rests against mine.

I grimace and purse my lips. "Uh...I don't even know where to begin."

Bastien touches my cheek, getting me to look at him again as I lose myself to my thoughts. He offers me another smile, tilting his head and searching my eyes. And then he leans in and kisses me, brushing his lips against my mouth in a whisper of affection that leaves my body craving more.

"Lyric," he says softly, easing away from me but still staying close enough to rest his forehead to my temple and share my breath. "You didn't fuck up. I know you think you did, but just because that's how you feel doesn't mean it's true for me. You had your reasons not to tell us about Flynn. No one blames you. Look at the shitshow around us. I'm sure you'd have told us when you didn't have to deal with everything else. I do not blame you for going into survival mode, especially with the treachery among the packs."

"But—"

He cuts off my argument with another kiss, trying to fill me with his tranquility. How he manages to remain so calm? I have no idea. "I'm sorry for interrupting you, but I don't want you to try to reason with me about why I should be angry or upset with you. I'm not."

"I claimed Radek," I blurt, unable to keep the words to myself. "You should be pissed off that I called him mine before I had done so with you. It was fucked up."

He chuckles and sighs, scrubbing his scruffy cheek with his free hand. "While it was unexpected and rather...weird, I can't be mad. We made a deal, remember?"

I blink a few times. "But I hated the guy. The deal was if I liked another, not because I got tired of his asshole attitude and made him bow." Because that was my stipulation in agreeing to try to manipulate the games so that Dax, Bastien, Sterling, and Sagan could join my pack. I wasn't just going to accept it. I wanted to leave it open for if I did find someone else I liked. But that person would've never been Radek.

"Some things we just can't control," he murmurs. "No one had any idea. The claims have always been the men choosing the women. It's how we manage to blend packs, remember?"

"But Dax and Sagan let me claim them at the same time

they claimed me as theirs." I shift with my thoughts.

"I can't speak for them, but your claim was more affirmation to them, knowing that you agreed to accept them. At least, at the time it was. Sterling confirmed it was more than that. Apparently, something about you is different, but don't worry. We will figure it out."

"Fuck, I hope so. What I felt with Radek—" I shake my head, pushing the memory away.

"Wasn't supposed to be like that. Not even the mates of the leaders experience such a connection." He twists his lips with his frown.

"Lucky-fucking-me," I mutter.

"We will do whatever we can to ensure you never have to experience such agony again, Ma Belle." Bastien caresses his fingers against my cheek. "We only want you to ever feel what brings you the best life has to offer. The bond you create—try not to let what happened with Radek ruin it for you."

I bob my head, taking a breath. "It's easier said than done. I just keep replaying his death over and over again. My heart hurts. My soul feels tired. It's hard to explain."

"Why don't you let me take care of you then?" He shifts and reaches for the bag he set down at his feet. "Try to eat something while I tend to your injuries. I'm sure they don't help."

I stare at the blistering skin of my hands from removing the spelled muzzle from Dax. The pain in my heart is far greater than the wounds that I hadn't even noticed hadn't healed.

Bastien doesn't wait for my response and pulls out a container full of familiar foods from the Mortal World. Surprise washes over me, and I pick up the veggie-filled sandwich and bring it to my lips.

"How the hell did you get this? This is from my favorite sandwich shop by Ripped Fitness," I say, taking a bite, humming at the delicious familiar flavors of the place that reminds me of home. Of my life in the Mortal World.

"Flynn brought it," Bastien says, pulling a couple of bottles of some sort of ointment from the same bag to set on the bed beside us. He wastes no time getting to work, pouring the liquid into the palm of his hand and clasping my free hand by my wrist.

"But how did he...?" My words trail off with my question. He wouldn't have known without help, and there is only one person who knows my favorite sandwich shop and exactly what to order me. Caz picked me up food all the time. "Fuck, Bastien. Caz is—"

"Caz really wants to talk to you, and you should hear him out, Ma Belle," he says softly, continuing to massage the ointment over my tender skin until my blisters magically fade.

"But Bastien, he was there with the alpha-mates. He—" I clench my jaw, trying my best to suppress my raging emotions before I snap at Bastien. It's not his fault. He doesn't know what I know or has heard what I had heard. "I can't right now. I want to murder him, and it wouldn't be fair to Viviana having to lose a son after she lost her mate, no matter how awful Calhoun was."

I set the sandwich on its wrapper, my stomach knotting, no longer wanting food. There is just so much going on that my mind wants to shut the world out. I can't think about anything else right now. I have too many questions and no answers. Like what happens now? Why are we in Storm Haven? Is Luke dead? What about the others? What about Paige and the witch? Fuck.

Bastien cups my cheeks in his hands and clutches my face. "Take a breath. Your mind is racing."

I do as he says and inhale a breath with him. Bastien presses his forehead to mine, working through my spiraling emotions with me until all I can think about is how close his lips hover in front of mine, how his body now nestles between my legs as he kneels to get ultra-close. I can't stop thinking about how much his presence consumes my attention, drawing me to him like a magnetic pull I never want to resist.

I kiss him, wanting nothing more than to push the universe away and pretend it doesn't exist outside of the two of us. Bastien makes it so easy to forget, his calm emotions blanketing over me to slow my heartbeat only to have his building passion send it into overdrive.

He reacts to my affection, kissing me deeper, needing to give me everything I want in this moment. And suddenly, all I want is him. I want to remember what his lips feel like exploring my body. How his hands feel gliding across my curves. I want to feel his mind and soul open completely for me, allowing me to savor exactly what I do to him.

But I want more than that.

I know I shouldn't even think the words. I've done enough damage, wreaked enough havoc, but my soul screams for me to stop resisting the pull I feel for this man, so full of adoration and care. So full of everything I could ever want from a future pack mate. From a lover and friend.

Mine. I want him—no, I need him—to be mine. The thought burns so hotly through me that I push Bastien back onto the floor. He hums at my fervent desperation to rip his shirt off him, my fingers bunching the fabric until I manage to yank it over his head to kiss the spot over his heart, now racing and thumping seemingly just for me.

Bastien tangles his fingers through my hair, trying to guide me back to his mouth, and I follow his lead to give him what he wants. I kiss him with everything good inside me, wanting him to feel my soul on a new intimate level without the constant heartache and anger. Without my confusion and morbid thoughts. I only want him to feel my soul as it is in this moment as I think about him and only him and our lives together and how it's one thing that will complete me after feeling as if a piece of me broke off and disappeared.

"Lyric," he murmurs against my mouth, dragging his big, warm hands down my back until he reaches the hem of my shirt. He yanks it off and touches my breast, caressing my nipple with his fingers. "Let me make love to you, my beautiful, hypnotic, dazzling mate."

I bite my lip between my teeth and nod my agreement. I want this more than I thought possible. I can't wait any longer, not after everything we've gone through. I was worried about dooming my guys because of a claim, but it's not like that. That's my human rationale trying to explain away my feelings to stop me from giving in to my innate need. My unrelenting desire to bond with men I realize I don't want to live without. And now that I claim them, I will do better. Be stronger. Because I can't ever let them down. This guarantees that I'll be careful. That I'll be everything they need me to be as they are everything I need.

Bastien deepens our kiss, stroking his tongue over mine softly, sensually, like he wants nothing more than to savor the taste of my mouth. Sliding his arms around me, he lifts me off the ground with him and carries me to the bed. He sets me on my feet and trails his hands down my sides and to the curves of my hips, slowly teasing my humming skin as he undresses me. Taking his time, he kisses his way down my stomach, drawing his tongue in a line down my middle. I brace my hands to his shoulders as he works his way lower and eases my leg onto his shoulder like he wants to see my knees weaken with the gliding of his tongue.

I gasp and moan, massaging my fingers into his broad, muscular shoulders, my knees trembling from the pleasure he creates with the passionate strokes of his tongue to the sensitive skin of my body. Wrapping his arm around me, he holds me in place by my ass, kissing and licking and sucking my clit in complete desperation to bring me to my peak.

I intake a sharp breath at the explosion of mind-blowing tingles, stealing my breath and curling me forward over Bastien's shoulder. He lifts me as he stands and eases me on the bed, a smile lighting his whole face. I pant and rub my legs together, my body craving more of him.

Stretching out my arms, I silently beg him to hurry back to me, the space between us suddenly the most torturous thing in the world. He moans deep in his throat, drinking in the sight of me as I lie bare and exposed before him. The sound is so incredibly sexy that a shiver rushes through me, my body reminding me exactly of the pleasure he's capable of.

He tugs down his shorts, revealing he wears nothing under them, and I scoot forward to lace my fingers around his hard body, guiding him to me while I memorize the smoothness of his skin, how his cock flexes in anticipation, and how I know with his thick girth and all those inches it keeps between us that I'm in for something incredible.

Bastien smiles at my thoughts as they wander to what he'd feel like inside me this very second and how much he'll enjoy it. His desire crashes into me in a hot wave, the anticipation of taking things to a new level now the most important thing to him in this moment. And it's not because he's just attracted to me, nor does he think of me as a prize to win. But this moment is important because he can give himself to me fully and completely—mind, body, and soul—as I can to him.

Bastien kisses me again, moaning as I stroke his hard-on, pleasuring him to work him up until he can't take my teasing any longer. He surprises me by grabbing the backs of my legs and tugging them out from under me so that I land on my back on the soft bed. His heavy-lidded eyes devour me, roving over every inch of my body. My chest heaves in anticipation, and I wonder what he likes and if he'll be sensual and loving or passionate and rough.

Bastien eases my legs open and kisses each of my knees before leaning down to kiss me as he aligns our bodies. Wrapping my legs around his waist, I open myself wider for him, panting at the sensation of his tip slipping into me, just feeling my body welcome his, so we can be as one.

He moans, pushing farther into me, just slowly, teasingly, wanting me to experience every inch of pleasure inside me. Goosebumps prickle over my skin, my body loving the hum of his voice against my mouth. Hearing him moan with the ecstasy of exploring and savoring my body turns me on even more. I had no idea how much I would enjoy hearing my name on his lips, how breathless he becomes, or how with each of his thrusts, he growls with an intense passion that prods at the wild nature of my wolf.

"Lyric," he whispers, linking his hand through my hair to bend my neck enough to kiss the tender spot beneath my ear. "You feel so good. So perfect. I've never experienced anything so right in my life. You were meant for me. The fates knew and ensured it."

Picking up speed, Bastien thrusts harder and faster, each of his movements touching every sensitive buzzing part of me. I moan every time our bodies meet completely, the sensation even more delicious, hot, more mind-blowing than I imagined. Bastien eases away to meet my gaze, but he keeps me close with his big hand supporting my lower back as he braces me in place. Our minds connect, our emotions tangling and twisting together until I can no longer tell if the intensity of the pleasure cascading through me is mine alone.

Bastien's movements rub against my clit, building even more pleasure until I arch back, my muscles tensing with my orgasm. Moaning with me, Bastien experiences the same wave of sensations. His fingers dig into my back as he uses his strength to create more resistance until I moan again, feeling as if I orgasm a second time as he cums.

And damn. I want this to be my life now.

Bastien groans and chuckles, hearing my thoughts as I remain completely open and unfiltered, loving how much he enjoys listening to exactly what runs through my mind. Rolling next to me, he wraps me in his arms, snuggling close, our legs entangled, our bodies flush together.

"I will do everything I can to ensure it is," he teases, kissing my temple before stretching to meet my lips. "You deserve nothing less than a life of passion, happiness, and allowing me to fulfill your every desire, Ma Belle. I can't get enough of you."

"Good, because I'm not through with you. I want more," I murmur, drawing my finger across his pec and to his abs, slowly tracing my way down his body.

"Whatever you want," he murmurs, rolling me on top of him, hard and ready to go at it again.

"Damn," Sterling groans, and something thunks against the door. "Maybe you might want me too, blondie. I can smell your sweet desire from a mile away. My boner radar led me all the way here from Night Forest, knowing what glorious treasure awaited me in your cock box. It's been rough. I need you." The bastard fakes a whimper on the other side of the door and scratches the metal. "Let me help."

Bastien chuckles and shakes his head with a laugh. The melodic sound of his voice fills me up, his amusement with Sterling matching mine.

"What do you think, doctor?" I ask, biting my lip, suppressing another laugh. "Are you open to taking on an assistant?"

The second the comment escapes my mouth, I burn with blush, something intended to be innocent, sounding oh-so-bad, yet something that excites me. Bastien laughs again and pulls the covers around us, hiding our view of the world.

"Whatever you want, Ma Belle," Bastien murmurs, his words surprising me. I mean...he's serious.

The door opens with a clank, the metal hitting the rock wall. I can't see Sterling, but I hear him shut the door and jog across the room, his footsteps as rushed as the excitement flooding from him to me.

I suck in a shuddering breath as the bed shifts, my whole body going out of whack. Sterling moans deep in his throat. His weight falls on top of me, sandwiching me to Bastien with only a sheet separating us. I crinkle my nose, his arms feeling weird as they hook around me, and Sterling playfully humps me, shaking the whole bed.

I screech and laugh, the realization cracking me up that he shifted into a wolf to surprise hump me just as I had done to him. The sneaky asshole. I shove him off and tackle him, pinning him on his back. He is one quick bastard. I don't even get a chance to tug the blanket off him before he shifts into his human self and tests the durability of the sheet with his hard-on.

"Fuck, this is amazing," Bastien murmurs, reaching out to brush his fingers over my shoulder.

Sterling shifts and meets his gaze, unfazed that the three of us are naked in bed after just Bastien and I made love. "Right? The world feels so perfect now that she's smiling and laughing." Raising his hand, he holds it up, motioning for Bastien to give him a high-five. "Good job. Welcome to the club."

I intercept the two of them, grabbing each of their hands to pull them to my chest. I slide off Sterling and separate Bastien and Sterling with my body, narrowing my eyes at them. Because no. Just no.

Sterling chuckles. "What? You should appreciate how happy I am that you claimed this guy here. Especially since you waited until after me."

"It's not a competition," I say, whacking Sterling across the chest.

"Tell that to my cocky-ass brother. Dax, too," he retorts, sitting up to snuggle his face right between my boobs. "Now, come here. I want my scent all over you. Bastien can't have all the fun in Dax's bed. Having him come back to this—fuck, this is going to be sweet."

"Where is he anyway? And Sagan? You said you were in Night Forest?" My brows pucker with my question. I feel selfish and bad for not asking sooner. I was so caught up on my own torment that I didn't even think about how Dax went through his own too.

Sterling pops out his bottom lip. "Please, Lyric. Don't do that. Dax is fine. He's strong. It's you we were all worried about."

I grip the sheets in my hand. "But I'm strong—"

A small tap draws our attention away from each other. Sterling quickly wraps the sheet around my body, and I know without having to ask that it's neither Sagan nor Dax. The door slowly swings open, and Caz pokes his head in without entering.

"The leaders have gathered," Caz says, keeping his gaze trained away from me like he can't bear to face me. "We gotta go."

Bastien intercepts my argument with a kiss and waves his hand toward Caz, sending him away. Brushing his lips to mine, he continues to kiss me until my muscles relax, and I no longer feel like murdering anyone.

Bastien eases away. "I know you're upset, but when you get a chance, please talk to him, Lyric."

Sterling releases a growl. "Give our mate time. She doesn't need the pressure. She's been through enough."

I sigh. "It's okay, Sterling. I'm okay. Let's just find out what the leaders want. Maybe they'll decide to change the games."

Sterling and Bastien remain expressionless, and Bastien says, "We can only hope."

Except with his words, I suddenly feel hopeless.

My instincts prickle, and I wonder if maybe the leaders aren't meeting to discuss the games or anything like that.

I know deep down that they want to discuss my claims. They want to discuss what happens to me.

16

GREAT SACRIFICE

"WE NEED TO SUMMON ONE of the high priestesses," Viviana says, sitting on the carpet with her legs stretched in front of her. "There has to be something we can do."

I stand on my tiptoes, watching the five elder leaders like a creep through a strange, magic window. This wasn't what I anticipated when I strolled with Bastien and Sterling from Dax's place. Flynn was the last person I had expected to see by Dax and Sagan's side, and it takes everything in me not to look at him now.

"And then what?" Trista stands from the arm of the couch she perches on. "We cannot afford to ask more from them. Look at where it got us."

I frown at her words and peek at Dax, trying to capture his gaze. His golden eyes remain locked on the viewing portal Flynn created for us to spy on the meeting not even all of the leaders were invited to. The four newest ones from recent games remain in their territories under the care of their packs. They're not needed for much of the games, considering all but one of their kids is way too young to compete.

The alpha-mates aren't with them either. I don't know where they are and refrain from asking. I need to stay focused on this discussion the best I can, despite not having a clue about what any of it means.

"I say we proceed as we always have and let things work themselves out," the fifth woman, Aurora of Eclipse Valley, says with a sigh. "What harm will it cause if we just award Dax a claim? He is a fine man and will offer Lyric the guidance she needs. And who knows. Maybe this was a fluke. The fates are fickle."

"You think this is fate?" Viviana asks, pursing her lips. "My mate is dead. Killed by your son, if I might add. Who knows what Lyric will do or what she will put into our sons' minds. Have you seen how miserable Caz is lately? He does not deserve a life of rejection. These games are supposed to keep the peace and strengthen our lines. They're not games meant for the heart, which Lyric turned them into. It is her duty."

I dig my fingernails into my palms. How can she expect me to go along with this without some sort of feelings? She's crazy.

"Give her a break, Viv," Trista says. "She was not raised as we were. Levi was always a romantic and Melody...she was so free-spirited. Loved endlessly."

"Loved reckless and dangerously, you mean." Viviana scrubs her hands over her face. "At least we were fortunate she had a daughter."

Wow.

Arms wrap around me from behind, and Sagan presses his chest to my back, not letting any space between us. He holds me tightly like he senses I'm on the verge of exploding or falling apart or maybe even starting a damn apocalypse by unleashing my hellish fury.

I mean, I've heard the stories about my mother and how during her She-Wolf Games that she and my dad bonded and he won her claims only to have the leaders of the time place my dad on Trista's pack due to some political bullshit within the territories. But now I wonder...there has to be more to it. I need answers, and I'm afraid I'm never going to get them here. Not because no one wants to tell me necessarily, but because no one can truly know. Except for my dad. And he's gone. He's gone, and I don't know if I'll ever manage to find him or get him back. I don't even know if I'll survive this week.

Clearing my throat, I finally manage to sort through my questions to pick the ones most important to me in this moment and ones I know my guys can answer. "What happened to your fathers? What about the pack leaders from before? Your grandparents, I guess. When Paige would've helped lead in a territory."

Now that I ask my questions out loud, they suddenly feel so important, and I will not let my worry about bringing back negative feelings on a subject that I know hurts each of them deeply because I feel as if within their grief lies the answers we need.

I shift on my feet and away from the spy-glass, allowing us to see and hear the leaders. I no longer care what they discuss. Nothing they say matters. They can't force me to do anything. They will see. Paige was right about me. I will not fall into line. I will lead as my dad taught me. I will make my mom proud. I will not let their downfall scare me from creating a future outside this sanctuary that hides more danger and secrets than I ever imagined.

"It was an attack," Dax says, tightening his mouth. "Happened after your parents left. There was a lot of tension caused by their disappearance, and the elder leaders of the time decided to put in an effort to bring your mom back."

"And as you know, gorgeous, when the gateway is opened, it grows weak in those places until the magic has time to heal it. It drew attention from those cursed by witches, bringing the lycans to us. They wanted our sanctuary." Sagan squeezes my hands.

"We were all young at the time, but many people accused the warriors of allowing the lycans in to kill the elders. Our fathers turned to the witches for help, but their help comes at a price."

I rub my lips together. "The Great Sacrifice or whatever?" I remember Radek mentioning it. "Your dads gave themselves to the witches to save Lulupoterra?"

Sterling runs his fingers through his platinum hair, his gray eyes narrowing with his frown. "Fuck no. Our dads were against calling the witches again. It was total bullshit."

"They didn't deserve that fate," Sagan adds. "Our mom lost two of her mates. It devastated her."

"Which we know was an obvious setup now." Dax growls, his deep voice reverberating through my very being. "I'm going to kill those assholes. My dad loved my mom. He loved her beyond the devotion and loyalty supposed to be found in a pack mate. It was never about power, and that's why he helped Levi. He understood."

I tip my head back and stare at the sky for a moment, their spiraling feelings rousing a sorrow I desperately need to cure. I extend my arms out. "Come here, all of you. I need to hug you right this instant."

"Except for that guy, right? I know he looks all broody and shit," Sterling says, eyeing Flynn as he stands and listens quietly. "But I mean, uh, I don't even know him. I need a date night or something if you want me to start—"

I whack Sterling on the shoulder. "Oh, shut up. You know I'm not going to hug him."

He chuckles. "You're right. You don't do anything out of fucking pity. I should know."

Sterling's so lucky he's hot, because otherwise I'd grab him by the balls for winking at me and slapping my ass. Sagan reaches his arm over my shoulder, and I expect him to whack him on my behalf, but that cocky bastard bumps knuckles with his brother.

Flynn clears his throat, standing awkward as hell next to us as my four pack mates hug their arms around each other with me sandwiched in the middle. I stand on my tiptoes and barely manage to peek at him from over Dax's shoulder. But I'm not ready to leave the safety of this muscle man cage.

"Can I have a moment alone with you?" Flynn asks, brushing his hair from his forehead.

Dax stiffens. "The fuck you can. After everything we've been through, Lyric—"

I grab his cock to silence him. "Can decide for myself." Pushing between Dax and Bastien, I have to force my way through their hulking stances as they both refuse to budge to make it easier for me. Fingers lock to the hem of my shirt, pulling me back until Dax slides his arm across my chest to pin me against him. Leaning down, he uses his nose to push my hair from my ear. He presses his lips against my lobe, his warm breath tickling my skin.

"What if he steals you away?" Dax asks softly, his voice rumbling at even the thought. "I know he wants you to leave with him."

"It's more than that. He wants her. I can sense these kinds of things," Sterling mutters.

I scoff and elbow Dax in his stomach, making him tighten his abs. Sterling is lucky as hell he's too far out of my reach. "You guys need to chill out. I think you're being overprotective toward the wrong person. If he was going to kidnap me, he'd have done so."

Sterling leans into Sagan. "She's ignoring my comment because she knows it's true."

"Can you blame the fucker?" Sagan asks.

I sigh. "Seriously, you guys?"

"What? You're hot. You're the best thing I've ever smelled—like paradise and rainbows and all that bullshit you know would taste mouthwatering if you could bottle it up. Shit, I want to bottle your love juice up and—"

Bastien and Sagan both hit him, Bastien whacking him in the back of the head and Sagan getting close enough to his balls that Sterling throws himself out of the circle. I squeeze my eyes shut and strut away from them, raising my finger to stop Dax from following.

He growls at me, crossing his arms over his chest, looking like he's about to throw me on his shoulder and shout that I'm theirs and Flynn shouldn't get my time. The cute, broody bastard.

Flynn raises his hand to touch my back but decides against it and drops his arms to his sides, thinking things through. I can't blame him. The tension behind us sizzles over my skin. And strangely enough, the nearly inaudible growl Sagan releases sounds so hot that I can't help but turn to look at him.

I don't know what comes over me, but I stick my tongue out at him. Maybe it's because despite the world exploding around us, we're together. It killed me to think I had almost lost them. Facing the She-Wolf Games alone, knowing what was at stake, nearly did kill me. But finishing first and winning on my own—I feel more powerful than ever.

"Which is sexy as hell," Sagan thinks to me, smiling at my teasing of him.

Flynn risks his limbs to touch the top of my hand, drawing my attention away from the guys and to him. His lavender eyes sparkle, his brows lowering with uncertainty. He looks as if he struggles to spit the words out. And damn it. It makes me nervous as fuck, deflating the lightness keeping me from sinking into the dark thoughts trying to sneak from the depths of my mind.

"Lyric, I have something I need to tell you," he says softly, like if he speaks normally, he might scare me off.

"You still think I should go with you?" I ask, crossing my arms over my chest. "Because I will...if and only if, you have a place that can accommodate all of us. I know you thought I was crazy for wanting to come back here, but I couldn't just leave my soul behind. It's hard to explain, because I don't know if it's love or just the intense feeling of belonging, but if I go, they go. They're my pack."

"They're your true mates." Flynn sounds so certain with his comment, his affirmation making my feelings over Dax, Sterling, Sagan, and Bastien seem less out there. My human rationale trained me against thinking such a thing existed—I've had boyfriends, lovers, and thought I'd one day have a husband, but I never expected I'd have a pack, and with my pack, a family. A connection. A bond that we all share.

"True mates," I repeat, needing to say the words out loud. "Yeah, I guess they are."

"But the witches that helped the packs...they've cursed the wolves to stop such a thing from occurring. At least, that's what I think." Flynn flicks his gaze behind me. "I won't know for certain unless you stick to my plan."

"You mean..." I want to vomit just thinking about it. "No way. No-fucking-way. I won't do it. I'd rather face lycans or witches or whatever in the Mortal World."

Because there is no way I will hand a day claim to Axel. That's weird as hell. For one, he's not in the competition. Two, he talked about Paige as if she already has a collar on him, even though she was one of my grandparent's sister. And three, just no. He's been trying to get his damn sons to flip me on my back and make me submit. He'd probably love it if I called him daddy, and I have no desire to explore that kink with anyone apart from—

"It's one day," Flynn argues, stepping closer, sensing Dax inching his way into our space.

He's trying so hard to be subtle, but considering he's tall enough to be my sunshade, he's not as inconspicuous as he thinks.

"Then you do it," I snap, crossing my arms.

Flynn raises his eyebrows and tilts his mouth downward in thought. "Actually, that's not a bad idea."

"What?" I ask in surprise. "How is that going to work?"

He smirks at me, and I think it might be the first time he's ever done so. And hell. He's so much cuter, his teeth straight and white, his eyes crinkling in the corners, smiling too. I gawk at him a little too long, because electricity flickers through his irises and he shifts on his feet under my attention, forgetting to answer my question.

"Shit, blondie. Did you just accidentally stake a claim on him?" Sterling mutters from behind me. "I don't like that creepy-ass smile. He looks ready to eat you, and I already called dibs."

I jerk my attention to glare at Sterling. "Do you want me to tickle you or something?"

He laughs, unable to remain serious. "Or something. You can do whatever the hell you want with that naughty tongue of yours but brace yourself. I'm a master at licking every sexy inch of your body. Your love juice will quench my damn thirst for you."

"Which I'm going to need," Flynn says, dragging my attention back to him.

"What the fuck? Uh, no," I say, baring my bottom teeth. Because how the hell will that work? I don't even want to think about it. Sterling's dirty mouth already makes me question a couple of things.

Dax growls, unable to contain his urge to stand close enough to touch, and links his fingers through mine. He towers behind me, his chest vibrating with his anger. "Hell-fucking-no. She's mine. Ours. You're not using any part of her for whatever the fuck you plan."

I knew that was coming. "What he said. That's a weird-ass request. I've already given dirty panties to that horn-dog once." I motion to Sterling.

"Hey, it wasn't for my kinks," Sterling argues. "Though I wish you'd give them to me more often for my spank bank."

I tilt my head and glower at him. "Really?"

"If you won't give me what I need, then give your claim to Axel," Flynn says, his voice deepening with annoyance. "Unlike that foul-mouthed sex fiend, I need your scent for a spell. I'm trying to help you, Lyric. This is important. I'd prefer it to be me over you. You've been through enough."

He sounds so honest, so sympathetic. I can't help but meet Flynn's gaze again. His pouty lip draws my attention, and I study his frown, kind of wishing he'd smile again.

Sagan groans. "You were right, Sterling."

"It doesn't matter. You know we made her a promise." Bastien steps closer and reaches for my other hand, needing to be by my side.

"I don't like it." Dax grumbles deep in his throat again, trying to pull me even closer to him.

I raise an eyebrow and look at him. "I don't like it either but maybe Flynn is right."

Sterling huffs and whispers, "Totally over her head."

"Maybe that's a good thing," Sagan says, leaning into him.

I ignore their comments, not in the mood to try to figure them out. Instead, I focus on Bastien and his tranquility. He is far calmer than Dax, Sterling, and Sagan.

"Just think about it, Lyric," Flynn says, looking to me, knowing that I will not allow anyone else to make the decision. Because I doubt they will like any of our options. "I'll cast a spell to fool Axel into believing I am you. When we're alone, I'll be able to extract any information he knows."

I blink a few times. "You're going to turn into me?"

He purses his lips, tightening his mouth. "I will make him think I am. I'll still be me."

Dax surprises me by hooking his hands to my waist. He lifts me off my feet, spins around, and hands me to Sagan like I'm a piece of furniture or some shit. He's so quick to get into Flynn's face, herding him farther away and out of earshot, that I don't even get a chance to react.

Sagan smirks at me, tossing me up, getting my body to instinctively wrap around his. His blue eyes search mine, and he squeezes my ass cheeks, trying to keep my attention on him. And damn it. I thought Dax was the only one who could manage to give me puppy-dog eyes. Sagan doesn't even have to say anything before I lean in and kiss him.

I ease away. "You guys are in trouble. I want to know what the hell they're talking about. It involves me."

"It involves us," Dax calls from behind me. "And as your mate, I will do whatever it takes to protect you. We don't know this asshole, and all of a sudden he's here, trying to help you, claiming he's doing it out of the kindness of his heart? Fucking lies. I will not agree to anything until I know exactly what he wants."

"He wants our fucking woman," Sterling says, stepping between me and Dax, cutting off my view of him.

I sigh. "He's not even a wolf."

"Exactly. There is more to it than him wanting to bang you." Dax's comment sends heat through my body, burning blush across my face.

"Seriously?" I don't know how much I can take of this unwarranted jealousy. I mean, Dax, Sterling, Sagan, and Bastien have all been a team in the last few weeks. They even accepted Caz getting a claim without a throw down. Is this how it'll be once their claims are official? Because this is nuts. We will be heading to the Mortal World, and I can't have a pack of muscle men threatening any man who even looks at me.

"Yes, seriously," Dax snaps.

Sagan sighs. "Uh-oh. Brace yourself, brother."

I throw myself back with his comment, forcing Sterling to catch me as Sagan loses his hold. I balance against his sturdy frame, catching myself before I eat shit on the ground. I expect Sterling to tighten his arms around me, but he hops back and covers his junk protectively, expecting me to put up a fight he knows he'll lose.

Dax, on the other hand, flips around in his spot and challenges me with a growl. His dare sets me off, and I ball my hands into fists and stride the dozen feet to him. It would be a helluva lot easier if I could get in his face, but there isn't anything to stand on out here.

"You need to let me handle this," I say, poking him in his hard pec. "I am your leader."

He snatches my hand, wrapping his fingers around mine to stop me from jabbing him again. "But I am responsible for your safety. You are the most important person in my existence, and I don't give a fuck if you can handle this shady fuckhead or not. I will do what I have to."

"What happened to the promise you made me?" I droop my shoulders, lowering my voice, adding a little bit of whine to my words. My strong will tests his, making him more stubborn, so I decide to take another approach. "You said you would stand by my side and not in front of me."

Dax's glower falters, his eyes darting from mine to the pout I puff out on my lips. I focus on keeping my mind clear, so he doesn't realize what I'm doing. He's so wound up, giving in to his nature, that this should work.

"So please. Let me handle this, Dax," I add, pulling his hand to my chest.

He continues to stare at me, his chest heaving, his wild emotions settling down the longer we stay close and silent.

He blinks a few times and narrows his eyes again. "Nice try. The answer is n—"

A blink of light sparks through the air, and Dax freezes mid-sentence. His hand remains locked around mine, even stronger in this freaky state. Silence falls through the air, the world around us lit in the magic Flynn summons to interrupt my argument.

And surprisingly, it pisses me off.

"Lyric, I—"

"Unfreeze them, now!" I say, raising my voice. "You can't just get in the middle of my argu—"

"No." Dax unfreezes, the light diminishing.

Flynn risks getting a fist to the face by stepping beside us. "Okay, you know what? You're right. I'm not doing all of this out of the kindness of my heart. Well, at least not completely."

"I fucking knew it," Dax mutters, eyeing me. Cocky bastard.

"Then why?" I try not to let Dax's smugness get to me.

"I can use this information to my advantage. Things have

been a bit...complicated in Magaelorum, and I think the witches providing you protection here are involved. More and more lycans are showing up, bringing too much attention. They're trying to tip the balance in their favor."

Dax releases my hand to cross his arms. "So they want their own territory in Magaelorum?"

"They want to abandon it completely, but you know what they can do." Flynn stands taller—actually, I think he grows taller—to meet Dax at his eye level. It's freaky as hell, watching him bulk up right before my eyes. Now I can't help wondering what else he can change.

I don't ask, though. It's a struggle, but I do want to know more about the lycans and what he's talking about. "What can they do?" I ask.

"What's in it for you?" Dax says at the same time as me. I flick him, knowing that I shouldn't have let myself get distracted, because Flynn knows he has to convince my pack mates.

"To clear my coven's name," Flynn responds.

A dozen questions spin through my mind. Clear his coven's name? He never mentioned any of this.

If only a whistle didn't sound through the air at the same time the leaders emerge from the building.

Flynn disappears from sight.

"Oh, Lyric. You're just who we were looking for," Trista says, padding her way in our direction. "We've decided to allow you time alone instead of forcing you to pick a competitor to hold your day claim."

I slowly lift my gaze to look at her. Flynn's words sneak back to my mind, reminding me of what he wanted.

I consider denying him until I find out more information, because I have so many fucking questions now that I want answers to, but then he's also already willing to help me get some of them.

I gather my courage and finally say, "What if I want to pick someone?"

"It's not necessary to announce one of these guys as your chosen one," she says, glancing at Dax, Sterling, Sagan, and Bastien. "It's better if you don't."

"But it's not one of them," I say, steeling myself.

She frowns. "Really? Oh, the leaders will be thrilled to know you have decided on someone new. Who is it?"

"Axel of Stargaze Hill," I say, remaining expressionless.

"Axel? But he—"

"He hasn't claimed Paige yet, has he?" I ask, interrupting her.

"Well, no, but—"

"Then that's who I pick. You can tell the leaders and announce it. If anyone asks, it's because I've decided that I want someone with more experience when it comes to territory politics." I link my fingers together, wondering if we'll get away with this. Because Trista looks ready to deny me.

She flicks her attention to Dax, who remains expressionless.

"I suppose that would be okay, but I have to warn you. He's not used to someone so...independent."

I cross my arms. "I know. Maybe he won't be such an asshole if he realizes he can never break me."

"JUST RELAX," SAGAN MURMURS, KISSING my neck.

I scrunch my nose, trying to get my mind to chill but just knowing what we're attempting to do weirds me the hell out. It's one thing to be caught up in a moment of just being together without reason and only because we want to. It's a whole other situation when Sagan won the game of Rock-Paper-Scissors for the job of getting me worked up and turned on.

"I'm just...this is weird." I shift on the bed and peek at him.

"What if we do something else? We have a bit of time still. Want to go on a run? Wrestle? I can run to the dining hall and get you something to eat." He sits up and twines our fingers together.

"How about...you work yourself up for me?" I smirk as I say the words, blush burning over my skin. "I mean, if you want to...since there isn't a TV. I think I just need a distraction to get me warmed up."

Sagan's smile melts into the sexiest, lust-filled expression I have ever seen on him. Just the idea of getting his mind going excites me. He licks his lips and leans into me, pinching my chin to guide my mouth to his for a kiss.

"Will you help me?" he asks, his voice all rumbly, his mind whispering how badly he wants to watch me undress for him.

I puff out a shuddering breath, his wandering mind turning me on. I can nearly feel his touch caressing my skin, his fingers tugging at the hem of my shirt to pull it off. I scoot to the edge of the bed and stand up, turning my back toward him.

"Nice and slow," he murmurs, his lust crashing through me with his instructions. "I like it when you're a bit of a tease."

I peek at him from over my shoulder. "Is that so?"

"Mmmhmm."

"Well, it's a good thing that I can't undress completely. You're just going to have to enjoy only getting a peek." I ease my shirt up inch by inch, seductively swaying a bit like the tease he wants me to be. I tug off my shirt, revealing a fiery red bra made from lace and silk that dips low to enhance my cleavage.

"My favorite color," Sagan murmurs, his movements rustling the blankets. "Turn around. I need a better look."

I bite my bottom lip with a smile and swivel on my feet to face him. My heart picks up speed as he slides his hand into his shorts and tugs his raging boner out for me to see. His eyelids turn heavy, and he strokes the length of his cock, never taking his gaze away from mine. Combing my hair with my fingers, I shift it from my shoulders to give him a better view of the sheer material, my nipples now on full display with their arousal.

"My gorgeous woman," he says, continuing to pleasure himself in front of me. "Let me touch you."

I wag my finger. "Not yet."

He play-growls.

Turning back around, I shake my ass a little, loving the deep, throaty moan escaping his mouth. I ease the waistband of my yoga pants down, showing off the matching G-string. The bed creaks as he moves closer to the edge. Bending over, I give him a view of my body from behind. He spanks my ass cheek, the sensation sending tingles straight to my vagina, making me gasp.

"I want to touch you more," he murmurs, his words a breath of desire on his lips.

"You can't," I tease. "You can only look."

"This is torture." His voice hums with his moan, and I turn around to face him.

He's right about that. I love how sexy he looks, turned on by me, knowing how badly he wants to touch me, to taste me, to give me exactly what I want.

"Then come here," he says, listening to my thoughts. "I've missed being alone with you. These last few days have been trying. I want so badly to steal you away from here."

"Your brother might not like that," I say, meeting Sagan's gaze as his lust starts to fizzle, his mind taking him in a different direction.

Sagan slows his motions. "We would all go. I'd never leave him behind."

"Because you obviously need backup." Sterling's voice trickles through the door, drawing our attention from each other. "Get naked, blondie. I'm coming. Hopefully inside you. My sperm gun is locked and loaded."

Sagan chuckles and snatches me by my waist, tugging me to him. Sterling enters the room, his playful smile widening at the sight of me in Sagan's arms. It's in this moment that I realize Sagan isn't trying to keep me away from Sterling. He's holding me still.

I wiggle my ass on his lap, teasing him while only half putting up a fight. Sagan moans under my movements, shifting me until his cock flexes between my legs. Sterling closes the space to me and leans down, caressing his lips to mine.

"Looks like we might have to battle this out, brother," Sterling says, his teasing growl vibrating across my lips. "I don't think she's ready for double the peen."

My eyes widen at his words. "I'm not losing my ass virginity right now."

"So some other time?" Sterling asks, hooking his fingers onto my hips. "Because you know...unlike most men in the Mortal World, I understand you can't treat a rosebud like it's in full bloom."

I tip my head back and laugh, unable to keep a straight face at his words. He's totally serious and eager, his thoughts wandering to me on all fours as he proves his tongue is far naughtier than mine.

Sagan shifts my hair and kisses the base of my throat, drawing his fingers from my stomach and down my pelvis to explore my thighs. With one finger, he shifts my G-string out of the way and teases me with his touch, turning my laugh into a moan.

"She likes the idea," Sagan murmurs, his voice sounding as if it comes from smiling lips. I can't see his expression, but the wave of happiness rolling over me is enough to warm my insides even more.

"So maybe tomorrow," Sterling teases, kissing me again. His hands slip into my bra as he rubs his fingers over my nipples.

I hum and shrug. "It depends on how good you make me feel today."

"That's my brother's job. I'm here as back up." Sterling bends down and slides his hands under my legs, picking me up enough to feel my body align with Sagan's. "Maybe give a small helping hand."

I moan so fucking loud as I sink completely onto Sagan. Sterling eases my legs open to get full access to my clit. My breath quickens, and I lean my head back, craning my neck to kiss Sagan again. A part of me doesn't believe I'm doing this. Allowing these two men to work together to make me orgasm. Another much more dominant part of me asks me why I haven't done this before. Their attention, their desire and need to make me feel so incredibly good, makes everything even better. I was a bit worried after finding out that I'd have a pack of four men wanting relationships and lives with me. I was concerned that they'd fight for my attention or it'd be too much. What I didn't really think about was exactly how much more attention I'd get.

And now my body screams for more. More of everything. To indulge in the pleasure of the men who belong to me.

Sterling and Sagan each take turns kissing me, opening their thoughts completely. Their lust entangles with mine, their pleasure of knowing exactly what they do to me running hot and wild like the beasts in their souls.

I gasp and moan, Sagan lifting and lowering my body over and over again onto his while Sterling adds more pressure with his fingers, his consistent, rhythmic motion bringing me to completion.

I tense with my orgasm, the sensation a bit different yet more powerful than ever. I clench my legs through the electricity zinging through my body from inside to burn through me so that I feel the pleasure within every fiber of my being, from my head to the tips of my toes.

Sterling surprises me by ripping my panties free before kissing me once more. "Enjoy the rest of your time with Sagan, blondie. He's a damn lucky man, but not for long. You and I will make some good plans."

I can only nod and gasp and watch him leave. Sagan continues to kiss my shoulder, sucking my skin into his mouth, leaving a hickey. I lose myself to the pleasure and enjoy the whisper of his voice as he tells me how much he relishes our time and me, and how I'm the most magnificent woman in the universe.

Sagan moans as he finishes, hugging me close, letting me sink on his lap while we both catch our breaths. My body hums, my thoughts finally managing to sort through this moment. Our passion, the pleasure still coursing through me is enough to push away the purpose of this adventure. And damn.

Sagan eases me off of him and lies back on the bed, tugging me with him. "Let's consider the purpose as something else. Because it was for me. My sole purpose is to be here for you in any way you need."

I smile and run my finger across his bare chest. "Just tell Sterling that. I can already hear him now."

"I promise you we won't high-five...in front of you," he teases. "Just this once."

Propping up on my elbow, I meet his gaze. "You say that as if you think this is going to happen all the time."

He chuckles. "Definitely not. I just want you to know that I'm good with whatever. Because I know you're mine and I'm yours. And being together is all that matters."

"You're right. Together. How it should be."

"Do you really think so now?" he asks, hugging me close.

I clutch his face, kissing him softly, exploring his mouth while I open my mind completely, letting him feel the truth simmering inside me. "I do. It was hard at first, but this—" I point between me and him. "This is undeniable. I was able to do something that I shouldn't have been. I was given the chance to choose who I wanted to be with, and I chose you."

"I love you, Lyric," he says softly, pulling back to stare into my eyes. "I want you to know that. I love you."

I open and close my mouth in surprise.

He chuckles. "I know it feels too soon for you, but I just had to tell you. I worry about what might happen. I can't wait another moment without saying it."

Whoa. I don't know what to say or if I should try to say anything, so I kiss him again, filling him with the emotions his words awaken in me, his confession solidifying our bond in a way I know I should've expected and now can't figure out why I hadn't.

Sagan savors my affection for as long as we can before we have to get ready. The last thing I want is for Flynn to materialize here like the creep he can be, knowing exactly where to show. He knows we have a meeting place, but I think he will pop in when he wants regardless, like he now has the permission since his presence is known.

Flynn must be in my head or some shit, heeding the warnings I was throwing out telepathically as I enjoyed the rest of my time with Sagan. Now that we're out in the open, I kind of hope he's nearby like he promised he'd be, ready and waiting with magic in case someone comes hunting for me before the claim announcement.

Howls sound through the air as we enter the foggy forest, and I grip onto Sagan, unsure if it's because I want to protect him or if I want him to protect me. Maybe both. If only my bones didn't suddenly freeze at the sight of dozens of wolves heading toward the middle of Storm Haven. We slow our pace and cut in the opposite direction. Since everyone comes out of the shelters nestled into the side of a mountain and within huge rocks that keep the Storm Haven pack safe, we can avoid the main path everyone takes. Clouds darken the forest more, a chill in the air making me shiver. It's called Storm Haven for a reason, but Dax swore it isn't bad once you're used to it. The rains make it harder for the packs to track, which is one of the reasons why Dax is so excellent at it.

"Flynn didn't want to tell you this, but we're going to be testing his spell," Sagan says, tightening his hand through mine. "Once we're sure it will be successful, we will need to hide for a bit. Flynn will bring Axel to us."

"I get to watch his interrogation?" I ask, a bit surprised. I didn't think anyone would allow that douchebag man even near me.

"You're our pack leader. Once we know what the hell is really going on around here, we're leaving what happens next with our futures up to you." Sagan peers around the forest. "We will always follow wherever you take us."

I open my mouth to tell him that I want to make the decision as a pack, but Flynn materializes with the flash of lavender light. Him and his timing, I swear. And now that I see him…I don't know what I was expecting—maybe to see a clone of myself standing before me—but nothing about Flynn seems different. My chest clenches as my hope sinks with my disappointment.

"Holy fuck," Sagan says, his mouth falling open. "Fuck."

I frown. "I know. It fucking sucks it didn't work." I place my hands on my hips. "You're lucky I had a good time, but if I find out you just played us for my panties, I'm—"

"What do you mean it didn't work?" Sagan says, interrupting me. "It's freaky. He not only looks and smells like you, but his mind *feels* like you."

"It's a doppelganger spell. You won't be able to see me as you see yourself because I can only capture how others see you." Flynn steps closer. "Usually witches wouldn't dare use it on themselves because it's not foolproof and easier to manipulate something like dirt or an animal, but I will not risk messing up. The only one I trust with magic is myself." Flynn smiles at me.

"So if you could please get your mate to step back before he tries to tackle me...that would be great."

Sagan ignores his comment and touches Flynn's cheek with the back of his knuckles. "Damn. I don't like this."

"Because your soul knows the truth since you've bonded to Lyric." Flynn whacks Sagan's hand before he can tug on his shirt.

I laugh and wrap my arms around him. "I'm going to mistake your curiosity as affection, which might make me jealous."

"I'm sorry," they both say in unison.

Sagan growls.

I laugh. "Shit, this is weird. I think we need to test it on one of the others. Just to be sure."

Tugging away from Sagan, I spin around and quickly shrug out of my shirt and shorts, preparing to transform into a wolf. I pounce on Sagan, standing up on my hind legs to lick his throat. This situation is so stressful that I could use a good laugh. Who knows what will happen next. I need to enjoy this crazy-ass situation before things explode.

Sagan chuckles as he graces me with a smile. Scratching his fingers between my ears, he leans down and kisses my nose.

I lick his chin, making him laugh and drag his hands down my back until he reaches around to rub his fingers into my belly. I play-growl at him, knowing how much he likes to tease me. A wave of warmth—what I recognize as his love—cascades over me in a waterfall of everything good about him. He loves me as a woman or wolf, his soul bonded to my being.

I push my paws into his chest and launch away from him. He doesn't even consider staying with Flynn, tugging his shirt off to join me in the form I choose for this moment. I dart through two trees and skid across the muddy ground, dirtying my blond fur.

Pouncing on Sagan, I tackle him, forcing him to get as dirty as I am.

Flynn follows us into the forest, keeping quiet as we lead him toward where I know the others wait. Four silhouettes appear within the fog, and I slow, wary at the sight of Caz with Dax, Sterling, and Bastien.

"What is he doing here?" I ask Sagan through our telepathic link.

"He's part of our pack." Sagan darts in front of me, cutting me off. "But don't worry. You have no obligations to him. He bowed to Dax."

"I don't trust him," I argue.

"But we do. We heard him out and still believe he's on our side." Sagan nuzzles his nose to mine, his closeness easing my anxiety. "You should hear him out when you're ready. And before you tackle me, I want you to remember that we don't trust Flynn. Consider it a compromise."

"Did Dax tell you to say that to me?" I huff a breath through my nostrils.

Sagan rubs his body to mine, circling me and nudging me with his head, licking my snout and trying to distract me by teasing my nature. "No, gorgeous. These are my thoughts. My pleas. I'm not asking you to claim Caz. All I'm asking is that you trust me like I trust you. If you think Flynn is okay, then I'll stand beside your decision to accept his help."

I growl at him. "Why do you have to be so reasonable? I hope you know it's not exactly the same. Caz hurt me. He lied."

"It wasn't his intention to ever hurt you. He feels like shit that things happened like this. He wasn't lying about his dad and the alpha-mates, not really. He hadn't gotten the chance to tell us before you discovered it...kind of like how we discovered Flynn." Sagan licks my face again, his words calling me out on my hypocrisy, but his emotions continuously remain calm. And it makes me feel bad. Like utter shit.

"You're right. When this bullshit is over, I'll talk to him," I say, returning his affection with my own, nuzzling my head under his.

A soft catcall of a whistle draws my attention away from Sagan and to Flynn as he saunters toward the others at the edge of the foggy lake.

Sagan chuckles at the fact that Sterling looks ready to smack Flynn's ass and lift him off his feet.

I pad my way closer, sneaking through the overgrowth to listen in on their conversation. Sagan remains glued to my side like he fears even a foot of space getting between us.

"Where's Sagan?" Dax asks, peering around. "He wasn't supposed to leave you."

"Lighten up. I can take care of my damn self," Flynn says, trying to impersonate me.

I groan. "They're going to know it's not me. I don't sound like that."

Sagan bumps his hindquarters to mine. "What are you talking about? He sounds just like you."

"Yeah-fucking-right," Flynn and I say at the same time, his voice in sync with my thought to Sagan. I missed what was said, and I can't stop the growl escaping my lips.

"Told you," Sagan teases. "Next time we'll have to bet on it."

I slink away from him, sneaking closer to the small group. Sterling totally checks Flynn out, his eyes darting down to his chest. It's weird as hell, because I know he's supposed to see him as me, but I'm a teensy bit jealous that he looks at someone else like he wants to hump the hell out of them.

Sagan follows along, his laughter sneaking into my mind as he listens to my thoughts. "I'm going to hold this over him forever."

"Bastien too," I say, trying not to make any weird noises they could possibly hear. Bastien watches Flynn like he's holding a piece of steak. I think with my claim so fresh to them, they might be a bit clingy, which I wouldn't mind if it wasn't Flynn.

"Come here, blondie. This space is killing my boner. I need to feel those perky tits against me before I go. Sagan is a fucking lucky bastard." Sterling holds open his arms, wiggling his fingers for Flynn.

Flynn hesitates, making Sagan laugh with a bark. I bump into him, pushing him back, and continue on my mission to get as close as possible without being spotted. Flynn gets his shit together and steps forward to hug Sterling.

Stopping short, Flynn eases his head back before Sterling can kiss him. "All right, man. If you insist. We gotta make this quick, though. I'm going to be late for the claim announcement."

Sterling frowns, his brows lowering on his head. Confusion lines his expression, and he flares his nostrils. Sterling narrows his eyes as realization sets in. His carefree demeanor stiffens, his muscles rippling. He looks ready to punch Flynn for messing with him.

So I pounce.

Standing on my hind legs, I attach myself to Sterling's back with my paws around his sides and surprise hump him from behind.

Sagan barks with his laugh, circling the two of us as Flynn gets out of the way.

Dax and Bastien howl with laughter, watching as Sterling struggles to get a hold on me to get me off. Caz looks like he's not sure if he should be amused or scared that I'll come for him next in less than a playful manner.

"Watching you flirt and check out Flynn made me so jealous," I think to Sterling, darting back before he locks his fingers to my fur to try to lift me up and over his head. "That pouty mouth of yours is mine."

Sterling tries to grab me, and I circle him again. "I knew it wasn't you."

"Yeah, right," I say, dodging out of his reach.

"My dick didn't even harden." He launches in my direction, missing me by a foot, and lands on his hands and knees.

He doesn't get a chance to get up as I pounce on him again, mounting him like I'm sure he'd love to mount the hell out of me, and hump him hard enough in my wolf form that I knock him forward and face-first into the lake.

I freeze in surprise, watching him sink under. The guys laugh hysterically, not even bothering to see if Sterling is okay. I inch forward to look into the glowing lake, my nerves bunching, because I know this fucker will try to pop up and grab me to pull me into the water.

"Shit, Lyric. Get back," Dax says, his voice going from light to deep and rumbly.

I don't get a chance to move as the water ripples and Sterling launches from the lake in his wolf form. He knocks me back, making me screech, and I laugh and bite into his fur, trying to roll him off.

"You fucker," I say, shaking my head to throw the water off my snout.

Sterling snatches me by the fur of my neck, dragging me away from the lake. "Run." He tries to push me up on my paws.

"Run, now!"

A huge wave erupts from the lake, cresting over us.

I don't get a chance to move or react.

With a roar, a lycan charges from the water.

It comes straight for me.

18

LYCAN ATTACK

BRIGHT ELECTRICITY SHOCKS THE LYCAN, knocking him off course. Dax and Caz launch at the lycan, snarling and biting, trying to keep the huge beast on the ground. I scramble to my paws and back away, keeping my eyes locked to the monster. Bastien and Sagan join the fight as Flynn sends another burst of power at the lycan. Watching the five of them work together while Sterling guards me protectively is unlike anything I've ever seen.

The lycan drops to its stomach, clawing at the soft mud near the lake. It struggles to pull itself toward the water as it tries to escape. Dax cuts it off and sinks his fangs into the back of the lycan's neck, exposing its throat. It screeches and thrashes, but it's no match for Dax's strength or Sagan's determination.

My stomach twists as Sagan rips at the lycan's neck, going for a kill bite. My muscles ripple and spasm. I transform into a human like my wolf can't handle the emotions flooding through me or the sight of the guys ensuring the lycan never gets up again. The sudden sickness threatens to leave me incapacitated and dry-heaving.

I've never seen anything like it. I don't know what I was expecting. Every lycan attack left me running and fighting myself. It ended with the lycans escaping or drowning. But in this moment, my pack teams up with Flynn to teach this lycan a lesson.

We're more powerful than it. We won't let lycans get away with coming in here and trying to ruin everything.

The lycan's sharp shriek cuts off, and I grip onto Sterling's fur to steady myself, using his muscular wolf form to stop from falling forward as my body threatens to give out on me. I remain frozen, staring at the dead body—or what's left of it—as Flynn mutters a spell that melts the beast into a pile of goo that slips into the lake.

Caz, Dax, and Sagan stand together at the lake's edge, focusing on the water as if they suspect another monster will explode from its depths. Sterling whimpers and pokes me with his nose before licking my cheek. I tighten my fingers into his fur, hugging him like my life depends on it. My body refuses to allow me to do anything else.

A warm hand touches my shoulder. "Lyric, hey. Look at me, Ma Belle." Bastien squats naked beside me, his body dirty with a mixture of mud and blood and things I don't even want to think about. He pulls his shirt over my head, his scent prodding at my soul.

"Is she hurt?" Flynn asks, stepping closer.

Bastien engulfs me in a hug and lifts me from the ground, forcing me to release Sterling. "I think she's in shock."

"She's overwhelmed," Sagan says. I hadn't realized he turned back into a man.

"A bit disgusted," Sterling adds, stretching his arms over his head, flexing his stomach muscles. "I'm pretty sure none of you guys are kissing her for a week."

A whistle sounds through the air, coming from somewhere in the distance. Everyone looks at each other as I continue to stare at the glowing lake. Something feels incredibly wrong. The last couple of times, it has been more than one lycan. So, where are the others?

"We have to go if we're going to get the information we need," Flynn says, touching my shoulder. "If you would prefer I stay here and you award Axel your day claim—"

I thrash my head back and forth. "No, it should be you."

"I'll stay and guard the lake," Caz says, his voice low like he's afraid anything louder might cause me to react.

Dax crosses his arms and looks at Bastien. "Stay with Flynn. I'll comb the area to make sure we didn't miss anything. The last thing we need is for another damn lycan to threaten the packs. Everyone's too on edge, and the tension is bad enough already. If any of our alliances fall apart, it'll leave the territories weak and open to more attacks."

"That's exactly what's happening," I say, the sudden thought consuming me. "I don't think the lycans just happened to get in. I mean, we know Paige is indebted to a witch. They are trying to break the alliances between packs to make sure we can't all rise together to fight back. Maybe they know what we're planning. Fire Mountain—"

"This isn't the work of the Fire Mountain Clan witches," Flynn says, rubbing his hands together, creating sparks between his palms. "Paige is indebted to the Nightstar Coven. It was one of their witches that I fought."

"They could be working together," Sagan says, standing super close to Bastien as he silently holds me.

Flynn shakes his head. "No, they're enemies. They wouldn't work together. They might be warring over taking this territory and trying to collar all of you."

My heart stalls at his words. "What? What does that mean?"

"You do know how they manage to curse humans to turn into lycans, right? Why do you think your species was thought to go extinct? Lycans form unbreakable allegiances to the witches who curse them. They bite and infect others and those who survive the transformation join the witch's supposed army. They're one of the few creatures to be able to access the gates that take them through the realms and back without the use of debilitating magic, because they're linked to the Mortal World. Whatever happened with your parents, Lyric, must've triggered a sort of beacon to alert other covens that the wolves are still around. I just—" He sighs. "We need to figure this out. The alpha-mates know something that the leaders don't."

I have so many questions, but what he says makes sense. Before my parents abandoned Lulupoterra, the wolves remained hidden in their sanctuary.

The five witches who helped them—including Fire Mountain—might not have been even doing it to help the wolf species. It's logical that they would only protect us to use us, and maybe now they finally think they can take what they've been protecting for a century.

"So, you just want to stick to the plan?" I ask, wiggling in Bastien's arms until he sets me on my feet. "Shouldn't we alert the leaders of the danger?"

Dax sighs. "I don't think so. I don't know who to trust. Even my mom is afraid to speak up against the alpha-mates. With Luke's disappearance, she feels as if she has no choice but to rely on her other mates for protection."

"The other leaders feel the same," Bastien says. "It's why

they ignore the rising tension and keep focusing on the games. Instead of acting first, they want to handle each threat as it comes."

"Shit, someone needs to remind them that they're just as strong and capable as their damn mates," I mutter, anger boiling through me. I thought they were powerful. I thought they had their shit together and knew exactly how to keep everyone in line. But really, they're doing nothing at all.

But I know they want to. I can see it. Feel it.

Sagan slides his hand around my waist and pulls me against his warm body. "I think that was your dad's plan. Hell, even if it wasn't, you will do it. Your arrival has already shifted things."

"We just need to figure out how to keep everyone together, before things fall apart." Dax clenches and unclenches his fists, cracking his knuckles. "So let's start there. We'll proceed as planned with Flynn working his magic."

I meet Flynn's gaze. "I hope you know I'm trusting you."

"And if you break her trust, I'll fucking break every damn bone on your body," Dax says. "If you even think about using this against us—"

"Calm down, tough guy," Flynn says. "How about you direct those threats to the ones already against you?"

I step between the two of them. "Can we just get through this?"

Flynn nods. "It's all I want."

"Good," I say, glancing at each of my guys. "Because that's

what I want too."

I hold both Sterling and Sagan's hands, standing between their rigid forms as we peer from a hillside at the gathering crowd far in the distance. Flynn walks alone, strutting right through the center of the competitors, forcing them to part around him.

"This is still so fucking weird," Sterling mutters softly. "That damn ass shake is a little too much. I don't like it. Only we can show your ass that kind of attention."

"But my ass is right here." I bump him with my hip. Trying to find something, anything, to calm my nerves, I decide to give Sterling and Sagan a little bit of attention since we have nothing to do except watch this shitshow unfold. "Or do you think Flynn's version looks better?"

I step forward and stretch my arms over my head before bending over to touch my toes, flashing them my ass as it peeks out from under Bastien's shirt. Sagan play-growls and knocks his arm into Sterling, shoving him back to stop him from getting to me first. I shake my ass a bit more, teasing them, knowing that neither of them will be able to control themselves. Sagan swings his hand and slaps my ass, making me jump. My knees quiver under the sensation, my body expecting Sagan to continue with his attention.

"Careful, blondie. Your teasing will get you in more trouble than a little spank. I owe you for the lake, you know. Don't think I won't mount that tight ass of yours, looking so ready to let my rocket into your sexy star."

The sudden silence drawing through the crowd snags my attention from Sterling and Sagan before they convince me to join them on some crazy adventure. I straighten my back and take a few steps forward, peering around.

Trista, Bridgette, Simone, and Viviana stroll from the protective circles created by their remaining mates to face the anxious onlookers. The fifth elder leader isn't present, nor are the newest four from the last couple of games.

"It is with great regret that we must inform you that the Eclipse Valley pack has withdrawn from the She-Wolf Games," Trista says, keeping her face expressionless. It's weird as hell to be able to hear her so clearly from this distance. But Flynn ensured it. "All competitors from Eclipse Valley must now leave the territory."

"What?" Fergus asks, his voice hollering over the murmuring crowd. "None of us agreed to that."

Trista links her fingers together. "It was Aurora's decision, and perhaps she will reconsider for the next games, once she remembers the purpose. The rest of us leaders could not in good conscience agree to her desire to cut Lyric of Lunar Crest from the games and hold a lottery drawing for the remaining spots."

"Well, why the hell not?" another man says, his voice practically snarling the words. "She has already made up her mind about who she wants and won't even give anyone else a damn chance. It's only fair if she can't play the games fairly."

"And with your damn son trying to sway your decision with an impossible claim—he should be disqualified." This comes from an Eclipse Valley competitor. Of course he'd be upset, since it's his home territory.

Simone waves her hands, getting the men to settle down. "We considered it. It was a hard decision to make, but Lyric proved Aurora's point wrong by requesting to award her day claim to someone currently uninvolved in the competition. This certainly shows that she is willing to compromise despite her growing bonds toward some of you."

"You must've threatened her. That's the only way that bitch would ever comply." I keep a mental note of all the assholes speaking against me to remember to kick them in the balls later.

Bridgette steps forward. "Her request came as a surprise to all of us, and was in fact not persuaded by other means. So please, everyone settle down. Perhaps you can take note of her choice and show her that you too are worthy of her interest."

I crinkle my nose and groan. "Ugh. I wish she didn't say that."

"Right? Giving all those fuckers hope. You're mi—"

Shoving Sterling, I cut off his comment. "Don't you dare say it."

Sagan laughs. "That's right. Because she's mine."

I tip my head back and stare at the cloudy sky, the dark gray color threatening us with a storm. Thunder booms through the air, and lightning glitters across the sky in jagged bolts, startling me.

The deafening noise prevents me from hearing the rest of the leaders, but whatever they say must be enough to settle down the crowd. Flynn pushes his way to the group of women and allows them to greet him with a hug and kiss to his cheeks. A part of me wishes I could see him as myself, but then again...no thanks. This is weird enough already.

The crowd shifts closer in anticipation, each of the men giving Flynn their full attention as if he's about to beg one of them to sweep him off his feet. He straightens his back, and I imagine he's purposely sticking out his version of my boobs to distract the horny bastards.

"Yours are way better," Sterling mumbles under his breath, listening to my thoughts.

I smirk and shake my head. "You're ridiculous."

"Lyric of Lunar Crest, it's an honor to stand before the first she-wolf to have ever won the games," Trista starts, touching Flynn's shoulder. His eyes flicker lavender, but no one reacts. I wonder if it's just me who can see it since I can peer past his disguise.

"We wish we could have gathered sooner and without the disappointing announcement of Eclipse Valley's abandonment of our traditions, but we hope that perhaps this moment will help change things to better our future." Simone touches Flynn's other shoulder, showing her support.

"Because our packs are stronger together. The blending of

our bloodlines has proved it with how powerful the competitors are today," Bridgette adds. She smiles at Antone in the crowd, who stands nearby, ready to jump in to protect his mother from whatever invisible threat that seems to always linger.

"So with saying that, as the former leader of Lyric's first pack mate and the alliance between Meadow View and Lunar Crest, it is with great honor to award this magnificent she-wolf's day claim to someone who was worthy once before." Viviana motions to the crowd, her mouth frowning despite the smoothness of her voice. "Congratulations to Axel of Stargaze Hill. Do you accept Lyric's day claim and the opportunity to blend your pack with hers as a new competitor in the She-Wolf Games?"

Utter silence draws through the crowd as all of the current competitors shift and move, searching around for Axel. The red-haired man stands erect at the back of the crowd next to Killian with Harlow, who hovers a good few feet away, her arms hugging around herself. She ignores the other guy, who I think is from Eclipse Valley, like just the announcement of Aurora breaking her alliance is enough to get Harlow to automatically reject him.

"Axel, please join us on the winner's podium and declare whether or not you are up for the challenge," Trista says, pursing her lips in annoyance when the man isn't quick to move.

Flynn places his hands on his hips, offering an adorable smirk that makes him look even cuter. "Or are you afraid you can't handle me?" he asks, poking at Axel's ego.

Sagan mutters something under his breath and Sterling hums his agreement, though I can't hear what either of them said.

"I know it's been a while since you had to show your worth, but I'd like to give a strong man like yourself a chance," Flynn continues, twirling his finger through imaginary hair I can't see. He looks utterly ridiculous as he cocks out his hip. "Unless you're afraid I might make you submit."

I sigh and cover my eyes with my hands. Flynn is definitely taking this a bit far. He obviously doesn't have any good sense of how to handle the beast of a man who would love nothing more than to pin me down and force me to do his bidding. The same man who is also hell-bent on one of his sons winning my claim because he's confident enough they could possibly break me.

One glance at his narrowed eyes proves that he's also willing to accept any challenge in regards to me. And fuck. This shit better work. The last thing I need is for him—especially as an experienced competitor—to think he even has a chance at winning my claim and also Lunar Crest.

Killian smacks his father on the back and pumps his fist into the air, goading him on. Other competitors break their silence and cheer, whooping and hollering, even catcalling Flynn to tell him to get ready to have his world rocked.

Axel jogs the rest of the way to the podium and grins, his whole face lighting up in a cocky-bastard smile. He rushes Flynn and scoops him off his feet, holding him like a damn blushing bride. The absurdity of it makes me laugh, because Flynn doesn't waver or flinch. He gives one helluva show, acting as me, and then he shocks the hell out of me by planting a damn kiss right on Axel's mouth, getting the whole crowd to cheer.

"I accept this beautiful she-wolf's day claim," Axel says, pumping his fist. He grins and winks at Flynn, energized by the cheering crowd. "Get ready to be mine, baby doll. I'll teach you what a real man is."

Fuck.

Sterling and Sagan each grab my hand and pull me a few feet back. It reminds me that we have to go to be ready for Flynn and Axel's arrival.

A scream rips through the air, stopping me from leaving my spot. The familiar voice freaks me the hell out, Paige's sudden appearance all too convenient. I brace myself for an army of lycans to follow behind her. I expect a whole coven of witches to materialize in the crowd to snap collars on all the competitors.

But she's alone, dragging chains from her wrists, and bruised and beaten, barely standing on her feet.

"Stop! Stop everything," she yells, shaking her fists. "I'm his mate. She can't give him her day claim. I am his, and we will continue as so, ruling Stargaze Hill."

Tension fills the air. Paige bends down and rests her hands on her knees, taking a few slow, deep breaths. The woman looks frailer than before, her body seeming to weaken, where the last time I saw her, she could still stand her ground. It's like the life has been sucked from her, leaving her looking more her age. The witches have done something since she had gone missing, and I can't help but think she's like this to make everyone feel bad for her instead of questioning what the hell she's gotten into.

Viviana rushes to Paige's side and touches her hand between her shoulder blades, leaning down to meet her eyes. "Where have you been, Paige?" she asks, flicking her gaze to the leaders. "We've been looking everywhere for you."

Paige's face twists into a frown, and she drops to her knees and begins to sob. "I was k-kidnapped. I j-just broke f-free."

I swear to the fucking universe that the leaders don't fall for her bullshit.

"What? Who kidnapped you?" Viviana asks.

Paige heaves a few shuddering breaths. She points at Flynn disguised as me.

19

Nightstar Witch

SAGAN LOCKS HIS HANDS AROUND my waist and lifts me off my feet. With a growl, Sterling transforms into his wolf, his shiny coat looking more metallic with another streak of lightning crossing through the sky. My chest clenches, my body buzzing with my natural instincts. My intuition screams for me to flee.

"What bullshit!" Antone says, his loud voice sounding over the murmurs of confusion. He marches closer, his skin rippling, his black wolf begging to break free. I try to search for Bastien, but I don't see him. I don't see Dax either. "Do you think the leaders are that stupid, Paige? You weren't kidnapped. Admit it. Lyric couldn't have done it. Why would she even want to?"

Paige cries harder, her acting skills far better than mine would ever be. The old woman, who usually looks far from a great anything to me, looks younger with her frown. Vulnerable too. I nearly feel bad for her just from the desperation in her cries alone, but then she bares her teeth at Antone in a leering smile. If she were in her wolf form, I'm sure she'd launch at him and try to eat his heart out.

"You can't see the truth because you've already fallen for the spell," Paige says, motioning to him. She replaces her fake fear with rage, her face reddening with Antone's accusation. "All of you have. I didn't say it was Lyric. I said it was *her*." She points at Flynn. "Him. They. It. Whoever the hell has replaced my poor, sweet niece. The coven of Fire Mountain has fooled you all. That's an imposter."

Oh, shit. How does she know? Even my guys believed Flynn was me.

"You have to believe me," Paige says, scrambling to get to her feet. She swivels and looks around. "This isn't Lyric. She'd never agree to this. She's too headstrong."

All of the leaders take a couple of steps back like Paige will suddenly attack them. A few of their pack mates join them to stand by them protectively. Axel frowns, still holding onto Flynn like he doesn't believe Paige.

But then he drops Flynn, sending him crashing to his ass. Sagan sucks in a breath, feeling my fear zing through me. This wasn't supposed to happen. It should've been easy. Now, Flynn faces the wrath of all the packs. They'd rather fight to the death than let him escape, and I'm not so sure I can make it to him in time.

Gathering power, Flynn sets the world aglow with lavender light, sending a tree falling in front of the competitors to cut them off. Howls and snarls hum through the air over the sound of another burst of thunder. Flynn pushes up to his feet and rubs his palms together. His eyes dart around the area as he mouths what I know is some sort of spell.

Axel transforms into a massive red wolf and launches at Flynn. His teeth glisten, his eyes reflecting the lavender light glowing within Flynn's palms as he lurches forward, stalking Flynn like prey. Axel collides into Flynn and knocks him onto his back, interrupting his spellcasting. The force of Axel's body snaps Flynn's disguise completely, and the world around him wavers in a strange haze. I tense, watching as the leaders and the rest of the packs finally see that Paige was telling the truth. And it pisses me off that she manages to stay one step ahead of us and is now able to twist things in her favor.

Something shifts in Flynn's expression, and his handsome face morphs, his teeth elongating, his jaw widening. Shoving Axel, he knocks the huge wolf back a few feet. But Flynn doesn't stop Axel for long. The wolf charges him again and smashes his paws to Flynn's chest, snapping his teeth at his face. Flynn roars and tries to bite Axel back.

I gasp, the shock of seeing Flynn in such a way freaking me out. "What the hell? I thought he was a warlock."

Because whatever happened to Flynn right now—it turned him into something humanoid, scary, almost like a cross between a vampire and some other beast. His eyes flicker with power, and Flynn summons another bolt of electricity. Smacking his hands on the sides of Axel's snout, Flynn shocks him with more power. Axel howls in pain, scrambling off as his coat smokes and smolders, burning from his face and down his neck.

"Erutpac eht flow retsnom!" Flynn yells, managing to get to his feet. He raises his hands toward the sky, summoning energy with his spell.

Axel's body jerks and shudders, his coat shedding into piles of fur on the muddy ground. His human form peeks through, though his wolf resists. His howl turns into a scream of anguish as whatever spell Flynn casts over him forces his transformation from wolf to man. Axel arches his back, his muscles rippling. I cringe at the tormented shrieking, the noise nothing I've ever heard come from a wolf or a man.

"Don't let him take my mate!" Paige yells, cowering against the tree like some helpless prey about to be eaten. She breaks a branch and throws it toward Flynn. "He will use him to collar us. He will get us all and ruin our lives."

Three giant wolves take action and catapult over the fallen tree. One latches onto Paige to pull her away and the others circle around Flynn and Axel. Sagan tries to pull me to him, but I resist his need to run away with me. A part of me fears the consequences of turning my back on Flynn and not helping him. Another part of me, the part that gives into my instincts as a she-wolf, screams to be fucking brave. He's only up there because of me. He's fighting the wolves on my behalf. He doesn't deserve risking his life. None of these wolves can take me down. Paige is the least of my worries. I can't let them get to Flynn and hurt him. I can't.

Breaking from Sterling and Sagan, I rush forward. I don't care if anyone finds out that Flynn is here because of me and that I didn't tell anyone. I won't allow Paige to play a victim as an innocent she-wolf dragged and chained by magic. She gave up whatever freedom she had for some convictions I just don't understand. She put herself in this position and should face her own damn consequence.

She claimed to be hunting me for years, trying to get me away from my father because she believed my mother ruined him and his teaching in her name would ruin me. She tried to kill me because she thought I'd end up responsible for more deaths. But it was her arrival that has caused all this bullshit. I refuse to let this go on any longer.

The leaders, the packs, and every damn competitor will see her for the backstabber traitor she is. I will not only stop her. I will force her to bow before me and give up the information I need to be the leader my dad trained me to be. I will do him proud. I will prove to the world that I am not ashamed of my mother. I will thrive, knowing I am Melody of Lunar Crest's daughter.

Thunder booms and lightning crackles, the sky illuminating with an eerie light not unlike what blasts from Flynn's palms. He manages to keep Axel and a few of the other competitors back, but unless he gets a chance to cast a spell that isn't one only to protect himself, he might not get to leave. He isn't invisible or hidden, popping in and out on a whim like he usually is. He's in full view and under attack. Outnumbered.

Picking up my pace, I dash forward as more competitors shift into their wolf forms. They devour Paige's instructions, turning to the woman who doesn't belong in control while the other she-wolves hide behind the muscular shields of the men who swore to protect them. And it drives me crazy. They believe Paige too.

Sagan and Sterling howl from behind me, trying to catch up, but it only pushes me to run faster on my feet. Their strength suppresses my fear of what will happen when I defend Flynn, because everyone will automatically assume I'm the traitor. I just hope my vagina is enough to stop them from trying to kill me. They're so obsessed with saving themselves from extinction that they might not want to end the life of another womb that could help out.

As much as it bothers me. As fucked up as it is to think about. I will take advantage of their ways in any way I can. I will not fall by the hands of some manipulating bitch, turned against her own kind—and for what? What does she get? Power? Protection? Whatever it is, I'll do whatever it takes to stop that from happening. I shouldn't care so much for people who want to use me, but it's not only that. These are my guys' packs. Family. They're victims of a lifetime before them and want to survive. But I will change that. I will give them more than this life. I will help them thrive. For my parents. For my pack and our future, for all the she-wolves who will come after me.

A shadow flickers in the edge of my vision, dragging my focus from the fight. I skid across the ground, trying to slow down without tearing off my skin in the process. But I'm not fast enough to stop. Something crashes into me, knocking me off my feet. My shoulder smashes into the ground as I try to protect my head. A heavy, furry body plasters against me, pinning me down. Crackling energy zaps above me, exploding against a tree. I startle and cling onto the wolf, trying to protect us both from the flash of power intent on hurting us. Sparks and ash rain down, and Caz drags me out of the way before a branch crashes on top of us. He shoves his head into my stomach, pushing me under the cover of some low branches to guard me with a threatening growl.

"Erutpac eht flow retsnom," a feminine voice says, ringing over the noise of the sky exploding above us. Static clings to everything, setting strands of my hair floating around my head. The clouds open up and a torrential downpour cascades from the sky. It's like a massive waterfall rains on us, trying to wash us away.

Caz scrambles back and on top of me once more, using his wolf body to shield me the best he can. Another crack of lightning steals my hearing, and I prepare to pull Caz back with me. I search the area for Sterling and Sagan, but I can't see them through the rain and darkness shrouding the forest.

"Erutpac eht flow retsnom," the hidden witch says again, her chant humming to my ears despite the cacophonous storm shaking the world around us.

Caz jerks on top of me, and a strange crunching noise twists my stomach. I try to pull him closer and out of the open, but he thrashes with a howl, breaking my hold. Caz whimpers and flops onto his side in front of me, his body contorting with the witch's spell. It's the same one I heard Flynn try to use on Axel. And fuck.

Fury ignites inside me, my muscles tightening, my mind focusing on a white-haired woman as she saunters from between the trees, her hands raised toward the sky. Rain pelts my face, soaking through my clothes. My body continues to buzz with static and nerves, but I don't back down. She focuses her attention on me and curls her lips in a sneer, contorting her beautiful face into something fearsome. Blue light flickers in the witch's eyes, consuming her pupils. She continues to chant, holding her hands up, shaking the world beneath my feet. Heat burns in my middle, but I fight against the sensation and grind my teeth. This is nothing compared to the pain I've been put through before.

"Lyric," she whispers, her eyes turning into slits. "Batoo lor retitina." Rain pours around her, but she doesn't get wet. I've never seen anything like it. I expect my body to fold under her spell. I expect to suddenly explode with the heat continuing to build. But nothing happens. The witch's frustration mars her face, her voice now shouting toward the sky. Whatever she attempts to do doesn't work, and it's enough to get me from my spot beside Caz.

"Lyric, no! You have to run!" Sagan yells, cutting me off before I charge the woman. He shoves his big wolf head under Caz's convulsing body, trying to help him up.

The woman's attention jerks to Sagan, and she bares her teeth, her expression turning sharp with lines, her teeth elongating not unlike Flynn's had. Jerking back, Sagan flies off his paws and crashes hard into a tree. The witch's focus on Sagan distracts her enough that she doesn't notice Sterling sneaking up behind her.

I dig my hands into the muddy ground and pick up two handfuls of dirt. I chuck it at the witch, hoping to break her concentration on Sagan while also giving Sterling a chance to attack. The mud sizzles against some sort of magical shield, and she flicks her hand at me. Something shocks me, capturing me in a strange force field that lifts me off my feet. My throat tightens, my whole body tensing. She might not be able to force me to change like she was doing to Caz, but she still has plenty of magic I don't know how to fight against. Pain explodes through me, stealing away my ability to fight, to scream, to do anything to protect myself from this psychotic bitch, hell-bent on killing me.

Sterling launches at the woman from behind, his fangs glistening with his snarl. She spins and holds her palms out, drawing energy straight from the air to build a shield between them. He yelps as he smashes into whatever magical wall she uses to protect herself from any of our counter-attacks.

The weight crushing and pinning me in place eases away, and I drop to my knees in the mud. Caz and Sagan join Sterling, and they surround the witch. She might be powerful, but it seems that she can only defend herself against one wolf at a time. Every time she loses focus, her magic falters. Sagan growls, seeing an opening, and manages to break through her shield, biting her in the calf. She tries to blast him with her power, but Caz attacks her next. Grabbing onto her wrist with his teeth, he yanks her hard enough that she falls to her knees. Sterling jumps on her back, using his heavy weight to pin her to the ground. I dash forward and yank her white, now sopping wet hair, pulling her head up to meet her gaze.

She grins, her wicked smile stretching across her face. "Lyric, batoo lor retitina. Shev leh—"

I slap my hand over her mouth, cutting off whatever the

fuck incantation she tries to use against me. "What the hell do you want? Why are you doing this?" I ask, my chest heaving in anger. "What coven are you from?"

"Dispo terro et prev," the witch says, jerking her head to free her mouth. She ignores me and tips her head toward the sky, screeching with a peel of laughter that scratches through my soul.

I throw myself back and cover my ears, unable to stand the noise piercing my eardrums.

She disappears in a flash of light, blinding me. Caz shoves his heavy body into mine, knocking me out of the way as a tree cracks and falls, the wide trunk hitting the ground where I stood. The world quakes from its force, and I tense, spinning around to see if the witch moved only to sneak attack me again. If it wasn't raining, I might be able to track her scent, but it's impossible. I'm nearly certain she broke the sky open to ensure no one could do so.

"We have to go," Sagan thinks to me, his bark snapping through the air. He nudges his head into my ass, pushing me to move. "Come on. It's not safe. We have to get to the lake."

"What about Dax and Bastien? What about Flynn? We can't leave him," I say, swiping the wet strands of hair from my face. I inhale a few deep breaths and peer at the blasts of light continuously blinking through the air like the lightning now crackles across the earth. "The competitors will kill him. You know they will. We need him. This is more than about the damn packs, Sagan. Look around."

"Right now, this is about us, and you're more important to me," he says, his growl rippling over me.

"We're wasting time, brother. Just—don't disobey our leader." Sterling knocks his head into Sagan's side. "She's right about the warlock. Look around. Look at this bullshit."

Sagan snarls and slams his big paws to the ground. "Fine. But we don't fight. We can't have them accusing us of treason."

Sterling releases a loud howl, calling out to Bastien and Dax. Another howl sounds over the thundering sky, returning his call. Caz limps closer, his thoughts silent to me—or maybe I lock him from my mind. I don't know. I don't try to fix it otherwise in this moment. I'm too tense. Too shaken. This isn't how things were supposed to be.

Caz trembles in pain, doing his best to stay upright. His back leg bends in an unnatural position, sending my heart into my stomach. It's like the interruption of the witch's spell left him half transformed and unable to shift either way, his limb broken in the process. Sagan pads his way to Caz and nuzzles his nose to Caz's injured leg. Caz releases the saddest whimper, his head bowing as he holds his leg close to his body.

"You need to stay here with Caz," Sagan says, projecting his voice to me. "He's too injured to fight. He couldn't even keep up if he wanted to."

"But you guys need me," I argue. "I can fight."

Sterling barks. "Please, Lyric. He needs your protection more. The witch could come back and try to take him."

I groan and squeeze my eyes shut, trying to fight my urge to argue. "I can't just stay here. I'll carry him. I don't want to separate."

"Damn it," Sagan swears, stretching his body until he shifts back into a man. Without another word, he hooks his arms under Caz's belly and lifts him up and onto his shoulders, balancing his weight while managing to keep one of his arms free. "Lead the way but don't go charging in. We need to wait for Dax and Bastien. They're coming."

I bob my head and motion to Sterling to take my side. He remains in his wolf form, mirroring my every movement, guarding me protectively as we jog through the trees and toward the chaos.

Flynn stands trapped against a boulder, his hands burning with his magic. Six massive wolves circle him, each trying to get through his protective shield. My gaze darts from Flynn, now heaving with exhaustion, his magic faltering, and to where Paige points her finger, yelling commands that the wolves obey. It's only been minutes since she arrived, but it feels like years have passed, and she already controls the packs across all territories. Just the thought pushes me harder and faster. This is it. She cannot win.

"I want you to go around and get to Flynn from the back. All he needs is time to cast his escape spell. Do something to grab everyone's attention," I say to Sterling, bending down to bunch his silver coat on his neck between my fingers. I kiss the top of his head. "And be safe, damn it. There's no one else in the world I'd rather surprise hump than your sexy ass."

Sterling licks my cheek and bolts away, but he doesn't make it far. A tree crashes to the ground in front of him, missing him by inches. He scrambles back, his hackles rising. Sagan steps closer beside me and whistles for Sterling to return to us.

An eerie silence falls over the world. The rain stills, the water freezing in the air in front of us like glittering orbs of magic as they reflect the light breaking through the clouds. My skin prickles with goosebumps, and I reach out for Sagan.

My hand burns against a magical shield, the air turning heavy and thick around me. I realize it's not the world that slows but me. The white-haired witch returns, chanting something I can't hear. Panic seizes my chest as two lycans blink into existence next to her. Their humanoid forms loom at least two feet taller than her and their eyes flash green.

I push my hands into the shield again, trying to break free, but I can't. It's too strong. I'm no match against it.

The lycans break away from the witch, one running toward Sterling and the other toward Sagan. My heart shatters into a million pieces as one swipes its long claws across Sagan's chest. Blood spatters and burns against the shield, and I scream and pound my hands to it. I can't let this happen. I can't let this witch and these beasts hurt my pack mates.

"No!" I scream, slamming my shoulder to the magical barrier as hard as I can.

It breaks under my force, sending me sprawling to the mud. The world kicks back on, and I can't get to my feet fast enough. The witch and lycans vanish in a flash of light, leaving Sagan and Sterling bleeding and unmoving in the mud.

A part of me dies.

20

War

"FUCK. FUCK. FUCK!" MY HEART splits right down the middle begging me to run in two different directions to get to Sagan and Sterling at the same time. How could this have happened? I should've protected them better, tried harder to break through the magic. I should've never let this happen to begin with.

The edges of my vision shadow, my world feeling as if it's falling apart and taking me with it. Agony threatens to send me back to my knees, Sagan and Sterling's pain radiating through me as if it's my own. Our bonds blister and fire cuts across my chest. I swear I can feel the heat of my blood spilling, though nothing happens. This is far worse than experiencing Radek's pain. I don't think I'll survive this. I'm not sure I want to.

"G-go g-get Bastien." Sagan's low voice shocks my heart, making me release a cry of relief. He groans from the ground, clutching his hands to the wounds ravaging his chest.

"I'll protect them with my last breath." Caz pushes from the ground, his body now transformed completely into a man. He struggles to make his way to Sagan. "Please trust me, Lyric. Please."

Sterling whimpers from the mud, but he doesn't speak to me through our mental link. He loses himself to his wolf as a way to push the world out of his mind. I can feel the disconnect, and I fear I might lose him if I go, but I know I'll lose him if I stay. It takes everything in me to leave them, but I don't know what I can do. I have nothing to staunch the bleeding. If I stay, I fear the witch will return. It'll be their death sentences.

Sucking in a breath, I gather my nerve, reminding myself that Bastien can help them and Dax can help me. I just need for us all to be together. To fight together. I swear to the damn universe we're never separating again. I will devour anyone who tries to rip us apart.

"Hang on for me, okay? I swear you better fucking hang on," I say, blinking my eyes, talking to the both of them. "Just think about all the fun we will have when this is over. I'll do anything you want."

With one more look behind me, I dash away and send out a call with my mind. I just hope Bastien and Dax are close enough to meet me. I have no fucking clue where they even are. Everything is so screwed up. The lycans ruined everything. I knew with them would come something worse. I should've just—

"Lyric, shit." The deep voice comes from the trees, stalling my racing thoughts. Thank the fucking universe. I slow, my heart filling with relief at the familiarity of Bastien's voice, but then Antone emerges from the trees instead of Bastien. And damn it. "Where have you been, Cherie? Are you okay? Come on. I need to get you out of here. There is a warlock—"

"Flynn is my friend," I blurt, bracing myself for Antone to turn against me. I curl my fingers into fists, positioning my legs into a fighting stance. It's in this moment that I wish Antone wasn't such a damn wild beast. I never know what to expect from him. "Paige is lying about everything, and now Sterling and Sagan are hurt badly, attacked by lycans. Caz has a broken leg. Everything is so messed up. I—I need your brother. Please, please. You have to help."

Antone's eyes search my face, a softness smoothing out his rugged features. "I believe you. Now, where are your mates? I have medical training too. I can help them."

I rub my lips together, bouncing on my feet. Commotion

sounds from just beyond the fallen trees piling up from the fight between Flynn and the wolves. It hasn't been more than minutes, but it feels like hours. Hearing the growls and Flynn's incantations sets me off even more. My chest clenches in pain and anger. I hate that I can't help everyone. "Head south. They're not far. Please hurry. I'm afraid the witch and lycans will return."

"Show me," he says, trying to grab my hand. "I don't want to leave you out here. Bastien will gut me if something happens to you."

"I-I can't. I need to find him. I need to find Dax, too." I send another silent call to them through our mental link, praying they'll hear me. They can't be far. I know they responded to our calls before. But the rain...shit. How will they track us?

Antone growls, his face turning hard in annoyance as I re-fuse his command. He looks ready to snatch me off my feet to carry me with him. I shuffle back and hold my hands up, trying to get some space between us.

He shifts on his feet. "Cherie, don't be stupid. Your life is more im—"

"They're more important to me," I snap, releasing a growl. "Stop wasting time and go, damn it."

A familiar howl cuts through the air, stopping Antone from charging me. He cocks his head, swiveling on his feet to stare in the direction the call comes from. For once, the universe is on my side. Bastien heard me. He sounds nearby.

Flaring his nostrils, Antone stretches his arms over his head a second before turning into a wolf. "He's heading this way," Antone says into my mind, circling me. "Just wait for him here. Please. You can't fight alone. If someone sees you, they might assume you're another witch."

I purse my lips. "I'll be fine. Just go. Hurry. I can handle myself."

With a howl, Antone bolts away, heading in the direction I left Sagan, Sterling, and Caz. I bounce on the balls of my feet and jog another two dozen feet toward the fight, getting a clear view of what's going on even with the fallen trees. And shit.

Flynn's protection spell falters, leaving him open to an attack. He yells out as Axel snaps his teeth into his ankle and drags him away from the boulder he uses to protect his back. Gathering more power, Flynn fights off the wolf again, but he can't seem to push himself from the ground fast enough before Killian charges him next. Another wolf, Dre, joins Killian and the two of them each grab onto Flynn, attempting to rip him in half.

My stomach twists as Flynn hollers again. This time, he can't manage to summon any power. He can't fight off the wolves as they injure him, wearing him down. If I don't do something, they'll kill him. I know they will. They're strategizing and teaming up to push through the magic until Flynn can't fight anymore.

Gathering my bravery and ignoring my good sense to wait for Bastien, I run toward the wolves. Dozens and dozens of the competitors watch as Flynn wears down until he can no longer summon magic. They howl and bark, waiting for some sort of command. It's like they're waiting for the whistle to blow that announces the start of the games before they plow forward.

"Finish him!" Paige yells, commanding the wolves to do her bidding.

Her hair flies in a gust of wind, her voice carrying over the clapping thunder. She looks strange as hell, like she's feeding off the power she has taken from the other leaders in this moment. They're nowhere to be seen, and it pisses me off how easily Paige just took everything.

A flash of light crackles overhead, setting Paige aglow. Her features harden, and I know in this moment that she's consumed by power. The witch's control her, using her like a puppet to do their bidding.

She steps forward, another burst of power raining over her, and a knife materializes in her hand. "Pin him down! I will take his heart. He must—"

Paige freezes in her tracks, her words cutting off. Fear widens her eyes as she catches sight of something—or someone—who is a threat. I halt in my tracks and follow her line of sight, spotting Bastien and Dax slinking through crowd. I frown in confusion. They were supposed to come to me, not get in the middle of the fight between the wolves and Flynn.

Another shock of power gets her moving, and she aims the knife in warning, getting Dax and Bastien to slow down. Axel and Killian drag Flynn in front of Paige like a fucking gift for their new queen, now unintentionally standing between Dax and Bastien and their sight on Paige.

"Let this be a lesson to everyone. The magic protecting us grows weak once again. We must call upon those who can help us and pay our dues. If we don't, this will only get worse. We must protect our species. If you bow to me, I'll ensure your future. The leaders are too weak. They deserve to be put back in their places," she calls, raising her voice. And hell. She knows exactly what to say to rile the wolves up. They devour her speech, and some even bow. "I trust that none of you will doubt me again. To ensure our survival, we must not let those with wild hearts destroy us. We must take action. We must do whatever it takes."

Dax howls, drawing Paige's attention to him. He bows in his wolf form and transforms into a man. Bastien remains close to his side, his white fur dirty and wet from the rain, but thankfully they both seem to be okay. I inch forward, taking advantage of the distraction their arrival causes.

"You don't know what must be done, she-wolf. Look around you. You have failed. You were supposed to get Lyric and instead an imposter stands in her place. Tell me where Lyric is, Paige of Hunter's Trail," Dax says, his voice sounding strange, his posture hunkering slightly instead of stiff and sturdy. My heart beats wildly, watching him strut naked toward Paige. "Where is the lost she-wolf?"

"I don't know," Paige responds, remaining in her spot. She waves at Flynn. "The warlock took her."

"That is untrue, Paige of Hunter's Trail. She is here. You will bring her to me. You've run out of time and must pay your dues."

Ah, hell.

"Wait!" Paige yells. "Wait, please!"

Silence settles over the world as haze swirls through the air. My mouth falls open at the flicker of blue in Dax's eyes. It's not him, and the fucker posing as my mate casts magic over everyone, except for me. It doesn't stop them, but it's like the world runs in slow motion.

"You are out of time," Dax repeats, flexing his muscles. "We will settle this now."

A flash of lightning zigzags across the sky, and the world erupts back into motion.

Paige shrieks and tries to run, but Bastien—or not. Fuck. Definitely not—cuts her off. Fear explodes through me as the realization sinks in. The witches posing as Dax and Bastien will attack Paige in front of everyone. These doppelgangers will end her life and in doing so, end my pack mates' lives too...

Fuck. I can't stop the fear crashing into me. They might've hurt Dax and Bastien already like the witch hurt—

Sterling and Sagan hurdle from the crowd in their wolf forms, snapping and growling to get some of the competitors to stand back. And hell. They're not my pack mates either. The fucking witch must've attacked us to set this all up. She wanted to ensure the ones backing me up couldn't do so any longer.

But she didn't take into account that I back them up too, and there is no way in hell I'll let things end like this.

I rush forward through the trees, my body tense and ready to fight with whatever I have left. I can't let these bastards ruin my pack's good standing. I will not allow this to go on. These fucking assholes will learn that they can't control us. Not with me around.

"Axel, help! They're allies to the warlock! That's why they've been fighting so hard to get Lyric." Paige's voice rips through the air. "Help me!"

Axel abandons Flynn and snarls, launching at Dax. I scream out, my muscles spasming with my uncontrollable transformation into a wolf. A growl sounds through the air, and I don't have time to brace myself as a wolf launches toward me. Dax knocks me off my feet and falls on top of me. His golden eyes shine in the sizzling lightning turning the world so bright I have to squint to see anything.

"You can't go out there," Dax says into my mind, his body wobbling as he struggles to get off me. Warmth seeps across my body, and I flinch at the sight of his blood on my coat.

"Fuck. What happened?" I ask.

"Traitors!" Paige yells, snapping my attention back to her.

I struggle to push from the ground, my heart thrashing in my chest, trying to break free as Sterling and Sagan's imposters charge from the crowd. They look clean and perfect, untouched by the rain, the mud, blood, or any of the fight.

The two of them intercept Axel, grabbing him by his furry back. Imposter Dax marches toward Paige while Bastien circles behind her, now in his human form. Flynn yells out a spell, and I expect the doppelgangers to explode or fall to the ground. I expect him to fissure their disguises to show the packs that they're not my mates.

But he disappears, abandoning the fight altogether.

And then Paige screams, her high-pitched wail tearing through my very being as Bastien's imposter holds her in place while Dax uses Paige's own blade to sink it into her chest to cut out her heart.

I heave and gag, my eyes burning with tears as the horrors taking place sear into my brain. Axel hollers next, and I can't stop from turning back to the fight to watch Sterling and Sagan's doppelgangers do the same thing to him. The shock of their actions leaves the packs frozen in horror, stopping anyone from trying to fight.

"Wolves of Lulupoterra," Dax's doppelganger shouts, holding Paige's heart in his hand. "Our truce is over. This is war."

Bastien lands on top of me before I can charge forward and clear my pack's name. I transform into a human, only to have Dax slap his hand over my mouth, stopping me from screaming out. I thrash and fight against both their strengths, but they force me to stay down. They force me to watch as their doppelgangers get away, leaving blood, bodies, and destruction in their wake.

"Take a breath, Ma Belle," Bastien whispers, stroking his hand up and down the length of my back. "There is nothing we can do right now. If we show ourselves, the packs will issue an execution. It's hard to prove our innocence with the murders in front of everyone."

"We need to get out of here." Dax slides his hands under me and lifts me up. "Where are the others? They were supposed to be with you."

I throw my arms around Dax's shoulders, making him grunt. I pull back and dart my gaze to his bloody, scratched chest. "We were attacked. A witch and lycans."

"So were we," Bastien says, shifting my hair from my shoulder. "Were you hurt?"

"Only through our bond." I swallow the burning in my throat. "The witch didn't hurt me. Some of her power didn't even work. She couldn't force me to transform like she wanted."

"She could come back. We should move," Dax says, flaring his nostrils as he sniffs the air.

Sun peeks through the clouds, setting the ground aglow with starbursts of light through the trees. Silence settles over the world, like the calm after the storm, but my body continues to clench with phantom pain, my heart fearing this is only the beginning. The collection of howls disturbing the silence proves it.

Adjusting me in his arms, Dax holds me so I cling to him like a sloth, allowing him to keep his hands free. I know I should walk. I'm probably the least injured out of all of us. But I can tell he doesn't want to set me down. His nature as my mate consumes him. And I would be lying if I didn't want to just rest and feel the safety his arms around me brings. I've been taught all my life to fight, to do things for myself, but right now? It's so comforting to just be taken care of. It's been so long since I've had this.

Something rustles in the forest, and Bastien dodges forward and growls, his white fur sticking up on his back, his choice to take on his wolf form for our protection. Antone emerges from behind a tree, supporting Caz's weight as he hobbles on one foot, his broken leg in a makeshift splint.

Antone helps Caz lean against a tree and bends down, opening his arms. Bastien hauls ass toward his brother and jumps up, landing with his paws on Antone's shoulders. I don't think I've ever seen them hug. Bastien transforms into a man and whacks Antone on the back. A part of me loves seeing such a bond despite my feelings toward Antone's hard-ass attitude.

"What, Cherie?" Antone says, curling his lip into a half-smile. "You want in on this?"

I twist my lips and shake my head. Maybe if he didn't open his mouth and ruin the sweet moment with his bastard attitude. I catch sight of Sagan and Sterling moving through the trees, probably circling to ensure it's safe. I drop to my knees and make kissing noises, clapping my hands together.

"Come here, my sexy, fierce babes," I say, my voice teasing.

Because they both look like they could use it.

Sagan dashes around Sterling, rushing toward me. I open my arms, bracing myself for him to knock me on my ass. But Sagan slows and lowers his body, releasing the cutest whimper. He flops over and exposes his stomach to me, making me laugh. I reach down to rub my hands across his belly fur when two paws lock around my damn neck and Sterling humps me from behind. I fall forward under the force and on top of Sagan. I practically cackle, my voice echoing through the forest. Sagan transforms faster than I knew possible and silences me with a kiss, clutching my face in his hands. Sterling's paws turn into hands, and he slides them lower and cups my breasts.

"Fuck, blondie. I've missed you," Sterling says, kissing my shoulder.

"It's been a couple of minutes," I say, hugging his arms to me so he can't move.

Sagan kisses me again. "Felt like forever, thinking we might have lost you."

Antone clears his throat from above us. Sterling rolls off me, taking me with him while Sagan pushes to his feet. Dax holds Caz's weight and Bastien peers around the forest.

"Cherie," Antone says. "I must ask that you take care of my brother and the rest of these assholes. They might think they know the Mortal World, but they don't know it as well as you."

His words swirl through my mind. The Mortal World. I never expected to enter it again so soon. But we can't stay here.

Dax was right. The packs will kill them on sight, but then, another part of me fears the danger we face going to a world unprotected by magic. I don't even know where Flynn is or if he decided to abandon this bullshit altogether. I wouldn't blame him. The wolves were going to kill him.

"She-wolf, I'm not ready to abandon you yet. I'm too invested now." Flynn's voice trickles through my mind like he's been waiting and watching nearby. Maybe he has been. "So come on. I can't keep open the gateway forever. The wolves are hunting us."

Dax cocks his head and twists to stare behind him. "He's right. Let's move."

"You can hear him?" I ask, surprise washing over me.

"We all can," Bastien says.

Sterling nudges me. "Damn it, blondie. Did you claim him too? What did I tell you?"

I crinkle my nose.

I don't get the chance to respond because howls call through the forest, drawing our attention.

"I'll hold them off," Antone says, hugging Bastien one more time. "Be safe, brother. I'll do what I can on this side, but take care of Cherie. Papa was right about her. She is going to change things. I can feel it." Turning to me, Antone smiles. "And remember, Cherie. If he fails you, there is always me."

Oh jeez.

I whack him on the shoulder. "Thank you for this. Take

care of yourself, Antone. Protect Harlow and Emerson. Teach them what you can. Prepare them for what's to come."

Antone nods, transforms into a black wolf, and howls once before darting away. I straighten my shoulders and meet the gazes of my pack mates, of the men my dad chose for Lunar Crest, but also the men I've chosen for my future.

"I need you guys to make me a promise," I say, motioning them to follow me as a bright light flashes near the lake. I can feel Flynn's magic humming through my very bones. It's the strangest thing how I can recognize him.

"You don't need to ask us to promise you anything," Sagan says, taking my hand. "We'll do anything for you."

I bob my head. "And I'll do anything for you. Especially fight. I want you to fight beside me. I want to claim you all as my pack, and I want you to claim me."

"Even me?" Caz asks, his voice lowering, the weight of his words wrapping around me.

"Even you," I repeat. "You're my mates. My future. My pack. No one will ever change that."

Because the doppelgangers were right about this bullshit life and their intrusion into our world. They will regret ever messing with me.

This is war.

21

Beacon

"IF YOU DON'T HOLD STILL, I'll make Sterling restrain you, Caz," I say, kneeling beside the couch in Flynn's Mortal World apartment. "You might not appreciate his boner like I do."

Sterling chuckles and crosses the room, leaving his protective spot by the door. "I can't help it that my puff pounder remembers that you made it a promise to do anything. My boner radar is throbbing in anticipation for what I assure will be an amazing time."

I jerk my attention to him and glare. "Keep your damn buster thruster in line, Sterling. The world is already a pain in my ass."

He chuckles. "Don't be so negative. Your teensy peach ring will welcome me in just fine."

"You sound like a professional ass trainer. I'm not sure how I feel about that." I smirk at him. "I might need some references from your prior experiences."

Sterling groans so fucking loud and dramatically that I can't help but laugh. It's enough to distract Caz so that he only flinches a bit when I start massaging the healing balm Flynn concocted into his leg.

"You do that for me, and I'll consider it...during my season. If you can make me orgasm first, keep all comments to yourself, buy a shit-ton of lube, and ensure no one intrudes on the moment, I might agree," I add.

"Fuck yeah, blondie!" Sterling says. "You're going to love it so much that—"

I whack him. "Chill. I said I *might* agree."

"Damn." Caz hums under his breath, my comment totally exciting him. "Maybe you should make the offer to me. Sterling might be a bit too excited. I, on the other hand, would guarantee at a minimum of five orgasms."

I bonk my head on the couch cushion. I surprise the hell out of him by tapping his growing erection with my index finger through his pants. "I suppose that sounds nice."

Sterling throws his hands up. "Seriously? You guys haven't even banged. You sneaking in foreplay with each other? How could I miss that? I don't think I've seen you kiss apart from our tie, and now you're here offering that sweet star to him. Fuck, blondie—"

I laugh and smack Sterling's arm. "Are you seriously trying to stake a claim on my ass?"

"Damn right." Sterling pulls me away from Caz and onto his lap. "I know you feel bad for trying to bite his cock off, but there are other ways to apologize."

"My way is just fine," I tease.

Sterling shifts my hair and kisses my throat. "Is it because his cock is smaller?"

I expect Caz to growl or smack Sterling, but he tips his head back and roars a laugh. Reaching his arms out, Caz tests me to see if I'll go to him, even if he thinks it might be only to tease Sterling. I let him pull me onto the couch, the ridiculous lightness of this weird conversation making the world feel less scary and crazy. I'd give anything, even a little ass play, to lighten things up. Who knew? Maybe because their new obsession and excitement might be contagious.

"Big dicks don't get all the benefits," Caz says, hugging his arms around me.

I shake my head with my laugh. "Caz, you say that as if you're like half his size. Whip them out. I need to see again, but

I'm nearly sure it's only by an inch, which is still intimidating."

"At least Dax hasn't asked," Sterling adds.

I laugh and groan, turning over to face my back toward him. Caz smiles at me, adjusting me in his arms to settle his legs between mine while making more room on his side. I'm careful not to jostle him, even if he doesn't complain about his leg any longer. A smile lights his face, his eyes searching mine, our sudden closeness consuming me.

"I am really sorry for everything that has happened between us, Lyric," Caz murmurs, stroking his finger along my cheek.

"I'm sorry too. The way I acted...I suck. I was just so hurt, thinking you betrayed me. Because I care about you, Caz. I didn't realize how much I did." I rub my lips together, leaning in closer. "I'd like to try again."

"Damn, kiss her already before I do." Sterling gets off the floor and lies behind me, turning me into the meat of my pack mate sandwich.

I laugh as Sterling tries to turn me over, but Caz tightens his arms around me and closes the space, hovering his lips an inch away from mine, testing to see how I respond without kissing me in case I don't want to. But I do.

I don't know if it's because I finally feel safe and content, the closeness of both Caz and Sterling smothering any chance of fear to sneak through me, or if it's because my heart and soul align, knowing that Caz is mine, but I brush my lips to his, giving into the deep-seated craving inside of me.

Caz kisses me deeper, teasing the seam of my lips with his tongue until I let him stroke his tongue to mine, soft and sensually, sending my body buzzing. Sterling moves my hair and brushes his lips to my neck, and I shift and kiss him next, wanting to split my affection between them. Four hands travel across my body, caressing my buzzing skin inch-by-inch.

"Is this okay?" Caz asks, working his lips over my jaw. "I don't want you to feel like you have to do anything ever with me. Your claim is enough."

My heart swells with his words, and I cup his face and kiss him again, sending a whisper of a plea through his mind to keep going. I want more. I'm ready for more. It's all I can think about.

Caz moans at my thoughts of him and uses them to guide him along in what I want from him. I imagine his warm hand slipping into my panties like he's never done so before. I imagine him massaging my sensitive skin to take care of the sudden ache rising from my desire. Every inch of me is incredibly turned on that I also imagine Sterling tugging down my waistband to screw me from behind, his hard cock already teasing me between my legs.

"Are you sure, Lyric?" Sterling asks softly.

"Mmmhmm." I ease my hip up and let him tug my pants down.

Caz kisses me passionately, trailing his hand over my hard nipples through my shirt and slowly, torturously, works his way down my stomach. We both moan at the same time his finger eases my body open a bit as he strokes my clit. Sterling molds his body to mine, kissing my shoulder and snaking his hand under my body to sneak his hand up my shirt. Pressure builds between my legs as he aligns his body to mine, testing me with his tip to discover how ready and wet I am from this moment.

Caz stifles my moan with another kiss, and I reach between us and rub my hand over his bulge until I make my way inside his pants and pull his cock out to jerk him off while he and Sterling both pleasure me.

We lose ourselves to our passion, and I savor the sizzling sensations burning across my skin. I gasp with Sterling's quickening movement and Caz's hand adding even more pleasure to my body until I cum before the both of them. I cling onto Caz with one hand, still working him over with my other. I enjoy the sound of their soft moans, the heat of our bodies together and so close that I can feel Caz's heart thumping against my chest as Sterling's races against my back. I love every moment of their affection, of their deep-seated need, and how good we all feel with our emotions entangling until Sterling finishes. Caz doesn't take long to orgasm after, the three of us caught up in each other's pleasure.

"I've never been so happy in my life," Caz murmurs, continuing to kiss me. "Your affection, your attention, it's indescribable."

"I'm in love," Sterling murmurs, nuzzling his nose to my neck. "You're it for me, Lyric. My life feels complete."

I shift onto my back, wedging more between them so I can meet both of their eyes. "My life *is* complete," I say. "If only the rest of our pack would hurry the hell up and return. I need all of you here, within my reach, so I can ensure it always stays that way."

The door to the single bedroom of Flynn's apartment creaks open and Dax fills the doorway with Sagan, Bastien, and Flynn behind him. Sterling tugs my pants back up and heat rushes through my face, realizing they might've arrived when I was wrapped in passion. Damn warlocks and their alternative form of travel.

"We could smell you guys from a mile away," Bastien says, keeping his voice even.

I crinkle my nose. "Really? Ugh. Please don't mention it again."

Dax crosses the room and plops on the floor next to the couch and bends over Sterling to meet me for a kiss, not even caring who I'm between or if the others watch us. I sigh against his lips, my soul practically purring at his closeness. I hadn't realized how much even their short absence would affect my very being.

"We have to, Lyric," Dax says, easing away. "Your body is like a beacon and more so for the damn competitors."

"If any of them come to the Mortal World, it'll be easy to track us down," Sagan adds.

Bastien reaches over and touches my cheek. "Especially with

how worked up you are right now."

"Then maybe you guys should back up. You all start it." I adjust my top and sit up. Turning to Sterling and Caz, I boop my index fingers to their noses. "Bad horn-dogs, bad."

Sterling tries to snatch me, and I roll off the couch and hop to my feet. Sneaking from his spot by the couch, he tries to cut me off on my escape towards the bathroom. If I'm releasing fucking cock bait, I need to shower. Because shit. Nope.

Flynn combs his fingers through his hair, pushing strands from his face. He clears his throat and enters the small kitchen, pulling a couple of containers from the cabinet. Bastien joins Sagan on their new mission to get to me, and I dash toward the bathroom. Once they get started, it might be hard for them to stop. It feels way too good not to give in to their playful moods, especially after everything we've been through.

Bastien beats me to the bathroom door and locks his fingers through mine, tugging me to him. Caressing his lips to mine, he shuts the bathroom door, locking it before any of the others can join us. I kiss Bastien sweetly, ruffling my fingers through his brown hair, making it hard for him to turn on the hot water. Setting me on the counter, he eases away and looks through Flynn's cabinet, pulling out a towel.

A knock taps on the door. "Hey Lyric, I have something for you to bathe with. It will help temporarily until we can figure out how far your scent reaches, and I can figure something else out," Flynn says, his voice muffled.

I hop off the counter while Bastien grabs some washcloths. Opening the door, I greet Flynn with a raised eyebrow. "Please tell me whatever you have isn't going to stink."

Flynn chuckles and holds up a glass bottle with a ruby liquid. "Most definitely, but at least I won't have to worry about you all making too much noise around here."

Sterling pops up beside Flynn. "I think you underestimate my need to bone that meat tunnel of hers. You'd understand if you—"

I flick Sterling in the forehead. "Shut the hell up."

Sterling doesn't get a chance to retaliate or try to push past Flynn. A chime jingles from the living room, and Flynn shifts on his feet and glances down the short hallway and toward the front door. He motions to the guys to head into the bedroom, and Bastien tugs me into the bathroom and locks the door. He shuts off the water and positions himself protectively in front of me. Everyone in the universe seems to be our enemy, and no one is willing to take any chances.

"Oh, hey, Martin," Flynn says, his voice lowering. "What can I help you with?"

"There was a noise complaint. Someone heard a dog bark and saw you with a Great Pyrenees or something. You know pets are against the rules," a low, masculine voice says.

"Wasn't me," Flynn responds. "Whoever said so must've been mistaken."

"Can I have a look around?" The man asks.

Bastien tenses, his muscles rippling in anticipation. I link my hands to his shoulders and pull him into my chest, running my fingers down his pecs to hug him from behind.

"Look, it's late and you need to give me notice before coming into my apartment. Lease says twenty-four hours." Flynn's voice remains even, and I'm relieved. I'd be annoyed as hell if someone wanted to barge in on my place with no proof.

A deep, guttural growl reverberates through the air, sending my arm hairs on end. Bastien rips through his clothes and transforms into his wolf form, preparing to attack. Something crashes outside the door. Flynn hollers some sort of spell, and glass shatters, the sound deafening.

I thrust the bathroom door open, my mind refusing to get trapped in this damn small space if there is a threat. I gawk in surprise at Mr. Remington transforming into a lycan right outside the door. And holy fuck.

"Give Lyric to me, and we won't have a problem," Mr. Remington, my old fuckhead apartment manager says, his guttural voice creeping me out as it escapes his beastly muzzle. "Ms. Larson, don't put up a fight, and I'll leave this asshole warlock alone."

Dax releases a growl. "You're dead, lycan."

Mr. Remington's eyes widen in surprise, and he flicks his gaze from me standing in the bathroom doorway and to Dax in front of the bedroom door. Bastien weaves between my legs, and Sagan, Sterling, and Caz exit the bedroom in their wolf forms to back up Dax.

"I want to do the honors," I say, fisting my hands.

Mr. Remington roars and scrambles back, realizing how outnumbered he is. Rushing after him, I jump on his hairy back and sink my middle fingers into his eyes. Dax and Caz circle in front of us, knocking Mr. Remington off his feet. Anger burns through me, the need to murder this douchebag the only thing I can think about. Howls sound from behind me, and Bastien, Sagan, and Sterling charge past me, launching toward another lycan—and not just any lycan. This is Todd, the dickwad from my complex in Evergreen Beach. And he's not alone.

Two more lycans emerge from behind the building, snapping their grossly frothy jowls. And I can't believe this shit. They shouldn't be here. How are they here? Who are these other assholes?

One of the lycans rushes Sagan and kicks him hard enough in the snout to send him tumbling head over paws to land on his back. I scream and punch the back of Mr. Remington's head, using my force to launch to my feet. I crash into the lycan going after Sagan. He falls forward and skids across the pathway. Sagan darts toward me and bites into the lycan's side. Sterling joins his brother and sinks his fangs into the lycan's throat.

"Lyric, behind you!" Dax's voice erupts in my mind.

"Crayat liptrist lycans gota calia tu!" Flynn shouts, sending a bright flash of light through the air.

I shield my face, using the lycan's body to get up with one

hand. The lycans screech and cover their eyes, stopping in their tracks.

Mr. Remington snarls and swipes his claws, trying to get Dax as he closes in on him. Flynn chants his spell again. Another burst of power pops through the night.

The lycans decide to flee instead of fight, the pack of them obviously new and unskilled when it comes to fighting. Caz and Bastien snarl and chase after them, determined to take them all down. My skin ripples, my muscles begging to let my wolf free to join them.

"Lyric, no. Command your pack to let them go," Flynn says, his voice erupting in my mind. "Don't go after them. It's not safe."

"But—"

"We can use them. I can track them and find out which coven they belong to." Flynn steps forward, releasing a whistle into the air when I'm not quick enough to call my pack back. "Something is definitely wrong. I've never seen lycans work together."

Shit. And there are even more.

"Caz, Bastien! Let them go. Dax, Sterling, Sagan, come here," I say, projecting my voice into their minds instead of yelling.

My guys saunter their way from where they ran, and I reach out to scratch my fingers into Dax's thick, mahogany coat. Sterling rubs his big body to the backs of my legs, and Sagan,

Bastien, and Caz continue to look around the complex.

"I need you guys to search the apartments. I know at least one of them lived here. He owns several complexes around here," Flynn says. "I just need something that belongs to one of them. I will track them."

I lick my lips and nod, motioning to them to go on. Dax is the only one who stays. He transforms into a man and moves in close, twining his fingers with mine like he can't resist touching me.

"We need to find a new place," Dax tells Flynn.

Flynn bobs his head. "I agree. We also need to figure out a plan. I need to prepare."

I clear my throat. "I want to find my dad."

Dax tightens his jaw. "Lyric, that's dangerous."

"Our life is dangerous. You promised me, Dax. You said once the games were over, we'd get him. And the games are over." At least for us. He knows it. "He can help us."

"I'm going to need something that belonged to him," Flynn says, keeping his voice low.

"What about me? I'm his daughter," I say, shifting on my feet.

Flynn rubs his palms together. "Something of his or your mother's would be better. If they bonded like I think, she'd be closer."

I groan and twist my hair in my hands. "I left everything behind. I don't have anything." Hopelessness washes through me.

Dax squeezes my fingers. "The den. There were some of your mom's belongings in the den in Lunar Crest."

"You can't go there," Flynn says, his mouth twisting. "You barely made it out."

Dax straightens his shoulders. "She won't be. I will go alone."

I glower. "The hell you will. We will only ever do things together. Understand? You are my pack mate. We are stronger together. More fierce together."

"You'll die together," Flynn says with a groan.

I heave a breath. "We won't. We have you to help us. We have more than anyone else to lose. We won't go down without a fight."

"Hell yeah, blondie!" Sterling says, howling through the night.

Sagan bounds toward us, carrying something in his mouth. He purposely jumps onto the dead lycan and uses its body to launch closer. Caz and Bastien make their way to us from around another building.

"If this is how you want to do things, Lyric, then I think we all need to agree," Dax says, bringing my hand to his face.

I straighten my shoulders. "Are you in, Dax? Are you going to be my backup?"

"Damn straight." He turns to the others. "Ready to prove ourselves to our mate?"

They all howl and dart around me in a protective circle.

I turn to Flynn. "What about you, warlock? You going to help my pack?"

Flynn looks around and slowly nods his head. "Like I said, she-wolf. I'm not ready to abandon you yet. Let's get these damn traitor covens. Let's show Magaelorum and the Mortal World what you're made of."

"Strength," Dax says.

"Ferocity," Sagan adds.

I smile. "And the power of the Lunar Crest pack."

The world better brace itself. We'll change everything.

22

The Hunt

"HUSTLE, GORGEOUS. WE'RE ALMOST THERE." Sagan nudges his snout to my ass cheek, nipping me hard enough to get me to run faster.

"Damn, Sagan. You want me to whack you on the nose?" I push my legs to run harder, my breath heaving.

He nips my other ass cheek and dashes forward too fast for me to swat at him. Dax jumps from a boulder and lands on his paws next to me. He bumps me with his huge body, herding me toward the icy river.

"Hurry up, blondie! The bastards are everywhere." Sterling yips from the river's edge, pacing back and forth.

Bastien whistles between his fingers, treading in the river, the water flowing around him but not sweeping him away. Light glows under him, the gateway open and ready to take us to the Mortal World.

"Fuck, behind you guys," Bastien says, pointing in the direction the soft thuds of paws on the ground sound from. "Dax, cut them off."

"No!" I yell, forcing myself to haul ass. "We stick together. No one fights."

Dax growls and bolts past me, picking up speed. Sagan joins him, leaving me alone a few feet behind them. Howls rip through the air, and I clench my fingers into fists, suppressing the fear rising through me.

None of us wanted to return to Lunar Crest, but there was something we needed—Flynn needed. But damn it. The packs have sent two or three of their warriors to guard the place, taking over what was supposed to be my home.

Sterling splashes into the water, jumping toward Bastien. The two of them sink under and disappear. Propelling from the river's edge, Sagan launches toward the middle of the river, remaining in his wolf form like his brother. Bastien pops back to the surface and grabs him by the waist, disappearing once more.

"Hurry the fuck up, Lyric," Dax snaps in my mind as a

growl escapes his mouth. "You first."

I smack my hand to his hind quarts. "No, you first. And take the bag."

Dax jerks his head toward my outstretched hand and yanks the bag out of my hand, carrying the strap between his teeth. He picks up speed, racing ahead of me to kick off a small boulder to fly toward the middle of the river. Bastien waits with his hands outstretched, and Dax crashes into him, sinking them both under.

"Don't let her get away!" Fergus shouts through my mind, his howl signaling the other wolves of my whereabouts. "You know what's at stake."

What's at stake? I don't even want to think about it.

Pushing the thought from my mind, I rush into the icy river water. A shadow crosses over the rippling water as a wolf catapults above, landing in the river. I tense, my body screaming, my heart nearly exploding.

"Cherie, you better fight me," Antone says, his voice trickling into my mind as he bares his fangs. "You weren't supposed to be here. What the fuck were you guys thinking?"

I charge forward and crash into him, locking my hands around his huge body. "We needed something from my mother's den."

Antone knocks his huge head into my side, pushing me toward the middle of the river. "Just hurry the hell up and get out of here. Don't come back. If you're caught—you can't get caught."

I cling onto his furry neck, spotting a couple of wolves dashing through the trees. "What's going on, Antone? You have to tell me. I need to prepare."

"The leaders issued a hunt to bring you back. The winner gets to choose three pack mates and will have a pack leader position. You will be their omega, Cherie. Your punishment for your—"

Fury explodes through me, and I shove Antone in anger, breaking away from him. He growls and swims forward, pretending to chase after me.

"Tell the damn leaders we'll be coming for them, understand?" I say. "Tell them they don't need to hunt us. We will return by our own free will, and when we do, they better fucking be ready."

I swing my hand out and punch Antone away as Fergus reaches the river. Diving under, I swim away from the surface, my mind whirling with anger. I can't believe what the leaders are doing.

What the hell are they even thinking? This is all so crazy, and the last thing I actually want to do is fight them. But a huge fucking part of me will if I have to. I will not be part of any more of their damn games.

"Give me your hands, Ma Belle," Bastien says into my mind, his voice sending a wave of tranquility through me to capture and cage the turmoil and annoyance radiating through me.

Stretching out my hands, I continue to kick my legs, my lungs now burning from the lack of oxygen. Sharp teeth sink into my ankle, startling me, and one of the wolves drags me up a foot.

I scream out underwater, inhaling a breath instinctively. Bastien grabs my wrists and tugs me down. Light flashes through the water, and Bastien shoves me toward it, using me to propel up to get to the wolf.

The world flips and warm air engulfs me. I cough and spit, expelling water from my lungs. Dax hooks his hands under my arms and lifts me from the creek. Energy hums through the air, and I cling onto Dax's naked body.

"Where's Bastien?" Sterling asks, his voice cutting over the humming water.

"He was right behind me," I gasp, sucking in another deep breath.

Flynn swears, drawing my attention to him as he stands at the creek's edge, facing his palms toward the water. "I can't keep it open for much longer. If anyone besides the six of you tries to come through, the gate will crack and snap open. They'll be able to follow u—"

A wave erupts from the water, cascading over us. Dax spins away and shields me protectively.

"Close it!" Bastien shouts, his voice ringing through the air.

Light blasts through the forest, turning the world so bright it looks as if the sun comes to Earth. Flynn falls forward, hitting his knees to the muddy ground. He hangs his head between his arms, his hands the only thing propping him up.

I hop from Dax's embrace and splash through the creek, the shallow water only reaching my knees. Sliding my hands around Flynn's waist, I pull him up and grin. "We did it!" I say, digging my fingers into his shoulders. "I can't believe we fucking did it!"

Sterling and Sagan howl at my excitement, closing in around me. I hug an arm around each of them and pull them close, ruffling my fingers through their fur. Bastien and Dax close the circle around me and Flynn.

Dax whacks Flynn on the back. "You're not so bad for a warlock," Dax says, dropping the bag of my mother's things in front of him. "But don't ever ask our mate to do something this crazy again. They could've killed her."

His words knock the excitement right out of me, and I tip my head back and look up at him. "They wouldn't have. Antone gave me a warning. He said something about the leaders issuing a hunt, which I'm pretty damn sure includes the Mortal World. The winner who captures me gets Lunar Crest and his choice of pack mates...along with me."

Bastien growls. "Fuck. They must be getting desperate if they've issued a hunt. This is more than about getting you back."

"It's about the witches," Flynn says, keeping his voice low. "We need to find the ones who created the shield around Lulupoterra, and soon."

Caz's howl cuts through the air, stealing my attention from

Flynn. The ground shakes and a deep snarl reverberates through my bones. I don't even have a chance to get to my feet as Caz barrels through the trees.

"Run!" he yells, skidding to a stop in front of me. "I couldn't keep them away."

No one gets a chance to move before two huge lycans smash through the trees. One launches at Caz and tackles him to the ground. He yelps and thrashes, biting at the lycan's chest, trying to injure him.

Flynn throws a ball of energy at the other lycan, sending it sprawling across the ground.

Dax grabs my hands, hauling me to my feet. Sterling and Sagan attack the lycan pinning Caz, and Bastien transforms to join Flynn.

Neither Dax nor I see the third lycan coming.

The monster rams into us, sending us flying through the air. Dax flips, forcing the brunt of the fall onto me as he tries to protect me with his body.

The lycan roars above us and slams his dagger claws so deep into Dax's back that they also sink into me.

I scream and try to move, but Dax sinks onto me, his heavy weight stealing my breath.

The lycan growls above me, sending its frothy saliva across my face. I can't move or fight. I can't do anything but watch the lycan slam its dagger claws into Dax's back again and again.

Dax's blood splashes my face.

The lycan hauls Dax off and throws him toward the creek.

Bringing my arms to my face, I try to protect myself the best I can.

The lycan launches at me.

To be continued...

Other Reverse Harem Novels by Ginna Moran

THE WOLFPACKS OF SHADOW MOON ISLAND:
Wild Wolves
Savage Wolves

THE VAMPIRE HEIRS WORLD

La Vega Vampire Showstoppers
Vampire Nights
Bloody Nights
Renegade Nights

The Divine Vampire Heirs
Blood Match
Blood Rebel
Blood Debt
Blood Feud
Blood Loss
Blood Vows
Blood Holiday

The Royale Vampire Heirs Series:
Rebel Vampires
Rebel Dhampir
Rebel Match
Rebel Heir
Rebel Fight

Academy of Vampire Heirs Series:
Dhampirs 101
Blood Sources 102
Coven Bonds 103
Personal Donors 104
Blood Wars 105

THE MATES OF MAGAELORUM WORLD

SERIES IN THE MATES OF MAGAELORUM WORLD

The Pack Mates of Lunar Crest:
The She-Wolf Games
The Wolf-Mate Trials
The Omega Hunt
The Witch Chase

Fated Mate of the Dragon Clans
Caged by Her Dragons
Freed by Her Dragons
Saved by Her Dragons

SEVEN SINNERS WORLD

The Seven Sinners of Hell's Kingdom:
Her Personal Demons
Her Deadly Angels
Her Darkest Devils
Her Sinful Saints
Her Twisted Sinners

Acknowledgments

I WANT TO GIVE A huge shout out to my incredible team. To Felicia, Noel, and Katie, you ladies rock! Thank you for all your hard work and enthusiasm you give my novels. I'd also like to thank Heather and Brittany (and again, Felicia) for everything you do to help me run my reader group. It's my favorite place on the internet, and it's because of your support.

And speaking of my reader group, everyone a part of Paranormal Center for Matches and Mates deserves a shout out as well. You all bring me such happiness and I love your crazy vibes! XOXO.

About Ginna Moran

GINNA MORAN IS the USA Today Bestselling author of over seventy novels including the popular The Pack Mates of Lunar Crest and The Seven Sinners of Hell's Kingdom reverse harem novels.

She always carried a fascination for all things paranormal and wrote her first unpublished manuscript at age eighteen. Her love of the supernatural grew stronger through her adult life, and she now spends her days with different creatures of the night. Whether it's vampires, werewolves, dragons, fae, angels, demons, or mermaids, Ginna loves creating and living in worlds from her dreams.

Aside from Ginna's professional life, she enjoys binge-watching TV, crafting and design, playing pretend with her daughter, and cuddling with her dog. Some of her favorite things include chocolate, mermaids, anything that glitters, learning new things, cheesy jokes, and organizing her bookshelf. Ginna is currently hard at work on her next novel and the one after, and the one after that.